THE MAN WHO WALKED AWAY

BY THE SAME AUTHOR

The Shape of Things to Come
Drastic
Genealogy

THE MAN WHO WALKED AWAY

a novel

MAUD CASEY

B L O O M S B U R Y

NEW YORK • LONDON • NEW DELHI • SYDNEY

Published by Bloomsbury USA, New York

All papers used by Bloomsbury USA are natural, recyclable products made
from wood grown in well-managed forests. The manufacturing processes
conform to the environmental regulations of the country of origin.

LIBRARY OF CONGRESS CATALOGING-IN-PUBLICATION DATA HAS BEEN APPLIED FOR

ISBN: 978-1-62040-311-2

First U.S. Edition 2014

1 3 5 7 9 10 8 6 4 2

Typeset by Hewer Text UK Ltd., Edinburgh
Printed and bound in the U.S.A. by Thomson-Shore Inc., Dexter, Michigan

I travel not to go anywhere but to go. The great affair is to move; to feel the needs and hitches of our life more nearly; to come down off this feather-bed of civilization, and to find the globe granite underfoot and strewn with cutting flint.

ROBERT LOUIS STEVENSON

TRAVELS WITH A DONKEY IN THE CÉVENNES

It all began one morning when we noticed a young man . . . crying in his bed in Dr. Pitre's ward. He had just come from a long journey on foot and was exhausted, but that was not the cause of his tears. He wept because he could not prevent himself from departing on a trip when the need took him; he deserted family, work, and daily life to walk as fast as he could, straight ahead, sometimes doing 70 kilometers a day on foot, until in the end he would be arrested for vagrancy and thrown in prison.

DR. PHILIPPE TISSIÉ

LES ALIÉNÉS VOYAGEURS (1887)

PART ONE

Someone Comes

I T WAS AS THOUGH he had always been there, haunting the landscape, if only you were paying attention.

"If it were possible to *see* the final movement of Beethoven's string quartet Number 16 in F major. That's what he was like," said the violinist from the Leipzig Orchestra. The man he saw walking along the Weisse Elster River reminded him of the note Beethoven wrote on the score underneath those eerie opening chords: *Muss es sein? Muss es sein?* And the note he wrote under the joyous faster chords swelling in response: *Es muss sein!* The walking man was the question and the answer. Must it be? Must it be? It must be!

It wasn't unusual to see a man out walking; even as the railways spiderwebbed their way across Europe, people still walked to get somewhere and to get nowhere. But the people who claimed to have seen him—this was later, after he became known as *le voyageur de Docteur*, after he disappeared altogether—agreed there was something different about this man. Everyone who saw him said so. "Oh, yes, I've seen *him*," said the woman in the lowlands who spotted him making his way along a ridge as she hung wash out to dry for her brothers away carving Tournai stone into baptismal fonts. The coal miner in Liège, blinking into daylight, saw him walking in the valley; the baker in Coblenz saw him cross two of that village's four bridges; the hotel maid in Mulhouse, that Alsatian city of a thousand chimneys, glimpsed him from the window walking through the public square as she snapped a clean sheet across a bed. "Even when he was right there," she said, "he was somewhere else." He shimmered, on the cusp of appearing. Or was he disappearing?

It was not surprising that the violinist saw him walking along the banks of the Weisse Elster. The walking man was often spotted near rivers—making his way up and down the hilly streets of Poitiers at the confluence of the Clain and the Boivre; striding through Bayonne at the confluence of the Nive and the Adour; through Valence d'Agen by the Barguelonne; through Maastricht by the Meuse; through Cologne by the Rhine; through Prague by the Vltava.

If anybody had asked, the man, whose name was Albert, would say the song of his body walking was a silky mist. Nobody asked. *Il revient*, the rivers called to him. He returns. The silky mist was his constant companion as he discovered himself walking, not knowing how he got there, under the soft spring sun, into summer's glare, through the muted fall, and into the hard chill of winter when the trees are bare.

When Albert walked along the paths to forges; when he walked the tracks to mines and quarries; when he walked the causeways from village to farm to town to city; when he walked along the trails to market for glassmakers and the merchants of salt, flax, hemp, linen, and yarn; when he walked along the administrative highways; when he passed recruits and vagabonds, rag-and-bone merchants and chimney sweeps; when he walked along pilgrimage routes to miraculous fountains or the chapel of a healing saint; when he walked past men shouldering their dead along roads overgrown with tall grass to the cemetery; wherever he walked, he was filled with a wonder so fierce it was as if he were being burned alive from its astonishing beauty. When Albert walked, he was astonished. When he walked, he was the steam engine, powering himself like a great ship. He was the telegraph; he was the phonograph; he cut a swath through the second half of that century of invention and endless possibility. Still faster, he moved faster, faster than time.

1

AN EARLY SPRING WIND skitters across the river and up onto the docks of this port city so shapely and grand it was once called the Port of the Moon, a port whose grandness made it vulnerable to the greed of the triangular trade, African men and women for the sugar of Santo Domingo. The women working the docks pull their doors shut tight. Making its way up the narrow, winding streets that lead to the center of town, the wind blows a woman's black oilskin hat right off her head. She slips out from underneath the long cape of the man escorting her home from a party, gently setting down a cage that carries a sleeping dove. A group of straggling, school-bound children herded by their mothers laugh as the woman runs after the hat skidding along just out of reach. She laughs too as the wind rushes past, past the children and their mothers, past a group of men on the way to the docks, knocking a casket of wine from a merchant's cart into the street. The wind rushes past them all.

Past the statue of Diana dragging the fallen stag, past the statue dedicated to the soldiers who died for their country, past the men lucky or unlucky enough not to work the docks as they

settle in at the café tables. It pushes open the doors of the cathedral, whipping around the spires, taking a spin around the bell
tower, where it becomes trapped, shivering the bell from the
inside out. Muted ringing echoes through the city.

Then it breaks free, blowing through the public square outside
the Palace of Justice, past the small stone church where the witchy-
looking woman stands guard to harangue anyone who will listen
and those who won't on the subjects of good and evil. "Do any of
you know the difference?" she asks. "Do you?" She does. The wind
blows past her too, arriving at the large iron gates of the asylum.

Across from the small stone church, in the long shadow of the
cathedral, the asylum lies at the intersection of the city's prosper-
ousness and the humble daily striving of its citizens. Long ago, it
was a place of refuge for pilgrims en route to the tomb of St.
James in Spain; now its red brick façade is infused with the
magnificence of a building once dedicated to something divine.

Outside the iron gates the wind still swirls; inside the courtyard the air is still and warm. There is a careful orderliness to the
little compound of the asylum—the dining room neatly dividing
the women's wing from the men's wing and the chapel—resting
on this generous slope of land on the edge of the city, its bound-
aries marked by a stream that flows into the river. From inside
the courtyard you can hear an occasional train, and if you were to
look out a window on the upper floor you would see the stern,
stony statues of the justices sitting on top of the Palace of Justice
across the park. You would see the city buzzing with people,
scurrying with heartbreaking purposefulness along the thin,
winding streets. But there would be no need to look out the
window because the asylum is a world unto itself.

The Director, a veteran of the last war (a war we *almost* won,
he likes to point out cheerfully), is responsible for making this
world. He is a high-chested man with a ruddy, mottled face who
often appears seemingly out of nowhere, particularly impressive

for a tall man always carrying a garden tool. He believes in the good effects of nature, music, and physical fitness on the insane. He is a man for whom the ancient Greek origins of the word *psychiatry*—the medical treatment of the soul—have always rung true and so, a vegetable garden, a piano, and the regimen of daily exercises he conducts in the courtyard every day except for Sunday (and some weeks even on Sunday).

"Well, that's that," says Walter, a patient who smells mysteriously of pudding, though pudding is never served because the Director forbids sweets, believing them to be one of the causes of the last war. "Even when I turn my back?" he asks. "Those people?" he asks Marian, who wouldn't eat pudding even if there were pudding because the sun has stolen her stomach.

"Are they there?"

Though she cares for Walter, she doesn't have the energy to prove him wrong. She is without a stomach; whether people are real or not is not her first concern. "Well, then," she begins, wandering away in search of the rest of her sentence. "Well . . ."

From the window, Walter sees the asylum's young doctor pedaling past on his bicycle. "Fleetingly improvised concoction," he whispers.

The Doctor keeps his eyes on the road in front of him in order to steady himself. Pedaling past, he remembers, not for the first time, that the asylum was once a hospital for lepers. On bad days he thinks of the patients as leprous pilgrims, pieces of them falling off as they journey to who knows where; on bad days, doomed, weary visionaries, all of them. "You've only been here a year," the Director often reminds him. "Give it time." But there are days when all the Doctor can hear is the suck of need, when the patients seem so tired it is as if the recent war has caused an epidemic of fatigue, a generation born into exhaustion.

But today is not one of those bad days. Today the optimism the Doctor felt almost one year ago when he first began his work at the asylum has returned. He is filled with gratitude simply to have been born in the age of mental medicine when there is all of this thinking about, well, thinking. This morning, the asylum seems to him a beautiful, simple vase that gives shape to people who would otherwise spill into an indistinct puddle. Though his good mood may have something to do with the fact that today he will not be going to the asylum at all. Instead, he will take the train all the way to Paris to hear a lecture by the son of a wagon maker who has made of himself a great doctor. A man who receives letters from admirers addressed simply to *The Great Doctor, Europe.*

But it is, most of all, the Doctor's bicycle, a recent purchase, which is responsible for his good mood. Since he was a child, he has dreamed of having one of his own, but it was only recently that he could afford it. A pinch, but he has never once regretted the purchase; the bicycle has reignited a childlike quality in the Doctor. Click-clickety-click. There is a system to his pleasure when he rides; his pleasure is the system. He begins always with the bones: stripped of their flesh, hollow and pockmarked, beautiful coral washed ashore. The elegant clavicle and scapula; the gently curved sections of the spinal column: cervical, thoracic, lumbar. The sacrum, the spine's punctuation. The slender, long fibula next to the stalwart tibia, that sturdy leg bone, only the second largest but which bore more weight than any other. The delicate birdlike bones of the feet: tarsals and metatarsals. The exquisite phalanges, quivering with the movement of the machine, or is it the machine quivering with the movement of his bones? Cranking away—click-clickety-click—the machine itself a miraculous body. Some nights the Doctor dreams of pedaling and he wakes up, his ankles already sore.

His good mood might also be attributed to the lingering effect of last night's visit to the docks. He woke in the night from his dreams of pedaling, filled with a restless hunger that made his shabby apartment appear even shabbier—the small kitchen

dusty from disuse, the ends of a loaf of bread left uncovered nibbled by mice, his bedclothes hopelessly tangled. Even the book by his bed didn't entice him—he has recently been enjoying an account of a man and his donkey making their way through the country in Cassagnas. He left his apartment and headed out into the night. Though the Doctor has never once been inside the bar underneath his apartment, the bartender always waves to him. He waved last night but the Doctor pretended not to see, continuing on past the Place de la Bourse, past his favorite monument—unfinished, the haunch of a great horse waiting for its rider to be built—past the small cemetery filled with tree stumps like amputees, cut down to make room for more dead. He hurried past, down to the docks, where only a few gas lamps flickered dimly, all the way to the brothels.

"Trouble sleeping?" the woman said when she opened the door. What relief, her pretty tousled hair. His restlessness was given a focus and a task. He muffled the tick, tick of his father's pocket watch on the dresser with his shirt, his waistcoat, his jacket, until there wasn't even the dullest echo of that painful sound. The cathedral bells rang up into the sky, disappearing along with her dress, and then he was gone with the bells and the dress, gone into the tang of sharp perfume, into the soft, warm, fleshy relief of her.

"There you are," she said, taking shape beneath him once again. "Better now?" He had said those same words the day before to Marian, who was weeping over a stolen kidney. The theft caused another patient to wonder if, by divine miracle, she too had had a kidney stolen.

"You'll be fine," he said to Marian, leaving Elizabeth to Nurse Anne. "Take her away from the others or we'll have an entire asylum of kidneyless patients." He gave Marian a bromide and sat with her until she fell asleep; when she woke up he put his hand on hers. "You are better now," he said. And she *was* better. Medicine's power, secreted away in these small, rehearsed

gestures—the steady, unwavering touch, the certain tone giving the ethereal *if* a solid spine: *You are.*

"Yes," he said to the woman lying next to him. "Thank you."

And for a moment he was better, but as he made his way home the restlessness returned. It was everywhere—in the rows of houses shuttered for the night that seemed on the verge of bursting; in the statue of Diana still dragging the fallen stag, in the statue dedicated to the soldiers who died for their country. When he reached his building, the restlessness was there in the swollen, drunken voices of the same two men huddled at the bar night after night. "Come on, don't be a stranger," called the bartender, but the Doctor remained a stranger, climbing the stairs to his room where he put the kettle on for tea, collapsing in the armchair by the window to read the same page from his book until the man in it had knocked walnuts from the trees that lined the road two, three, four times. The fifth time, the Doctor gave up and looked out the window at the stars, so many mysterious pinpricks of light. The kettle boiled, whistling his restlessness: *What do you know? What do you know?*

Click-clickety-click. The statues of the stern justices stare stonily down at him from the top of the Palace of Justice as he pedals past. *And? So? What do you know of medicine?* Just wait, he thinks. He watches as the woman, her oilskin hat clutched to her chest, runs to catch up with the handsome man holding his cape open to her as the dove flutters in the cage at his feet. The Doctor knows *he* is not a handsome man; he is aware his crowded features give him the look of someone who is perpetually worried.

And? So?

"Oh, shut up," he says out loud, but the wind snatches his words, carrying them all the way back down to the river.

The locomotion of the train hurtles the Doctor along the iron tracks to Paris, rumbling through his feet, up his shins, into his

thighs, the base of his spine, and then up each vertebra until he is breathing it. It fills him with a keen sense of anticipation of the sort he hasn't felt since he was the same age as the children who laughed as the woman retrieved her oilskin hat. The same *what next* feeling he had as a young boy waiting for the great Léotard, son of a renowned gymnast, a man who wore a spectacular form-fitting outfit, to come pedaling through his hometown on the bicycle with its high front wheel (the same bicycle that planted the seed of longing in the Doctor's heart). The occasion was the great Léotard's unprecedented forty-mile bicycle ride, and the Doctor waited with his parents along the side of the road with a throng of others, all of them staring at the horizon, willing something to appear. The night before, the great Léotard had performed a miraculous trapeze feat at an elegant banquet hosted by a duke. Racing into the dining room on his bicycle, he squealed to a stop just before he reached the table, then executed a perfect somersault over the heads of the unsuspecting diners.

When the great Léotard finally did whir past that day in his spectacular form-fitting outfit, the boy who did not yet dream of being a doctor, who dreamed only of being an acrobat in a spectacular form-fitting outfit, gripped the hands of his father and his mother. He was a boy of great imagination, according to his parents. "Sometimes too great," his father said when he forgot to do this or that because he was dreaming of a life beyond their small town, one that didn't involve his father's dry goods store. He was so excited when the great Léotard rode by that he closed his eyes to imagine the man somersaulting over their heads, landing precisely, sublimely, in the seat of his magical machine. He imagined the great Léotard turning to him and saying: *Come with me and we'll somersault over thousands of heads.* With his eyes shut tight, the only thing the boy experienced of the great Léotard and his magical machine that day was the whir of the wind on his face. But that glorious invitation! *Be this great.* It has stayed with him ever since, tugging him forward.

Today, the glorious invitation tugs the Doctor all the way to the City of Lights to a hospital altogether different from the simple vase of the asylum. This ward for insane women that was once a gunpowder factory and before that a poorhouse is complete with the first chemical laboratory, rooms for electrotherapy and hydrotherapy, a photographic laboratory, and a lecture hall that holds an audience of six hundred. The Doctor will soon be one of those six hundred, including doctors from Berlin and Vienna and as far afield as Riga, all come to see the great doctor discuss one of his cases as part of a lecture about the disorder that has condensed centuries of medicine.

"Hysteria," the great doctor declared in a recent journal article, "will find its place in the sun." The truth is it has already found its place. It has given a name to the young woman who collapses in fits, thrashing and grabbing at her throat as though she were being choked, and to the girl caught pleasuring herself in public, laughing uncontrollably though one side of her body has been struck with paralysis. It rolls along the new railway lines, its name whispered in café cars. At society parties, women play at having attacks—making faces, arms extended, rigid and strange, as if they were being crucified. A character in a recent novel even suffers from it.

Those doctors from Berlin and Vienna and Riga? After hearing the great doctor's earlier lectures, they returned home to their own hospitals and now there were patients in Berlin and Vienna and Riga performing beautiful *arcs de cercle* and falling into exquisite paralysis. The Great Neurosis, as the great doctor sometimes calls it, is contagious. It is impossible to ignore, this disorder whose origin, the great doctor claims, may be traced to a physical defect of the nervous system, the result of an injury or of neuropathic heredity but whose manifestation is a mysterious alteration of unknown nature or location in the central nervous system. Ingenious: a lesion that is invisible! How could the Doctor ignore it?

The metal face of the train spews steam as it pulls in and out of stations. The light shines through the roofs of the stations, speckling the bodies of the bustling, pomaded men carrying suitcases and the perfumed women towing young children behind them. The Doctor watches as people walk out of the steam and then disappear back into it again. At the next station, a group of children run after the train as it pulls out, waving as it chugs away. "Wait for us!" they cry as if the train is something wondrous and magical, and it is. Progress is beautiful and the Doctor yearns to be part of it. The train makes its way north, connecting towns and villages not unlike the one where the Doctor lived with his parents—his parents who as children had drawn water from wells and lit their houses with tallow tapers, for whom sending a letter was a great luxury, who dreamed of Paris but never had the opportunity to visit. The train is an extraordinary vision they are all having together.

It pulls into the next station and the next and the next with a great puff and *shhhh*, as though relieved to have finally arrived at its destination. The exhalation of warm, wet steam rushes through the Doctor and then it is gone, replaced by the squeal of the brakes, so loud that at first he doesn't hear the man speaking to him. He is startled to find someone sharing his compartment at all, never mind this vision in Scotch tweed, wearing a wide-brimmed felt hat, double-soled shoes, and gaiters.

"That's a fine timepiece," the red-cheeked man says again, pointing to the Doctor's hand. His words rush out as though, finally, a great dam has broken.

It is only then the Doctor realizes he has been clutching his father's watch. He returns it quickly to his pocket.

"The day of two noons," the man says.

The Doctor nods, though he has no idea what the man is talking about. He looks out the window, hoping this will convey the enormity of his desire to be left alone. He had hoped to spend some of the train ride thinking through the case of Rachel, an asylum patient who believes she has a frog living in her stomach who demands she play the piano. Out the window, there is a field full of cows, a river full of fishermen casting lines from small boats, a forest full of trees, a thick, dark tangle. He closes his eyes, pretending to sleep.

"At midday, the clocks set back to coordinate the railroad schedules?" and the Doctor decides the man is not someone who might appear one day at the iron gates of his asylum after all, unless being boring were suddenly declared a pathology. He is just another person determined to give a lesson. "Twenty-four time zones? The day of two noons? The universal day was established, like the slicing of a pie."

The Doctor opens his eyes, looking at the man in a way he hopes conveys exactly how little he wants to engage in this conversation.

"Owning such a fine timepiece, I assumed," the man sniffs, "*incorrectly* that you would be interested." He riffles through his bag as though searching for something.

"Oh," the Doctor says. "But of course I am." He wants to be left alone, but he also doesn't like other people's sadness. He has been trained after all to fix it. Out the window, another dark tangle of trees, another open field.

"There has been talk, you know," the man says, his cheeks glowing just a bit redder. It doesn't take much to renew his hope. "People dying of apoplexy caused by the rapidity of these newer, faster trains. I don't usually ride the train." He pulls a little green book from his satchel and holds it up—evidence! "A Baedeker's," he says, as if the name isn't right there on the front cover for the Doctor to read.

"Are you touring?" the Doctor asks, and the man smiles. There is a certain satisfaction in asking the right question.

"I *am*," says the man, as though he is saying, *Finally*. The Doctor sees in his eyes that the floodgates have opened and there is no closing them. "The roads are changing the world, my friend.

If the whistle of the train engine is awakening us from slumber, then the road is a giant, wondrous hammer to the head!"

"That sounds painful."

"For instance, the wonderful roads to Engstlenalp."

"I have no doubt." The Doctor knows nothing about the roads to Engstlenalp, but he has done his conversational duty and he does not feel obliged to ask.

"I've packed two sandwiches. Always travel prepared," the man says. He offers the Doctor two thick slices of bread in between which is nestled a slab of mysterious meat.

The Doctor, though somewhat afraid of the mysterious meat, is ravenous. "Thank you." In his rush to get out the door after his late night, he didn't pack much food for the train ride, which, with his new traveling companion, threatens to last forever. The mystery meat sandwich turns out to be delicious despite, or maybe because of, its mysteriousness.

The man takes the Doctor's appreciation of the sandwich as permission to regale him with his travels—there is a great deal more than the wrestling match not to be missed in Engstlenalp. The baths at Lamalou, the chateau on Lake Geneva, the opera house in Budapest. He is only getting started. After a while his voice is no longer a great rush bursting forth from a broken dam but a constant, steady stream swallowed by the rattle and sway of the train rumbling through the Doctor's feet and shins, his calves and the base of his spine, up each vertebra, into his lungs, his heart, his head.

Nestled in his pocket, his father's watch ticks its own rhythm into the Doctor's nesting palm. "There is time enough," his father said after the great Léotard whirred by. The Doctor cried that night because there was no longer anything coming up over the horizon and around the corner into town. The moment had passed. His father returned from a long day of work at the dry goods store to find his son weeping into his mother's lap. "There is time enough," he said, though he never did say for what. "Here," and, reaching into his pocket, he pulled out his pocket watch. "Take it. So you can see how much time there is left." Its tick, tick, ticking, was meant to be a comfort and a reminder.

But there hadn't been enough time.

It was ignorance that caused his mother to die from fever all those years ago, her bedroom filling with unimaginable heat. He hated that his father didn't understand the heat rising off her or how to cool it, and he hated himself for hating his father. Even when his father thrashed in the same hot bed a year later, there was lingering hatred in the boy as the smallpox blisters became sheets of their own, pulling the outer layers of skin from his father until he was no longer his father but any body unraveling.

" . . .And, of course, there is the funicular in Lyon not to be missed . . ."

The world grows dark as the train hurtles along the iron tracks, continuing on its way north, and soon a gibbous moon illuminates the darkening world, casting shadows in the trees, dappling the lakes. The Doctor's knees ache from sitting too long, but he is afraid to move for fear it will excite his traveling companion. Still, he cannot help but shift a little.

The red-cheeked man startles awake and continues, "And the vineyards of . . ."

The train pulls in and out of stations, puffing and *shhhh*ing. In between, the trees of the forests blur together. The Doctor's restlessness is stripped away with his fatigue, and there is the cold root of it. He doesn't want to be one of those for whom more trees will be cleared in the cemetery too soon.

". . . And I've forgotten the Baths of Urhasch . . ."

The light of the moon fills the compartment; it fills the Doctor until he feels he will burst.

2

To keep from being afraid, Albert sometimes says to himself, *Fascinating!* Or, *Magnificent!* Or, *Yet another escapade!* Even when he is lost, he is not lost. No *one fine day he found himself in a public square.* No *it seems* or *it appears* or *not able to say how he got here.* He *is,* he *is,* he *is.* He is *here*: walking somewhere on the road to Poitiers and Longjumeau, Champigny and Meaux, Provins and Vitry-le-François, Châlons-sur-Marne, Chaumont, Vesoul, Mâcon.

Years pass differently on the road. When Albert discovers himself walking, not knowing how he got there, through Budweis and Prague and Leipzig and Berlin, he is thirteen, selling umbrellas for the salesman in La Teste. He is seventeen, spending those first nights newly orphaned in the rotten hollow of a fallen tree, and then eighteen, nineteen, then twenty. He is all of those Alberts. He is himself and himself and himself again.

"...The biggest year for the construction of hotels in Switzerland..." At a nearby table in a tavern at the foot of the Cantabrian Mountains a man makes casual conversation, and "Berne" whispers its way into Albert's head. *Berne, Berne, Berne,* the word as delicious as a cake, and soon he discovers himself, not knowing how he got there, in Berne. For no reason at all, he discovers himself walking through Tournai, through Ostend, through Bruges, through Ghent, through Liège, through Nuremberg, through Stuttgart, and Mulhouse. His blood circulates astonishment to the tips of his fingers and his long nose, throughout his large head and his absurdly large ears (he knows: They are absurd), through the curves of his shapely calves as he walks through Delft and Amsterdam and Zwolle.

When Albert walks, people treat him like a prince; they are that kind. Even the men who put him in prison have been gentle. *Your papers?* He is always without papers. "Smell me," he says, holding out a sleeve to a gendarme who arrests him, his face braced for the worst. "I am not a vagrant." Surely, Albert thinks, a man as clean as he cannot be considered a vagrant. A man with a mustache as meticulously combed and trimmed as his, a vagrant? He is always very clean. Cleanliness is not easy when there is dust and, after it rains, mud to contend with. Even in fields of corn, of cotton, of olives, in the fields filled with sheep, cattle, and hogs (not all of them friendly), he manages. On the road, there are lakes and ponds and rivers. He has resorted to large puddles of rainwater, but he is always clean.

The gentleman at the French consul in Düsseldorf gives him five marks; the consul in Budapest gives him a fourth-class ticket to Vienna; the one in Leipzig gives him seven florins and a lodging ticket; the French ambassador in Prague takes up a collection and buys him a pair of shoes. *Yet another escapade and yet another escapade and yet another escapade!* The mayor of somewhere else entirely puts his arm around Albert's shoulder and says, "Now go home to Bordeaux. There's nothing better than returning home." But to Albert, kicking a fallen apple through the tall grass of another cemetery of toppled, crowded gravestones, home is never more home than when he is leaving, and he is always leaving, tugged like a balloon into the air.

There are those, like the man in charge of the mud baths in Dax, who don't believe Albert has a home even when he tells them again and again he is not a vagrant. Though he might be gone days or weeks or months, though the small cottage he once shared with his father is ramshackle, though its windows rattle in the wind off the harbor, though the bedclothes are tattered, though a mysterious mold grows in the kitchen, though the mice who dance in the pots are raising children in the stove, it is still his home. Once when he discovered himself there, his father's old friend the lamplighter offered to help. He tied Albert to his bed with rope. "To keep you safe," the lamplighter said, tightening the ropes around Albert's wrists and his ankles with hands that smelled permanently of gas. "He would have wanted me to keep you safe," the lamplighter said, and he began to cry. "I know," Albert said. There was something comforting and familiar about the way the ropes held him, but then he woke up somewhere else into some other day, not knowing how he got there, the stray thread on his trousers and his chafed wrists the only sign of the heavy rope. He was not angry or surprised. There was no holding him. There was no keeping him safe.

In Mont-de-Marsan there is a poster above the bar in a public house—a soldier and, trailing behind him, a corps of infantrymen on bicycles waiting to be led into battle. Cyclists are called *les marcheurs qui roules*. When Albert walks, he annihilates distance like a bicycle; he has no use for wheels but covers as much distance. *Un marcheur qui roule tout seul*, Albert doesn't need a war; when he walks he is a hero who has performed deeds of improbable greatness, and though he can't remember what they are, they are surely magnificent. When he walks, it doesn't matter that he can't remember what they are.

When he walks, he is no longer only moving toward death; he is no longer only dying. The gift of life is in his bones. The birds in the sky above him are utterly bird, the shadows cast by leaves totally and completely shadow. Their beauty is indisputable. They *are*. They are *here*. He *is*. He is *here*. Ripe fruit falls to the ground at his feet, offering itself to him. From the riverbeds comes the song of frogs. When Albert walks, he has been kissed. When he walks, his existence is complete and his body is divine; he is elemental as the sky drenched with sun, then infused with red dusk, then night-dark, then sun-bright again.

He walks for days without stopping, without eating, without sleeping, in order to feel the gift of astonishment.

He drifts on the fringes of days where a fog mutes the tick-tock, tick-tock others adhere to so rigorously. *Is it time to go? What time is it? Why is there never enough time?* These are not his questions. When he walks, days and weeks and months are nothing but scurrilous rumor. He trammels winter, spring, summer, fall, as if they were idle gossip.

Where does the time go? Vanished into the woods between Bordeaux and Toulouse? Splashed into the deep black water between Marseille and Blida? Flittered into the sky with the sparrows between Geneva and Strasbourg? Is it somewhere on the side of the road from Vienna to Budapest? It is such-and-such-a-day, people say to him. We are *this* day. We are *here* on the great clock of history. Albert, here you are, in this moment, *right here*, can't you see?

No, he cannot. The world is enamored of time—its shapely hours, its miraculous minutes, its svelte and speedy seconds. The entire world, that is, except for Albert.

This is how it goes, how it has always gone: He begins to fade and then a terrible thirst comes upon him and his body is overcome with restlessness. He must drink water, lots of water. Six, maybe ten glasses of water in a row, and still he is thirsty. He sweats through his clothes and he trembles, filled with a terrible itch. There is a ringing in his ears and in his legs, his hips and his groin; it crescendos, until it becomes a song. He's crescendoed all over Europe: behind the black blots of fir woods near stone cattle tracks; enveloped in the smell of moss and damp stone behind a cathedral; in the dark marshy open, all of nature invaded by a fog.

What will you do? The urge to walk is the answer to this question. It falls upon him and lifts him into heavenly oblivion until he disappears, and when he reappears he is walking again, somewhere else entirely, the sky darkening toward night when before the sun was just rising. The terrible itch gone.

What terrible itch?

Then there are the times when his body begins to fade and that terrible thirst comes upon him, when his body is overcome with restlessness and he is still thirsty even after he has drunk lots of water, and there is a ringing in his ears, and the terrible itch finds its way into his cock, which he prefers to refer to as his beautiful instrument. And so he plays his beautiful instrument. Always gently, as if he is greeting it—hello, *yet another escapade!* The buzz in his legs, his hips, and his groin, he achieves a steady cadence, holding the buzz inside, allowing the song to take shape. Always privately—he is a decent man! Behind this copse of trees or that one, and once or twice behind the cathedral, where it smelled of damp stone and moss. The song crescendos, an especially glorious crescendo, singing back the roots of his bristly hair, the slope of his long, strange nose, his thin mustache, his unusually large head, his absurdly large ears, his exquisitely muscular calves, his carefully trimmed toenails, and his beautiful feet. For these beautiful feet he seeks out clumps of the softest moss, luminous and blue, to pad his mended shoes.

Somewhere outside of Limoges, a man gives him a pair of shoes and he puts his old shoes to rest, burying them under a tree. He bows his head. "Hail Mary, full of grace," he says the way he dimly remembers his mother did long ago, before Albert was left all alone with only this silence waiting to be filled.

Please let it be filled.

And when he walks, it is, fleetingly. For years, Albert's journeys have been fleeting illuminations along a pitch-dark trail: he discovers himself at the Baths of Urhasch in the Canton of Appersell, watching a wrestling match on the side of the road surrounded by ruddy-faced men; he wakes to find himself lying on the platform of the Paris train station, light glinting through the roof, illuminating his body and the metal face of a train spewing steam as it pulls in and, soon, all around him, the feet of bustling people just arrived.

But when he stops.

When he stops, out of the mist near the Société Française in Berlin where he is given papers and new shoes, the face of an enormous dog, followed quickly by the body of the same enormous dog, tumbles him to the ground. The bite is painful, but worse is the man's face hovering above him. "You must be hurt," the face says. *It always hurts*, Albert wants to say, but why begin a sentence he can't finish? The look on the man's face says it must be a problem of translation; he is right, though Albert understands German well enough. How can he be expected to make himself understood in any language when the words trail off from public square to public square, if whole pages are missing from his life?

When he stops, sometimes he discovers himself at home where the mice dance in the kitchen and his friend Baptiste's father forbids Baptiste from speaking to him, where the bedclothes are tattered and moldy and the neighborhood women who once brought him food turn their backs on him as though he is an utter stranger.

When he stops, having discovered himself in this public square or that one, his arms and legs ache. For a fleeting moment, glorious relief: *My body is still here!* That he has woken up in Lausanne in the same body as in Toulouse! That he has the same legs in Dortmund as in Liechtenstein! It is a miracle to wake up somewhere else entirely, still him. But then the tick-tock hammer of time smashes down again. Fascination? *Vanished*. Magnificence? *Vanished*. Escapades? No more. When he stops, it is as if he never existed at all.

This morning, when he discovers himself in a public square, he is an anonymous hunk of rock rumbled forth from the earth, severed from its molten lava past. "It appears . . ." and, "It seems . . ." There are no finished sentences. "Fascinating!" he says, though it is not fascinating, not fascinating at all. He is not *here*. He is not, he is not, he is not. He is nowhere. It is as if the gift of astonishment never existed at all.

What gift?

There are no stars, only the moon disappearing into the morning as the townspeople wake from murmuring dreams into the smell of bread and a day that will be whittled out of hours whittled out of minutes. There is an ache in his thighs, in his back; still, even as he appears he is disappearing like the moon but unlike the moon he is not beautiful, he is only disappearing.

"Have you lost something?" A woman with skin like an aging peach—a soft, pink sag and fuzzy down along her jaw—bends to put a bowl of milk at the base of the monument to some great general. She smells of a life lived outside without soap, of hay and rich soil. Albert inhales deeply, narrowing his focus until he is the smell itself, until the question—*Have you lost something?*—disappears.

"They're starved," the woman says when Albert says nothing. He is grateful she doesn't require him to have a conversation, that she is happy to speak both parts. She wipes her hands on her skirts, nodding toward the cats who appear to be slipping out of the cracks in the cobblestones. They canter toward the milk, slithering between Albert's legs, flicking their tails.

"It appears . . ." he says, "hunger has made them quick."

This woman—her sagging, soft skin, her comforting smell—will soon be gone, along with the swarm of mewling cats.

"Where have you come from?" the woman asks.

He has no answer. The words fade with the disintegrating moon, an outline in the morning sky. It is not an idle threat; everything will disappear.

"It's not far, where I'm from," wanting to offer her something, this woman who does not tell him to go away. He is not an idiot. This is what he would like to say.

"Careful," the woman says as a cat hisses, batting at Albert's leg. "They can be vicious when it comes to getting what's theirs."

He wishes he were a cat filled with such purpose. Every morning to canter across the cobblestones on padded feet toward this woman. Albert wiggles his toes. They are a reminder: *You are here, you are here.* His feet have started to blister; he can feel another blister forming, the hot pinch of skin rubbing against the papery leaves with which he pads his shoes when he can't find the soft blue moss.

"Uh-oh," the woman says, looking over his shoulder. "Here we go again." As she hurries away, the cats gallop after her, tails whipping back and forth as they dart between the legs of the townspeople—men, women, and children—who have gathered at the edges of the public square to see the stranger. The milk from an overturned bowl seeps into the cobblestones.

At first the gendarme standing in front of Albert is the sum of his parts taking shape in the morning light: crisp uniform, large, loose cheeks quivering over a stiff collar; his mouth moves so emphatically his cheeks cascade and quiver as he comes to the end of a sentence Albert hasn't heard the beginning of.

There has been talk. The recent war has caused great concern: men at risk of no longer being men, women at risk of no longer being women, children at risk of never being children in the first place, at risk of never being produced, the family at risk of extinction! The gendarme, whose sentence continues even after he is finished speaking it, a ripple across the lake of those cheeks.

"I admire the cleanliness of your uniform," Albert ventures, because this sort of flattery has worked in the past and because the man's uniform *is* spotless and terrifically stiff. Albert balances there on the pin of its cleanliness, its crisp collar yoking him to the earth.

"Thank you," the gendarme says, his sharp countenance softening for just a moment. He prides himself on being neatly dressed, on being an exemplary representative of the state. Then, coming to his senses, he stands taller. The buttons on his jacket sparkle. "Let me put this very, very . . . what's the word . . . succinctly? The future of our country is at stake, sir. We lost so much in the last war—men, direction, pride. Here you are, a vagrant! You, sir, are a menace."

"You have, it appears, confused me with someone very important," Albert says. "I am *not* a vagrant." *He is not. He is not.* The gendarme's face has grown redder than the ripest tomato.

The crowd assembled on the steps of the church lean forward for a better view. They long for more than the smell of bread and a day whittled out of hours whittled out of minutes. Having never been cracked open, they long to be. The baker shares a few of his freshly baked croissants, biting the end off one himself, releasing a tendril of secret heat into the air.

Albert swirls along with that tendril, preparing to disappear into the air. Poof! But first.

"Aha!" the gendarme cries, turning to the crowd, pointing to Albert's jiggling foot as though it is proof of his menace.

Albert is pale and swaying from his efforts to be still.

"You appear ill. Are you all right?"

Albert is not all right.

"I must go," he says. He wants to go home. He wants nothing more than to go home and find his father sitting in his chair, smoking his pipe. How long has it been—years, or years and years, or perhaps years and years and years that are not gone, only misplaced? Years that have grown heavier in that other place; years that might crush him with their heaviness if they ever found their way back. Oh, he has grown so tired.

"Don't go!" a small girl shouts as he turns to walk away.

The gendarme takes Albert by the arm.

"I am not a vagrant," he says again, though doubt has inched its way into his voice.

He is not. He is not.

"Of course not," the gendarme says, rolling his eyes. But the crowd is not with him.

"Let him go!" they cry. They don't like the gendarme with his sparkling buttons. They prefer the man who has interrupted the rhythm of their day.

"Fascinating," whimpers Albert as the gendarme leads him away. The townspeople on the church steps rise and walk back into their days. "Magnificent," whispers Albert. "Yet another escapade." He is not afraid. He is not afraid. He will not be afraid.

In the jail cell where he is held overnight, time hides under the wafer-thin mattress. It seems, *what?* It appears, *what?* Albert falls gratefully into sleep, only to wake with a stiff neck and a belly covered in the rash of bedbug bites familiar from other nights spent in jail.

Before the gendarme releases him the next morning, he grips Albert's arm. *This,* his grip says, is how important his duty as a man and a citizen are. "You are a disgrace," he says.

This time, when Albert begins his journey home (Which way? Which way?), the only sound is that of a merchant's cart rattling along a distant road. The sky fills with charcoal clouds that darken the whole world and Albert too. Harbingers of nothing, the darkening clouds are reminders that every night the black sky will obliterate even these ominous smears. They remind him that even if the urge to walk arrives to save him, even if he could make it appear to lift him up and sing him into astonishment so that he forgets the misery of his waking life, he will only wake again to discover himself alone, balancing on the head of another pin.

The urgency always comes unbidden. But oh, when it does come, he is overcome. *Oh, Albert.* He is beautiful in this song, even to himself. A silky, silky mist. Lifted into the air, his sadness becomes part of the clouds, eventually raining back down on him transformed, spilling from the branches of poplars turned pale gold when winter's coming. The rain comes too fast to drink; still, it quenches his thirst.

When was he ever thirsty?

What was the question?

3

THE AMPHITHEATER IS HOT and loud with men with high
aristocratic foreheads and aquiline noses, men from families who never doubted their sons would become anything less
than doctors. Or so it seems to the Doctor from where he sits on
the hard wood benches, wedged between these anointed foreheads and noble noses, so certain of their right to be here, while
his low forehead and pudgy nose aren't sure at all. How could
they be sure when they were too busy vying for space on his
already crowded face? He knows his crowded features give him
the look of someone who is perpetually worried, of someone who
has toiled. He has. Surely there must be others who were not
born into the profession. Surely there must be others who spent
the night in a hotel, shabbier even than their shabby apartment,
in order to crash this party. Others whose parents taught them
the value of humility. Then he remembers: The great doctor
himself, the son of a wagon maker whose specialty was decorated
carriages, has toiled too.

He comforts himself with this as he scans the faces of the
men who surround him, from Vienna and Berlin and as far afield
as Riga, whose dignity can't mask their eagerness. Their eyes are

fixed on the center of the theater covered in sawdust to absorb the blood should there be blood. In the center is a synoptic chart on which is scrawled *in the throes of a fit* and *hands during paralysis*, underneath which lie three plaster casts. The first bears the impression of a contorted face; the second is in the shape of two hands rigidly entwined; the third is enormous and so smooth, so fleshlike, it causes the Doctor to look again. Even after he realizes it is only a cast and not the body of an especially pale woman, it looks so fresh he suspects the woman crawled out of it moments ago.

The heavy suck of greed pulls at his coat; it tugs at his skin. *Please*, say the greedy eyes of the high foreheads and the aquiline noses, fixed on the sawdust-covered center of the amphitheater, *let there be just a little blood.*

He tells himself he is being ridiculous. All of this waiting has made him impatient—was waiting also a part of the lesson they were being shown today? He has greed of his own, after all, pulling from the inside out—where did it expect him to go? He can hardly move a quarter of a centimeter, with men crowded shoulder to shoulder on either side of him and the bony knees of the man sitting behind him digging into the small of his back.

"I was a friend of his son, you know," says the eager man with the digging knees. There is something medicinal about the eager man's cologne—like carbolic soap but with a trace of something fishy—or perhaps that is the cologne of the man next to the Doctor. All of the waiting, eager men in the amphitheater have started to blur, one enormous body, ripe and bony. There are the knees of the man sitting behind him again.

"And his *house!*" Monsieur Eager is saying to—the Doctor can only assume, since he cannot turn around—what must be his eager companion. "Dark alcoves, tattered gothic tapestries, melancholics suffering from syphilis squirming on thirteenth century prayer stools. We—that is, myself and my dear friend, his son—ran around dodging the millionaires from Germany, Russia, America, England, Turkey, who come for prescriptions for strychnine or the thermal cure at Lamalou . . ."

Tomorrow there will be a bruise from those digging knees, the Doctor is sure. The ember of irritation that has been burning slowly under his skin becomes a hot flare. He doesn't want to be marked by the bony knees of this shouting fishy man. In an effort not to melt into the amphitheater of eagerness, the Doctor turns his head as much as possible in order to give Monsieur Eager a look that says, *Please, be less eager with your knees.*

Monsieur Eager looks directly at the Doctor—is he pressing his knees even more firmly into the Doctor's back?—as if to say, *And what of it?*

A shrill squeal from somewhere beyond the doors of the amphitheater saves the Doctor from wondering why he even bothered. Every eager head in the amphitheater turns.

"It is the great doctor's South American monkey," Monsieur Eager says, standing to deliver the news, delighted at the opportunity to educate.

Ahhh, says the amphitheater. A few men nearby laugh knowingly, as if they understood all along. *But of course*—a smug nodding of heads—*the great doctor's South American monkey!* The Doctor has heard the rumors: the monkey in a high chair at the great doctor's dinner table chewing bananas and stealing food from people's plates. He puts his jacket back on and takes it off again for the pleasure of digging his elbows one more time into the ribs of the smug nodders on either side of him. He focuses again on the replicas in the center of the sawdust-covered amphitheater, the weight of their possibility. Anything might happen. *This* is why the Doctor has come.

Anything might happen because this man whose monkey dines at his table has planted a flag for the centuries. He has taken an ancient word and made it new again. Anything might happen during one of these famous unplanned lectures they have all traveled so far to see, in which everything unfolds in the moment, in which everything is yet to be discovered. Anything might happen because they are all here to see the great doctor: this man who not only treats millionaires from Germany, Russia, America, Poland, England, Turkey, but lectures on syphilitic aneurysms, cerebral syphilis with gumma formation, meningitis, progressive optic atrophy, who began the first neurology clinic, and now has six thousand patients in his charge, in what he calls his museum of living pathology.

"Prepare yourself: This is the Versailles of pain," the aristocratic forehead in front of the Doctor whispers to the aquiline nose beside him. The Doctor hears it: a warning, a promise, and a wish.

"I've heard he's made a diagnosis of an eighteenth century woodcut," the aquiline nose says, laughing. "Perhaps he'll diagnose a piece of wood for us. His entire office is painted black, you know. The furniture too."

The great doctor is so great he inspires the kind of envy that disguises itself as dismissal. But the Doctor hasn't come all this way to dismiss him. He may not agree with the great doctor's theory that the volatile emotions of the women he treats suggest a disorder of neurologic origin, an invisible lesion that is evidence of a moral crisis. But he understands the complexity of making visible to others one's own vision of reality. This is what drew the Doctor into this line of work in the first place; it's what drew him to the asylum and the philosophy of moral medicine, with its attention to the emotional life of patients, where invisible lesions aren't the only answer. The patients' own poignant effort to make visible to others their vision of reality, this nearly impossible translation, is the larger concern around which the Doctor's life revolves. Why, for example, did Rachel mention *The Flying*

Dutchman and begin to cry for her mother the other day? Why did she stare at her hands for hours on end? Why does she believe a frog lives inside of her? She looks at the Doctor as if she were speaking in intelligible sentences, as if he should know. And then there is Walter, who stops the Doctor in the hallway to ask with great urgency, "Is the woman in the painting my wife?" The Doctor's life is devoted to understanding these efforts of translation whose source cannot possibly be an invisible lesion, or only an invisible lesion, but an invisible life. Every day, when the sun sets and the hornbeams and the lavender bushes that line the public square outside the Palace of Justice appear to be on fire with the red light, the Doctor thinks of the view Richard must have had as he stepped so casually out of an upper-story window of the asylum. The attendant, George, hadn't realized what was happening. "That awful, wet thud," he said before dissolving in tears. George, the largest, hulking attendant they had, who could sling a grown man across his shoulders, suddenly tiny with grief. "They are on fire," he claims Richard said just before, though how could he be sure? It happened so quickly. What did it matter anyway? All that was left was the jutting bone and the blood crawling stealthily away across the cobblestones as if it, like his family who dropped him off one day and then never returned, wanted nothing to do with him anymore. There had been talk around town after that—the Director is too lax, too permissive, these patients need to be restrained, not coddled. But those who were so critical never seemed to have any answers except returning to the days when mental patients were locked up in chains.

The Doctor may not agree with everything the great doctor is up to, but he has inspired him to deeper thinking about the intimate lives that exist underneath the great doctor's diagnosis. The intimate, invisible life *in addition* to the invisible lesion. This is why the Doctor is here. The great doctor has never suggested anything he has not also attempted to demonstrate, so let him make his case.

The great doctor's monkey squeals again. "That poor beast, locked up somewhere," says the high forehead sitting in front of the Doctor, a man whose back has been suffering from the Doctor's own eager knees.

Why is the great doctor not here already, *making his case?*

The monkey squeals again and, as if it is his cue, in walks the man himself, the great doctor.

"There he is," Monsieur Eager announces, as though no one else can see. Everyone leans forward, an amphitheater of knees digging into an amphitheater of backs.

There he is, the humble son of a wagon maker, now the great doctor. The man who has been endlessly discussed and dissected, who has refashioned an ancient word until it is as exquisite and ornate as one of his father's decorated carriages.

He is rotund. Stumpy. *Tiny*, really. The cast of the woman's body is enormous next to him. It could swallow him whole. *So this is all,* thinks the Doctor. Even as he feels a small zing of satisfaction, he is disappointed.

But then the great doctor speaks.

"I hope I haven't kept you waiting long." His voice is a sturdy house into which he invites each one of them. *Come in. Wander around. Take a look in my secret closets.*

The audience laughs nervously, as though it is they who have kept *him* waiting.

"What, then, is hysteria? What is its nature? We know nothing about its nature. Nor about the lesions that produce it. We know it only through its manifestations. Be forewarned: I will not lead you down a well-delineated path."

Dense and muscular, each word adds a centimeter to his height and removes one from his sizable girth. A grandeur hovers around him, a gentle Parisian mist. The Doctor feels the dewy wonder of it on his face; it washes away the smirks from the faces of any detractors.

"I have not pushed aside the thorny bushes that make this journey difficult," the great doctor says. "This lecture is for the benefit of those among you who have not already completed your medical training. I have no embarrassment in finding my way in front of the rest of you."

"He has the head of Napoleon," Monsieur Eager whispers to his neighbor.

The comparison is apt but the Doctor knows, even as the spell is being cast, the close resemblance, that fierce elegance, is carefully cultivated.

"The girl we will examine today suffers from intermittent cramps, trembling, convulsive attacks, and the paralysis of her right leg," the great doctor says. "For the past several days we have waited and watched. We have not interfered."

"She is very fond of ether, I hear," Monsieur Eager whispers.

"Is she clairvoyant?" whispers his companion with his aquiline nose. "I've heard some of them are clairvoyant."

Shhh.

"You cannot claim to have really seen something until you have photographed it," the great doctor says, gesturing to a tall, skinny man hovering in the corner, a pair of spectacles perched precariously on the top of his pointy head.

The tall, skinny man, in the midst of unfolding a tripod, appears to have been magically transported from the grand photography annex the Doctor has read about—a glass-walled studio, dark and light laboratories, a wealth of equipment. Platforms, beds, screens, backdrops in all colors, headrests that serve as vises for those patients who can't hold still to allow a photographer to capture a close-up of ears, eyes, nose. There are rumored to be gallows from which to suspend those patients too distressed to hold themselves upright, which fold up tidily along the wall of the studio at the end of the day.

"*I* am nothing more than a photographer," says the great doctor, "inscribing what I see."

But the great doctor is nothing like *this* photographer. Everyone in the amphitheater can see that. Beneath the camera's black tenting, the photographer's thin legs are indistinguishable from the thin legs of the tripod; from time to time mistaken for the spindly wooden legs of an inanimate object—a piano, for example. His shins are bruised because just the other night, in a restaurant where he'd gone with his wife, someone distractedly and repeatedly swung a foot under a table, mistaking his legs for those of a chair.

"Why you say nothing," his wife said when he showed his bruised shins to her later, "is the bigger question."

The bigger question is easily answered. The photographer prides himself on his talent for fading into the background. It is an art, blending into a room until he is a small flake of paint on the wall, a splinter of wood in the floor, a dust mote in the air. The great doctor wants him to find proof of what he is looking for but the photographer isn't after proof, he is after the question of the spirit enacted in the anatomy, that smoky ghost caught just for a moment in flesh and bone. Before the photographer became a photographer, he had gone to medical school. He had been on his way to becoming a man of science, though, contrary to what his teachers thought, he did not take up photography because of his mediocre grades in anatomy or because he couldn't stomach the sight of blood. He keeps it to himself but what he truly believes is that there is something else to taking pictures beyond recording the facts. Every photograph captures an irretrievable moment. Photography's precision, its science, is what has made it so appealing to men of medicine. Still, in every photograph there is also the mystery of a life moving through time; in every face the photographer captures on a photographic plate, a flicker of something. A life force? A spirit? He doesn't know, but in the corner of an eye, in the twist of a mouth, in the blur of a head turning or an arm flailing, there is something that cannot be contained. *This* is what photography can do. This is what photography is *meant* to do. It eludes him, as art should.

There is something in the photographer's face when the great doctor says, *I am nothing more than a photographer*, that catches the Doctor's attention, a look that says back, *If only you* were *a photographer*. The Doctor recalls a recent article accompanied by the photographer's portraits of the great doctor's women. There was a portrait of a young woman, writhing so parts of her were blurred yet she still looked directly at the camera. The Doctor found himself looking into those eyes, far more composed than her body. The difficulty of portraying the *expressions of the passions* in the face and body. This is how the great painter Charles Le Brun had described the classic problem in painting. But there, in the photograph of the young girl, the photographer had captured the movement of the soul on the body. This tall, skinny fellow lurking in the corner, looking as though he might at any moment become entangled in his equipment, was the man who had done that. He had made the girl's illness visible.

The photographer may pride himself on his ability to disappear but his equipment is very much in evidence. There is a great deal of clunk-clunking as he unwraps another plate from its cotton swathing. The great doctor clears his throat in his direction. From the scowl on his face, it is clear this is not the first time he has cleared his throat in the photographer's direction. The Doctor hears the message too: *Too much clunk-clunking and you will be banished.*

"The reason we have not interfered for these past few days," the great doctor is saying in that sturdy house of a voice, "is that with cases such as this, it is possible to provoke a second attack.

Why provoke such an attack? you might ask. In order to observe whether a symptom that at first seems fixed—cramping, trembling, paralysis—might be changed. Hysteria has its laws. I am merely here to observe them." He looks from eager face to eager face to eager face, and anyone who wasn't a believer is now.

As much as he hates to admit it, the Doctor feels his sharp edges dissolving, becoming part of the great body of eagerness as it waits for whatever the great doctor is about to offer. Then, as if Monsieur Eager has conjured the dust from the tattered gothic tapestries in the great doctor's house, there is a tickle in the Doctor's nose. What can he do? There is nothing to stop it: He sneezes violently.

Shhh! The entire amphitheater turns on him.

The great doctor scans the crowd slowly, an owl—has his head turned all the way around? The Doctor is sure it has. His father's watch tick-tocks in his pocket so loudly that everyone in the amphitheater must hear it ticking off the excruciating seconds as the great doctor locates—hoo-hoo!—his face in the crowd. When he has, he stops and simply looks. And looks. And looks. A photographer after all, inscribing what he sees.

What does he see?

"I'm very . . . sorry," the Doctor stammers into the silence. Monsieur Eager's gloat penetrates the back of his head. It is so much worse than his bony knees. *See?* it says. *You never belonged here.*

Why should he be sorry? Why should he be afraid? Has he come all this way to perch on a sliver of hard bench, jabbed by pointy knees and suffocated by hot, aristocratic bodies, in order to be afraid? He has never been afraid. He has never had the time. His parents never dreamed he would become a doctor. After they died, there were the long nights in the Toulouse railway station as a bookkeeper's clerk and then there were the longer days as a deliveryman—shouldering heavy chandeliers through streets jammed with kitchen maids carrying baskets, and merchants with their unwieldy carts—while he went to school at night. Finally, he hopped aboard the *Niger* to become a cargo clerk on the Bordeaux-Senegal run. It was the ship's doctor who saw in him what he couldn't yet see in himself: the Doctor. He hadn't received that sort of attention since his parents were alive, attention that said decisively, "You look tired. You must go to bed." Or "Come eat. It's dinnertime." The ship's doctor was so certain: *You have a gift*, and so he quickly returned home and took a job as an underlibrarian for the medical faculty while completing his baccalaureate in the sciences. He has worked at the asylum for nearly a year, and only now is he anywhere near becoming the Doctor the ship's doctor predicted he might be.

He will not be afraid. And he will definitely not be sorry. He is not sorry at all. He stares right back. *Here I am. I am what you see.* (What did he see?) Another tremendous clearing of the great doctor's throat—*You too (hoo-hoo) will be banished*—and then, as if the Doctor and his sneeze did not exist at all, he turns away.

"Is there something immoral about provoking such an attack?" he asks the crowd. There is general nodding and muttering and a wrinkling of brows.

"After I observed many patients suffering from the same symptoms, I thought, how can it be that such events are not described in the textbooks? Then one day I was struck with a sort of intuition about them: They are all the same. What you are about to see is not a series of individual small attacks, but a single event comprised of phases that will unfold sequentially. I will identify each phase, provoked by applying pressure to the hysterogenic points, as it occurs."

An attendant hairy as a bear enters the amphitheater, wheeling a girl on a stretcher through the thin layer of sawdust. She is small and translucent, weak and fading. She seems, in fact, to be shrinking. But when she arrives in the center, she sits up. The air, hot and heavy and thick before, shimmers; it is electric. Was it the Doctor's imagination, or has the entire audience leaned forward at once? And then he is leaning forward. The girl is a magnet and all of them little pieces of metal drawn up.

"And now," the great doctor says, "I will give you firsthand experience of this pain."

The girl slides off the stretcher, landing firmly on her feet. She pulls a plump hand through her braids to free her thick tresses. She shakes the waves out of her hair as if she is shaking everyone out of the room. She caresses her hair, fingers her thin nightgown. All these women: The great doctor has cultivated a veritable stable. There has been talk.

"The neurologic tree has many branches," the great doctor says, "and each one bears a diffcrent fruit. You may not be able to see the tremor from where you sit, but it is there."

"One thinks," says the girl, looking in the great doctor's direction though he does not look back, "one has dreamed something but it wasn't a dream at all."

The great doctor turns away from her, looking out at the crowd, but it is as though he were alone in his grand home with its dark alcoves trying to remember where he misplaced one of his thirteenth century prayer stools. Finally he turns back to her. She is small but fierce. They are well matched. For a moment it looks as though they might wrestle.

The photographer waits to press the stereoscopic bulb. Photography requires exquisite patience. The heavy wet collodion plates take time to prepare. Only after the photographer has situated the plate; only after he has framed the shot; only after he has looked again; only after he has focused, and focused again; only after he has adjusted the light and then adjusted it again; only then does he squeeze the bulb.

"Look at that profile," Monsieur Eager says. "That spectacular nose."

A spectacular nose? As if a nose were any indication of great-ness, the Doctor thinks, still furious at his own for betraying him. Still, there it is, that spectacular nose. It is as though the great doctor has had a hand in its shaping, in the same way the Doctor has often felt that his own crowded features are some fault of his own character. As much as he wants the photographer to drop one of those large glass plates on the great doctor's Napoleonic head, it is undeniable. The spell has been cast. What will he do next? There is a reason the great doctor is the great doctor.

This time the monkey's squeal is followed by a resounding thump, as though he is hurling himself against one of the amphi-theater's stout oak doors.

"What do you know?" the girl asks.

In the girl's round face there is heat and anger, and a question the Doctor can't quite name. He is reminded of a demonstration he went to recently, given by the disciple of a man who was famous for his experiments on the facial muscles of rabbits. That night, he used a volta-faradaic apparatus to charge the skin of a woman with electricity. "A veritable living anatomy," the scientist had said, isolating the muscles in the woman's face: there, the muscle for bliss; there, the muscle for fear; there, the muscle for sadness. And then there were the moments in between the grand emotions: between bliss and fear, fear and sadness. It was that in-between look on the woman's face that fascinated the Doctor. There it is—that strange, searching look—on the fierce girl's face too.

Clunk go the photographer's plates as he changes one for the other, and then another flash of light illuminates the amphitheater: the mysterious question on the girl's face inscribed for eternity.

"Her world is without color," the great doctor says, nodding to the hairy-bear attendant, who brings out a wooden chair and presses the girl down into it. "But hysteria has the regularity of a mechanism. There is a choreography, like a dance."

The great doctor holds a hand up to the rustling audience—*silence*—nodding to the hairy bear. The only noise is the thump of the monkey hurling itself against the door.

If the Doctor squints, the girl's face is the face of any girl in the street, a sweet, pretty face that would make him look again. The question written there is not familiar, but it too would make him look twice. It reminds him of Marian when she was carried into the asylum after she woke to discover herself paralyzed from the waist down. She clutched her throat and described a great ball rising in it, choking her, but as he began to ask her even the simplest questions—*How are you feeling now? May I plump your pillow? Would you like a glass of water?*—her hands fell to her lap. As though he were holding up a mirror and in her reflection she saw for the first time her own exhaustion. The great ball in her throat subsided and she began to breathe normally again. She looked at him in the same way the fierce girl looks at the great doctor now. It isn't a question after all but a look of gratitude that might be mistaken for love.

"The first hysterogenic point," the great doctor says, nodding to the hairy bear, who places his hand under the girl's left breast. When the great doctor nods, the hairy bear presses.

The girl rises from the chair, twisting in one direction, wrapping both arms around one side of her waist; abruptly, she swings herself in the other direction, wrapping her arms around the other side of her waist. Then her muscles go limp and she falls to the floor, writhing in the sawdust shavings.

"First, the epileptoid phase marked by contractures and spasms."

The amphitheater is illuminated by another flash. The photographer exists only for the photographs themselves, the pictures that arrive years later, like a star's light; like a star's light, dark around the edges, its miraculous image shining in the center. Here, the squirming figure—had she held still, mid-squirm, for one, two, three seconds?—captured.

As quickly as she fell to the floor, the girl freezes; her legs go stiff and her mouth opens, sawdust shavings speckling her hair. Flash: an image of her stiff arms by her side, her entire body gone rigid.

A few eager men clap politely.

Shhh! say the same men who knew about the monkey, those who want everyone to know they know better.

"Tonic immobility. And now, the second hysterogenic point," the great doctor says. The hairy bear bends over, pressing the girl just below her ribs.

"Remember," the great doctor says, "we are not dealing here with simulation."

The girl has rolled onto her stomach, reaching behind her for her feet. Her face, a contorted mask that is no longer gratitude or love. The in-between, this is where the Doctor would like to pause; this is what he is interested in. He would like to ask the girl why she is wearing that contorted mask and what it means but stillness is not the point here. The girl has taken hold of her ankles; pulling, she becomes a bow, rocking. Then, just as quickly, the rocking stops.

Flash: an image of her with her back impossibly arched, her hair cascading behind her.

Ohhhh, says the audience, and even as he wishes for stillness, the Doctor hears himself *ohhhhing* too.

"The *arc de cercle*," says the great doctor. "We have arrived at the stage of large movement, in which the patient assumes contorted postures. The third hysterogenic point . . ."

The hairy bear reaches underneath the girl and presses the side of her waist, and her body goes limp. Then she is scrambling to her feet again, shaking him off. As if an invisible force is acting upon her, she begins to stumble.

"I have a spider in my eye," the girl says. Her eyes flutter; one eye fixes itself in a wink. Her movements are more and more illogical; she appears to be a jumble of limbs gathered from different bodies. A slow tremor shivers through her. She falls to her knees, hands in prayer, eyes raised. Flash: an image of her crying "Oh, God, forgive me," as she begins to weep.

"*Attitudes passionelles*," the great doctor says. "Here the patient reenacts past emotional events." On her knees, the girl makes the sign of the cross. "A statue of living pain."

With a quick jerk of her shoulders, she falls back as though someone has yanked her. She thrashes and twists. Flash: an image of her mouth making the shape for the sound the audience is making. O. Leaping to her feet, she thrusts a hip to one side and turns to the great doctor. Flash: an image of her as she says, "Get rid of the snake in your pants."

"Eroticism," the great doctor says.

The girl looks up into the audience. "When I am bored, all I have to do is make a red knot and look at it."

The Doctor thinks of Marian in the courtyard the other day, turning her attention to the single red flower triumphantly blooming among the green shoots in the asylum flower garden. The sun isn't the only thing that speaks to her: there are the trees, the benches, the figures in the stained glass, the Virgin Mary who, it turns out, is very concerned the patients are not being fed properly, and the red flower too. The red flower frustrates her because it speaks a foreign language she has not yet learned. If she could only learn it, she said, and he'd had to call one of the attendants over to prevent her from banging her head against the wall in an effort to shake the language loose. The beautiful red flower isn't beautiful to her; it is a red knot to be undone.

"I'm not sure what we have here," the great doctor says, aiming the same stern owly look at the girl that he had aimed at the photographer and then at the Doctor. *You will be banished.* Still, for a moment the Doctor thinks he may have lost control; the girl may no longer be willing.

"You don't want any more?" she shouts.

Flash: an image of her pausing as she begins to pull something from her open mouth, from somewhere deep in her throat. The Doctor believes her entirely capable of conjuring something; he is only waiting to see what that something will turn out to be.

"Darling," the great doctor says, as if she is his wife with whom he is having a quarrel.

The great doctor nods to the hairy bear who steps forward and puts his hand on the right side of the girl's waist and presses.

"Mother! I am frightened." The fierceness gone; she is just someone's lost daughter.

"Note the emotional outburst," says the great doctor.

"Oh, Mother!" the girl cries.

"Not quite regular as a mechanism today," the aristocratic nose in front of the Doctor whispers to the high forehead.

"The belt," the great doctor says to the hairy bear, who leaves the amphitheater. To the audience he says, "This is no ordinary pain."

It is hard to tell from this distance, but the Doctor believes he sees a smile pass over the girl's face. Certainly the girl's pain is anything but ordinary. There is that great distance between where she began and where she has arrived; underneath the surface pattern that allows for the great doctor's diagnosis, the messier life.

"The ovary compressor," the great doctor announces when the hairy bear returns with a device comprised of a leather strap and a screw. "It may be directed at a particular hysterogenic point, then loosened or tightened as needed." The hairy bear secures the belt around the girl's slender hips, pulling it tight, turning the screw to secure it, and slowly, very slowly, she begins to list from side to side, a metronome: *tock, tock, tock.* Slower and slower. *Tock. Tock. Tock.*

"She may enter the withdrawal phase now. This phase can last for hours. Even days. The belt will give her a bit of peace."

The girl's movement has become so slow it is almost imperceptible.

"But she can't wear it forever," the great doctor says.

The hairy bear hoists her up on the stretcher, where she goes completely still. Her light has gone out. Once again, she appears to be sleeping; once again, she appears to be shrinking.

The monkey thumps against the door.

"The regularity of a mechanism," the great doctor says. *The monkey or the girl?* the Doctor wants to ask.

"He is amazing," Monsieur Eager whispers.

As much as he wishes for the girl to rise from the stretcher, as much as he is puzzled by what has just happened, the Doctor can't deny it.

"Oh, Mother," the girl says again, lifting her head, then laying it down again.

Flash: an image of the girl collapsed, arms hanging by her side, her eyes looking back over her shoulder. Then the hairy bear wheels her out of the amphitheater, the girl's look still a dare: *Take a photograph. Here I am.*

The keening that comes next fills the amphitheater. It might be a tree falling; it has that momentum, the sense of anticipation in advance of something inevitable and loud. It is the girl, the Doctor thinks. It is the sound of her very soul. The great doctor will be proven wrong—the soul does not have the regularity of a mechanism, it is not so easily described after all. Even as he thinks this, he realizes it is a childish wish.

"That," says the great doctor, "is the monkey. He does that every time."

But the Doctor will remember it as the sound of the girl. On his way home, as the train pulls in and out of stations with its giant's puff and *shhh*, its mighty exhalation of warm, wet steam rushing through him like breath, the squealing of its brakes will echo that keening.

Later still, when he has arrived home, restlessness will drive him down to the brothels by the river, to the woman with the pretty tousled hair. The tick of his father's watch will disappear as the woman's dress swishes to the floor. "That does it," he will hear a man wandering the docks say, followed by the smash of a glass bottle. "It would be tragic if it weren't so funny," the man's companion will say. The woman will use her pinkie to trace a circle on the back of the Doctor's thigh. "There," she will say, and trace another circle. "And there." *There, there,* as if he were her child.

In the silence that follows, he will hear the girl: *Mother, I am frightened.*

4

THE PATH IS ROUGH-HEWN, a suggestion: *Follow me!* Stray tree branches reach across; the blackberry bushes grow thick on either side; and the vast webs spun by resilient spiders are invisible except just after it rains when drops of water dotting the webs glitter with sunlight. Still, while the Doctor rides the train back from the City of Lights to the Port of the Moon, the Director prepares to lead the patients down this path from the asylum to the creek in order to contemplate nature. Today, there is no sun. There is no sun and so Marian, who would not be willing to risk the loss of yet another organ to her great glowing enemy, is, to everyone's relief, very willing. The Director will lead the way as he always does, snapping off the stray branches, clearing the sticky strands of spiderweb with whatever garden tool he happens to be carrying.

The walk to the creek is always an adventure, but the Director feels his efforts are worthwhile. It is worth the scratches from stray branches to have glimpsed a fox slipping through the woods, hiding itself in a blackberry bush to boldly watch the group of humans make their way. It is worth Rachel's complaints about her muddied clothes to discover a bird's wing in the middle of the path in the midst of loose feathers, an idea of a bird. Much to Nurse Anne's dismay, the Director allowed Elizabeth, who likes a project, to carry the wing and the feathers back to the asylum on that particular trip. She likes a project but has never finished a single one; she has been fiddling with the wing and the feathers ever since.

More than anything, the Director likes to remind them, these trips are occasions for beauty. "The Koine Greek word for *beauty* contained the word for *hour*," the Director says, and most in the assembled group don't remember this isn't the first time he's enlightened them with this fact. Each time, a revelation. They are so often off in other worlds, complex systems of their own making. The first time he explained that beauty means *being of one's hour*, the bells of St. Eloi rang as if on cue and he watched their faces as the information became part of the larger scheme of signs and symbols. The constellations in each patient's mysterious night sky made it necessary for one of the attendants to accompany them—last night Marian had to be slung over Claude's shoulder and carried to her room because her left side went numb and she could not get up from the dinner table; the day before yesterday, Samuel required both Claude, whose enormous potato-shaped body contains surprisingly agile strength, and his son Henri, a man of less bulk but greater speed, to restrain him. But today he announced he wants to go outside. The Director knows that more often than not the complex systems win, and so he has asked Henri to accompany them on their walk to the creek.

The veteran's complex system is winning now, just when the Director thinks he has successfully gathered everyone to head out the door. "Fuck!" the veteran shouts again.

"His nerves," Walter says, nodding sympathetically. His own nerves, and the nerves of other morally deprived men such as himself, the veteran, for instance, often vibrated; sometimes they became blackened from too much vibrating and surely the others could smell the burning? But he has other concerns, such as distinguishing between the fleetingly improvised concoctions and those among them who are real.

"It's not the veteran's nerves I mind," Nurse Anne says. She nods to Claude, who takes the veteran's arm and pulls him close to his bulk.

The veteran prefers *the veteran* to his name, which no one is sure he remembers after watching two of his brothers die on the battlefield where he continued to fight only to return home to find his mother had died waiting for her sons to return home. Unless he tells people he is a veteran, who will care, who will even *know*, about the only thing he has done of which he is proud? Even if that thing meant leaving one of his brothers to die alone because he did not want to die too because he could not watch one more brother die. One was enough; one was more than he could bear, and why was he allowed to bear it? He has nightmares that cause him to twitch and fill him with a constant, relentless rage from which there is no relief, which is what he deserves, and why wouldn't his nerves be angry too? The name he insists on is reminder and punishment.

"Fucking fuck!"

The Director looks at Nurse Anne. *Let him be*, he tries to say with his look, *let him come outside and experience the beauty of his hour*, but she is stricter than the Director and doesn't believe the beauty of someone's hour is more important than learning self-control. "This cannot continue," she says. "Besides, he claims to have told Rachel he was going to shoot her in the face."

"Rachel doesn't mind," says Marian, peering suspiciously up at the cloudy sky. The sun often takes her by surprise.

She is right. Rachel has been occupied with the problem of her mother's hands. "Come, darling," Henri says to her. Darling. It's what the creature calls her too—the creature she calls the *frog.* That's as close as she can get to naming the thing inside of her. "Stay, darling," it whispers, wanting her to stay here, to sit at the piano and solve the problem of her mother's hands, to ignore Henri. Whose side is he on as he takes her away from the beloved piano and moves her forward so there is room for Samuel to stand closer to the group? She swats him away with her hand, and when she does she sees her mother's hands but they weren't moving; they were motionless in her lap as they sat in the matinee of *The Flying Dutchman.* They didn't move at all, even when Senna fell in love with the portrait of the phantom captain whose plight it was to sail around the world until he found a love so absolute it would break the curse. Like Senna, Rachel had fallen for the phantom captain too that day. She was always falling for the ghost. Had it started then or long before—the ghost inside of her, taking shape? If only her mother had lifted her hands from her lap, reached over, and—what? Rachel imagines sticking a fork in one of her mother's hands. They would not be so still then. The music filled Rachel that afternoon until she wanted to bite something. She wills her own hands to move now, but they are still too and her mother goes blurry. That other life seems like a dream. It might very well have been.

Like the dream of Claude using his bulk to nudge the veteran down the hall.

"I hate shit-licking nature," the veteran says, his mouth twitching.

"Finally," Nurse Anne whispers to the Director. "Some relief from all that *fucking.* Go now, while you can."

And off they go, marching down the birch-lined path: the Director leading the way, bearing his trowel like a scepter; then Marian, her face hidden by a hat and veil; then Walter, a head shorter than Marian, his arm looped through hers, to console her, he claims, though everyone knows it is she who consoles him; then Elizabeth, quick green eyes fierce and vigilant, scanning the world for a miracle; then Rachel, her hands smoothing her stomach to settle the impatient frog; and finally Samuel, his knobby frame drowning in the enormous coat he wears no matter the weather, frightened eyes drowning in his face, accompanied by Henri, a hand hovering at Samuel's back. The group makes its way down the hill to the break in the bushes that marks the beginning of the path where, with the grand gesture of a discoverer laying claim, the Director swipes away a magnificent spiderweb with his trowel.

Samuel yelps—the poor spiders, ruined. They will have to start over from nothing.

"Of course, this is simply intuition and conjecture," Walter is saying to Marian as he knees a waist-high fern out of the way in order to sidle up to her.

"Don't disturb my hat," she says.

"I'm trying to tell you something," says Walter. "I am nowhere near your hat."

"You are breathing on it," says Marian.

"I am breathing out of the other side of my mouth," says Walter. "What I'm trying to tell you is the very thought of the water has greatly increased my feeling of voluptuousness."

"You are still breathing on my hat," she says. "I feel you breathing on my hat." How could she know that her lack of interest only increases his desire to tell her about the nature of his voluptuousness?

All the way to the creek, Walter attempts to capture it in words. ". . . A softness inside of me, like rabbit fur, against my cheek but the inside of my cheek, a softness *inside*, not too furry, not choking fur, not a fir tree, for example, but expanding . . ."

When they arrive on the narrow rocky bank, the Director says, "Don't forget to take off your socks and your stockings as well as your boots."

Marian has already unlaced her boots and unhitched her stockings, making her way carefully along the string of mossy rocks toward what the Director calls the tiny waterfall, the place where the creek bubbles up over a pile of larger rocks. She has left Walter on the bank, midsentence—". . . expanding out and out, but not in a bad way. I am full of . . ."—but he is accustomed to this.

"Watchful reverence," says the Director, ankle-deep in the creek. "This." Using the trowel to gesture. "The leafy shadows of the trees, the cool water between your toes. That breeze. This is what we are here for. Samuel! Come into the water, Samuel."

Samuel stands on the shore, dipping one trepidatious toe.

"Henri, come in. He'll follow you."

But everyone knows Samuel will not follow no matter how much Henri coaxes him.

"It is surely a divine miracle," says Elizabeth, watching as her skirts float on the surface of the water. She leans over to push her floating skirts below the surface, where they wave silkily. "Ah, yes," she says, her sleeves soaked and dripping. "Yes. Yes." Another divine miracle. Her body is the site of divine miracles. Her face soiled with food? Divine miracle. A broken tooth? Divine miracle. Frostbitten feet? Divine miracle. She has no memory of bolting her food or banging her head against the table or putting her feet through the heavy bars of her window on a day so cold the trees were entombed in ice.

"Yes, Elizabeth," the Director says. "Strange and wondrous, this life. You never solve its mystery. Close your eyes. Everyone, close your eyes. Pay attention."

And they do, listening to this moment that smells like spring light. The songbirds: A phoebe? A wren? The wind rustles the leaves of a willow tree. Even when they cheat and open their eyes, this strange life remains mysterious—the light on the water, the silver, blue, green blur of dragonflies. Everyone held in the soft arms of quiet: Marian, who is afraid to be outdoors; Samuel, who is afraid of everything; even Rachel's frog goes silent. Walter, in his increased voluptuousness, standing right here, is as real as the sound of the water running over the rocks and the silhouettes of the tree branches that cut the sky. But maybe the realness is just a dream he is having? Still, there is the relief of distraction and forgetting—he has forgotten the crackling noise he hears each night in the wall of his bedroom. For a moment, there is relief. There it is.

They are all fleetingly beautiful; they are all fleetingly of their hour. They are here and nowhere else.

"Nature," the Director says, "is alive. It is where the visible and the invisible coexist. Watch with reverence, and you will see it."

And then time begins again. The great shapeless mass of fear—the one that has followed Samuel since he was a boy—returns. His parents, so sure they could manage him themselves, but then he was no longer a boy. He grew and he was no longer so easily managed. If Samuel could describe it, he might describe it like this: a shadow growing longer and longer, until everything becomes shadow, erasing the borders of the world, erasing his borders, until everything is part of everything else. He blurs into the sky and the sky into the wind and the others are smeared into each other and into him. He feels himself spilling into the creek. What is *himself*? There is nowhere to go to escape; he is already part of nowhere. *Nowhere*. The word fills him until he begins to shake. *Nowhere*. He stamps his feet in the creek to get the word out and the water splashes back. *Nowhere*. "I can't," he says. "It is too much." Henri moves toward him swiftly, wrapping his arms around him from behind. Henri has worked long enough at the asylum to have mastered the rough art of restraint, but with Samuel he is gentle until there is no other choice.

"Sammy, you are fine. You are fine."

"It is too much." Samuel's voice is a whisper through the trees. It is the rustle of the wind. "I can't."

Only the giant coat quiets him. "Here." Henri pulls it closer around Samuel, holding him with it.

"We should go back," Rachel says. She is the youngest and prone to weeping. When she begins to cry, Elizabeth moves away. Her own tears are a divine miracle. Rachel's tears are contagious and disgusting.

"Shoes and socks, everyone," the Director says.

"Samuel is too small for his emotions," Elizabeth says, her wet skirts dragging heavily behind her until she is back on the bank where a magpie picks at the laces of her boot. "Look, a 'pie!" she shouts as it flicks its long pointed tail at her and flies off chattering.

"Only one of those is bad luck," Marian says. "Two? A divine miracle."

"How do you know there wasn't another?" Elizabeth asks. "How do you know? Perhaps he had a more subtle companion."

"Don't worry about the dirt," the Director says to Rachel, who is reluctant to sit on the ground because the frog disapproves. The frog would like to return to the asylum immediately and this makes putting her shoes back on difficult; its desire is an ache in her muscles.

"How kind, Elizabeth," the Director says when she allows Rachel with her contagious tears to put a hand on her shoulder for balance. She is willing to risk infection if it means being touched.

"I, myself, am enlivened by a joyful spirit of hope," Walter says, popping a blackberry into his mouth.

"Well, good, Walter, good," the Director says, sounding relieved. "Very good."

"Will you take my arm?" Marian asks, straightening her veil. She misses him when he is not at her side pestering her.

"Of course, my dear," he says, and they follow the Director, who walks ahead of Henri and Samuel, safe again inside his giant coat.

"Sammy's fine," Henri says, fixing Samuel's coat more securely around his shoulders. "You're tired is all. We're all tired."

Through the woods they go and back up the slope. Back along the birch-lined path, and then they are trooping into the common room in their wet and muddied clothes, clumps of creek clay on their shoes. "I see you've brought nature back with you," says Nurse Anne. "I suppose it might get lonely out there on its own." She eyes Samuel trembling in his coat and Rachel's freshly tear-streaked face.

"Wait," and she wipes the mud off Rachel's skirt before Rachel sits down at the piano.

These trips always end this way, in tears or something like tears, even when there is a curious fox or the beautiful wing of a bird. But for that fleeting moment of quiet contemplation, the Director will return to the creek again and again and again. He salutes Nurse Anne with his trowel; despite her scowl, he knows she believes it is worth it too.

"Who knew there was so much mud in the world?" she says. But she does trust him, this man who treats patients as children rather than animals, who prefers walks in nature to bloodletting, chains, and manacles, who has faith that patients may be restored through self-discipline in a place that is more a household than an institution, who knows he does not have all of the answers but believes he is doing his best. Rachel begins to play a Beethoven sonata; its bright key of E major suggests a desire to return to serenity, but first it wanders through improvisational wilderness. Marian curls into the armchair by the fire and Walter settles by her feet to continue talking about the voluptuousness he feels in the midst of nature. "Yes, yes," Marian says. "A furry, furry rabbit." Elizabeth has returned to the puzzle she undid this morning in order to start over again, and Samuel hovers in a corner whispering to Henri. Nurse Anne truly believes the Director is doing his best. It is why she is here. It is why she stays.

"You look very well," she says to Marian. "You too," she says to Walter. On her way past, Nurse Anne touches Samuel's shoulder, hidden somewhere in that giant coat. Order, the comfort of structure—this is what she has to offer. It's what keeps her own occasional desire to flee these people from creeping into her voice. She calms herself by thinking of that time on her way to and from the asylum, not there yet, not yet home, the time she has to herself when she thinks only of her body moving through the cool spring air—*this, this, this.* "Tomorrow will bring a new day," she says when Elizabeth, distressed over a missing puzzle piece, the piece that's always been missing, begins to twitch. Nurse Anne imagines tomorrow as a shadowy figure delivering a tiny wrapped gift and she almost laughs at the idea of unwrapping the new day: Fresh terror! But she doesn't laugh. She bends down, knees cracking, and tries to catch Elizabeth's shifting eye, which hovers around the blank space where the puzzle piece should go. "Tomorrow will bring a new day," Nurse Anne says again in her gentle, persuasive tone, and who could argue with that?

5

WHAT WAS THE QUESTION?
The only problem with oblivion is it doesn't last. Over and over, Albert has woken not knowing where he is—here, then there—not knowing how he got there. The sky filling with those charcoal clouds darkening the whole world and him too, and then he's fading again with that terrible thirst, sweating and trembling, his body ringing with the ache of it until finally the ringing becomes a song. Oh, Albert. He is beautiful in the song, walking, astonished, but the song keeps ending and the sky keeps filling with those charcoal clouds and he is so tired.

He walks through time as if it were as transparent as the bright spring air. But it is not. Tomorrow he will appear in the courtyard of the asylum across from the small stone church, but first there is Albert walking through time as if it had nothing to do with him.

Fascinating? Magnificent? Yet another escapade?

He discovers himself lying naked in the dark, not knowing where he is, not knowing how he got there. A fleeting illumination along the pitch-dark trail of his mind: there had been a shimmer on the verge of taking shape, and something unfolded deep inside of him, a pocket of space that opened and opened and opened until it was a hole through which he was falling. He fell through himself, and now he is here. "But you told me to wake you. Last night you told me," a woman is saying, her heart-shaped face losing its heart in her anger. "You said wake me. You said I need to get the train in the direction of Lectoure. It is not my fault you are angry." She slams the door behind her, and Albert lights the gas lamp to study the situation, first throwing back the covers to see what is left of him. All of it; it's all there. He touches his velvety cock, rising to meet his hand, ready for a crescendo that will lift him out of himself, save him from this terror of not knowing, of never knowing. The woman with the heart-shaped face was pretty even as her face lost its heart. A fleeting illumination: a woman lay down beside him once in a field where he slept, sent over by people standing around a fire. "They'll pay me if they can watch," the woman said, putting her hand on his beautiful instrument, but she wanted money, and besides, it is safer and easier for him to take care of his own pleasure, which he does while thinking of that woman and her quick hand, its smoky smell, and the swing of her large hips, her supple ass as she walked back to join the fire people. When he is done, when he is not fortunate enough to be lifted into the oblivion that obliterates the problem of now, what can he do but wash and dress in this hotel room he doesn't remember checking himself into? Reaching into his jacket pocket, he discovers a train ticket he doesn't remember purchasing. He wishes he could leave himself behind in the tangled sheets he doesn't remember sleeping in. *Stay here. Don't follow me.* But there he is, still himself, insisting.

"Do you know when is the train in the direction of Arcachon?" a man in the lobby asks the clerk. Hearing the word, Albert is suddenly very thirsty. *Arcachon Arcachon Arcachon.* The tremor moves through his toes into the arch of his right foot and when he tries to jiggle it loose, the urge leaps into the other foot. *Arcachon Arcachon Arcachon.* The ringing in his ears has become a song and off he goes until he is falling through the pocket of space that opens without warning inside of him into another unfamiliar place.

There are moments when he thinks he might be dreaming, that it has all been a dream from which he might awake. This is what he wishes when he discovers himself behind the horse and its rider on a muddy road with a rut six feet deep. Without warning they begin to sink. Albert's heart lifts at first. Surely this must be a dream. The rider kicks the horse, beats it with a stick, but the mud holds the horse fast, sucking it down. Kicking and beating are of no use and the rider is forced to leap off, to watch helplessly as the horse sinks up to its chest, its neck thrashing. Albert watches with the rider, who weeps as the horse thrashes and squeals until mud fills its nostrils and its mouth, until it is too tired to squeal. The horse's eyes stop rolling back in its head; they go still with hopelessness. *It is better not to thrash,* the eyes say.

Several men happen by in a carriage; with a rope they help the weeping rider drag the enormous body of the horse out of the sucking mud. After everyone has gone, Albert watches the still surface as though something might rise up out of it. *It is better not to thrash.* He is thick and deaf with sludge. He doesn't care anymore if the urge to walk comes or not. He is a shrouded version of a man who will leave behind only his simple, heavy body to be carried away. If he doesn't thrash, will someone carry him away, out of this life?

But when he finds himself in a shambles of a public square—not even a monument to such-and-such general—he has not been carried away, not at all. He is still himself, though he seems to be disappearing with greater frequency. How could he ever be sure, but it seems as if he is himself less and less. It is a town so poor the people wear vests with old coins for buttons and hats of worn black felt. Some people have no shoes at all. A large great-coat covers their misery.

"Would you like something to eat?" a child with a dirt-streaked face asks Albert, holding out a fat-fried potato in his pudgy hand. Nearby, his mother hangs clothes on a line. "He'll come back," she says through the clothespin between her teeth. She is speaking to her friend whose husband has gone on another bender.

"Or maybe he won't," the other woman says, "I should be so lucky." The way she laughs, Albert knows she doesn't mean it. There may be misery here, but every morning these women wake up into a family of the sort he will never have. To have a family requires being in one place. You cannot be the sort of man who ends up in Verdun with the echo of sheep bells in your head when you were meant to meet a woman who said she wanted to marry you at four o'clock somewhere else entirely.

"Would you like a potato?" the boy says, his hand still outstretched.

The boy's kindness is more than Albert can bear. Better that the woman hanging clothes should run him off or have him thrown in jail. Better to tell him he is not fulfilling his duties as a citizen, to accuse him of causing the nation's downfall.

What about love? It is somewhere else. Not for him. Never for him.

He wiggles his toe through the rustling leaves in his shoes. He hopes the child will understand.

Understand what? What day? What gift?

What was the question?

There is no explaining, so he does the only thing he knows how to do. Though his legs ache, though all he wants is to stop, he walks away.

"Wait!" the child calls after him. "Come back! I can make it smaller. I will cut it in half." The boy hurls the fat-fried potato after him in frustration. He was being kind the way his mother always told him to be. Why wouldn't this man receive his kindness? A bird, startled out of a holm oak, swoops down to where the potato lies in the dirt, spears it with its beak, and flies away.

"Come back!" cries the boy, a tug in his stomach. He is filled with a powerful longing he doesn't understand. He wants the man who is walking away to turn around more fiercely than he has wanted anything in his short life, but the man only becomes smaller and smaller and smaller.

"Stop your shouting," his mother shouts, and though the boy will eventually stop his shouting, though he will return to playing games—stealing his father's worn felt hat and dropping it down the well, for example—for days he will think about the man disappearing over the horizon. The boy's heart will be heavy with that image, and though it will fade eventually, it will return to him when he is a man and feeling melancholy. *What was that?* He won't be able to place it. It must have been a dream he had once long ago when he was a boy capable of conjuring such things.

"Don't go!" Albert hears the boy calling out to him, but it is too late. The bird with the potato in its beak flies past his ear. He hears the boy calling him even after he has walked so far away he couldn't possibly hear him. *Don't go!* As if there were a life for Albert there.

There is no life for him there. There is no life for him anywhere. This is no life at all.

He discovers himself fading with the light, trembling with cold amid the rubble of a cemetery wall half pulled down to make room for more victims of cholera. Though he doesn't know it, he is not far from home. He is not thinking of home. He wants only to sink into the mud. *It is better not to thrash.* Let him die right there in the cemetery. No one will have to drag him from a muddy rut; no one will have to shoulder his dead body out of town. Just dig a hole.

When he sees the lamplighter, grizzled and trembling with age, Albert believes he has gotten his wish: the man must be coming to bury him here where he lies.

"Is that you, boy?" the lamplighter says, pulling him up from the cold flattened gravestone where he has been lying. "I thought I saw a shape from the path that looked like a man. I wasn't sure if . . . it's been so long. Is that you, Albert?"

"Tell me you're not a dream."

"Stand up," the old man says. Albert is tired, so tired, too tired; he leans into the warmth of the lamplighter's body, the arm around his shoulder. "There is no need to cry. Come, now," the lamplighter says, pulling Albert to his feet.

He is so cold and stiff he can barely walk even with the old man's help, but he allows the lamplighter to guide him into the city, the home he is forever leaving, through the winding streets reeking of horse piss. He leans into the warmth of him as he escorts him past the public gardens with the Spanish chestnut trees under which the rats scurry, through the Cathedral Square where the men who live inside the tick-tock of regular days gather at the end of the work day, never worrying about wandering away. "Where has the time gone?" Albert imagines them saying to one another as he's heard other men say so breezily. They don't mean "Where is yesterday?" or "Where is the month of March?" Time has not really gone anywhere; it has not abandoned them, for example, in a cemetery to die.

"Look," a man Albert doesn't recognize says, though the laughing and pointing are familiar. "The man with the . . . *Oh! Oh!* My beautiful instrument!"

"What is wrong with you?" barks the lamplighter. "Go home. Leave him be."

Once more, kindness is so much worse than ridicule. Albert wants only to return to the cemetery. He wants to lie down and sink into the earth. Cover him with dirt; he will become the dirt.

But the lamplighter won't let him go and then they are passing the little church of St. Eulalie, where during the day men and women, so appealingly clean, whisper up and down the aisles, bowing their heads, kneeling and praying.

And then, *tsk-tsk*, out of the cold darkness of the church a cloaked figure appears into the shadows of dusk, clucking its tongue.

"I have seen you," hisses a familiar voice, throwing back a cloak to reveal her sharp eyes and clucking tongue. It is the witchy-looking woman who stands guard each day to harangue anyone who will listen and those who won't on the subjects of good and evil.

"Be quiet," the lamplighter says, though he knows as everyone does: She sees everything

"Behind the cathedral, abusing himself." Her loose neck jiggles as she speaks. "God curses you."

"God would not even bother to curse you," the lamplighter says.

"This man!" the woman shrieks at a group of men passing by. "He has committed unspeakable acts."

"It sounds as though you'd like him to commit them again," one of the men says, laughing.

The witchy woman grabs a bucket and hurls the filthy water. The lamplighter shouts and tries to pull Albert clear, but his clothes are drenched, the clothes he has taken such care to keep clean in spite of the dust and the mud of the road. He has walked great distances in search of rivers, in search of ponds.

It is better not to thrash. He will not thrash. He goes limp in the lamplighter's arms.

"You know nothing," the lamplighter shouts at the witchy woman. "Nothing." The filthy water has splashed him too, but it doesn't matter. All those years ago, when everyone else turned their backs, the lamplighter remained friends with Albert and his father. He had done what he could, but it wasn't enough. Once—it had been some time now, a year at least—he tied him to the bed, as Albert's father surely would have done had he been there, to keep him from walking but it hadn't worked. After that, from time to time, he would see the boy around town but recently he had not and he had come to believe Albert was gone forever. *Disappeared* was as much as he allowed himself to imagine, vanished over the horizon. To imagine the terrible end the boy might have met on the road, it was too much. Now the lamplighter has the chance to make it right as much as it is possible to make it right. He pulls Albert, heavy in his wet clothes, dripping with the filthy water, toward the large iron gates across the street from the small stone church.

"Are you taking me to the cottage?" Albert asks.

"You will be safer here." The lamplighter does not tell Albert that his home no longer exists, and Albert does not ask. The cottage where he and his father used to live, the cottage by the river, caught fire when a neighbor's gas lamp was blown over by the wind. A whole row of cottages, burned to the ground. He gives Albert a gentle push. "Go," he says. He is a kind man, a loyal man, but he cannot bear to involve himself again. It was years ago, but the time he tied Albert to his bed still lingers; it did no good. Nothing ever has. It is more than his goodwill this boy who hasn't been a boy for years needs, and so the lamplighter leans through the bars of the iron gates to call to a large man who appears to work here. "Will you let us in?"

A nurse who seems to glide just above the earth will take Albert by the arm and lead him through the empty courtyard of the asylum. "We will feed you," she will say. "But first you must rest." He will hear a woman crying out that her stockings have fallen down again; a man crying, "Fuck, fuck, fuck," and making the sound of a shooting gun; a doctor calling for a nurse; the bell attached to the giant clock of St. Eloi's ringing in the hour, and then another bell. Altogether, these sounds will create a new sound. Albert will listen to the new sound as the nurse leads him down a long hall. "We will find you a room," she will say, and this will become part of the music too.

How could he know that someday the word for the convergence of these sounds—*fugue*—will also describe the sound of his astonishment and his anguish, the sound they make when they are played together?

It doesn't matter. It has been so long since he has heard any song but his own; he had forgotten there were others.

Listen.

6

I N THE CENTER OF the public garden there is a lake, and in
the center of the lake float a gaggle of sleeping geese, heads
tucked beneath their wings. Each morning, the Doctor aspires to
ride his bicycle so smoothly that its mechanical whisper—click-
clickety-click—doesn't wake the geese. With great concentration,
he rides past the garden's newly imported Spanish chestnut trees,
the bicycle often trembling as it does now. The trees were a scan-
dal when they first arrived. The story went that in an effort to
keep up with that other gleaming city, the leaders of Bordeaux
had purchased the trees at enormous expense. As if to punish
this luxurious act of vanity, droves of rats immediately took up
residence in the rich soil, scrambling over one another to fight
for each fallen chestnut, upstaging the beautiful, expensive trees.

"Femur. Humerus," the Doctor whispers. "Supraorbital foramen." The sound of the words steadies him; it travels down
through his skeleton into the metal, whispering back to the
machine.

It's worth the few small bugs he swallows to recite the words
aloud. "Lacrimal bone," he says again, in an effort to erase the
sound of his sneeze in the amphitheater. Over and over, he's

replayed it. *Here I am.* He wasn't afraid. He wasn't sorry. Why had he apologized? He hadn't slept well last night after he returned from the docks, the keening of the great doctor's girl still in his head.

"Lacrimal," he says again. It is one of his favorite words: *Lacrimal, lacrimal, lacrimal.* The exquisite almond-shaped glands, an entire apparatus devoted to tears, keeping the eye moist and free of dust and also shedding the other sort of tears, the kind he was shocked to find himself shedding in the early morning hours. "Don't be a stranger," the bartender shouted as the Doctor climbed the stairs to his apartment when he returned from the docks, but he was a stranger, even to himself. There weren't many tears; still, he didn't understand them precisely. *Lacrimal.* Tears of a protective nature and the more mysterious kind passing through tiny openings in the corner of his eye, then into his lacrimal canaliculus, through a small sac and into his nasolacrimal duct, and into his nasal cavity. *Lacrimal,* one of his favorite bones: *Lacrimal, lacrimal, lacrimal.* The most fragile bone in the body. The hyoid bone—the horseshoe-shaped bone at the base of his tongue, which he did not think of as he ran his tongue over the woman's hip last night—was nearly as fragile, but the lacrimal bone was the most delicate. *Lacrimal.* An elegant word, really, and there, at its core, the mystery of the water that he found on his face in the early morning hours as he lay in his bed unable to sleep. *Mother, I am frightened.* The girl's voice, still with him, the look on her face that resembled love but wasn't love at all but a kind of decoy. A decoy that distracted from a question: *What is the story of my invisible life?*

"Lacrimal, lacrimal, lacrimal."

Click-clickety-click. The pleasure is the system; the system is the pleasure. If only he had invented the bicycle. Even to have invented the clever pedal! One day, some rich man had brought his *draisienne,* a mere toy, an oddity hobbyhorse made of wood, to the blacksmith for repair. How had Michaux known to use cranks to connect pedals to the front wheels? The sharp beauty of that idea must have sliced so cleanly through his mind. Pedals led to the use of ball bearings to make a free wheel, and then to the invention of individual spokes to link the hub to the rim. Soon after, wooden frames and then solid rubber tires replaced the wooden ones for better shock absorption, and then gears. The creation of the metal machine the Doctor rode now was a series of perfect discoveries. And now here he is, balancing miraculously on two wheels, an elegant example of the beauty of progress.

He rides out of the garden, past the flickering gas lamps soon to be snuffed out by the lamplighter (it is that early still). He imagines they are doing their flickering dance just for him. *Bravo, Doctor. Bravo,* they flicker. *Thank you,* the Doctor whispers back. *Thank you. It was nothing, really.*

Then past the stern stone justices on the top of the Palace of Justice: *And? So?* Past the witchy-looking woman outside the small stone church of St. Eulalie, who is in a particular twist this morning. "Unspeakable, the things that man has done!" she is saying, but when she sees him she says sweetly, "Good morning, Doctor." He has always appreciated that she interrupts her harangues to greet him politely.

"Good morning," he says, and as he slips off his bicycle and rolls it through the iron gates into the still air of the asylum courtyard, he feels once again the buoying optimism of the wind. His work doesn't require of him that he make a perfect discovery like Michaux's. He doesn't need to invent the clever pedal. He doesn't need to resurrect an ancient word and refashion it for the ages. What is required of him here is subtler than that. *Mother, I am frightened.* He needs to listen to the words. He needs to listen past the words.

"Stop that," says a familiar voice.

"But I haven't even begun," says the Doctor.

Marian sits on one of the wooden benches along the path lined with silver birch trees, as she likes to do on the mornings she is feeling bold. She sits with Claude, underneath one of the stained-glass windows left over from the asylum's days as a church, the Redemption window depicting the Ascension and Jesus on the road sparkling red, yellow, and blue to Cavalry.

"Why did you do that for no reason?" she asks. Last night the sun stole her other kidney.

Behind her words, for example, the Doctor knows, is a father, a wine merchant, who rejoiced when she agreed to marry a rival's son for the sake of good business, but when her new husband, anxious to begin a family, asked her why she was always too tired to make love, Marian confided her suspicion. When she slept, the sun, who had everyone duped into believing it had set, had been replacing her heart with a substitute heart. Behind her words is Marian explaining to her husband she had tried to stay awake all night in order to prevent the theft but she failed; behind her words are other words, "I am so tired," she said to her husband, and then her face, her arms, her legs, the entire left side of her body went stiff with paralysis. But her husband wasn't listening; he was busy packing her bag.

"How are you this morning?" the Doctor asks.

She gives the Doctor the withering look to which he has grown accustomed, a look that says she can't be bothered to explain something so complex to such a simple man. Claude nods to the Doctor. Claude's face is pouched; his red-rimmed eyes red-rimmed since the day he began the job. He unpins Marian's thick hair and tugs a fine-toothed comb through it until she closes her eyes, tilts her head back. He smiles at the Doctor, who, watching the miracle of Claude's posture—an enormous round man, he has elegant posture—is grateful that he is helping. He seems to be finding comfort even as he is giving it. The

Doctor knows a conversation with Marian can feel like a loose sock slipping down his leg after he has just finished pulling it back up. But this analogy is not even his own but something Elizabeth shouts when she cannot finish whatever puzzle she is currently working on: My stockings are falling down again!

"There's someone new," Claude says. "It's upset the balance."

"I'll be back," the Doctor says to Marian, nodding to Claude.

"Always vigilant," she says, eyes still closed.

"You're back," says the Director when the Doctor walks into the common room. The Director wields a rake as though it were a rifle, gathering everyone for a walk. "Come, everyone, up, up. Time to take some air."

The usual crowd is assembled. Walter plays chess with himself, sharing the table with Elizabeth and the half-finished jigsaw puzzle of the funicular railroad in Lyon that has been distracting her from the divine miracle of the scratch on her cheek long enough that Claude's son Henri was able to trim her fingernails this morning. At the piano, Rachel plays the last movement of Schumann's Kresleriana; her frog is in a playful, menacing mood.

Gliding down the long hall that runs along the living room and the men's bedrooms to the billiard room is Nurse Anne. The Doctor has never seen her standing still. Her walk is so swift and efficient that Claude and Henri have started a rumor among the other attendants that her feet don't actually touch the ground. As she floats in his direction, the Doctor thinks, as he often does, *She could be my sister.* Her features, like the Doctor's, are crowded on her small face; her brown-flecked green eyes a little close together as though she is always in the midst of solving a problem elsewhere even as she is in the midst of the one in front of her, which is usually true. When he first met her, he thought, *She could be my sister*, and then, *She would have been my unfortunate sister.* But the truth was she never would have been his sister, unfortunate or not. She arrived here from an entirely different world—educated at home in London by an eccentric wealthy father. (Had she said something once about a pet owl, or was the Doctor confusing her with a character in a novel he read recently?) Her father hadn't believed governesses were up to the task, so he took her around the world in order to cultivate her natural intelligence, but when she said she wanted to become a nurse and wear plain woolen dresses instead of marrying the flatulent cousin her father had chosen for her, he exploded. "There will be no slumming it in almshouses and penitentiaries. No cholera graveyard for you!" So she married the flatulent cousin until, as she explained to the Doctor, "I was up to my chin in linen and glass," and she left. In this, she and the Doctor *were* related; she, too, had walked out of a life. She also lives with regret. The Doctor has seen the bracelet she wears underneath her sleeve, woven from the hair of her father, her mother, and her two younger sisters, who disowned her when she became the lady superintendent at the Institute for Sick Gentlemen. After that she went to the front as a nurse and met a man near death who, instead of dying, lived on to father three children with her, so grateful she'd saved his life he didn't care that she hadn't received a proper divorce from the flatulent cousin.

"Someone new?" the Doctor asks.

"Yes," the Director says. "In the billiard room. Nurse Anne will introduce you," and he gestures to her with the rake he is carrying. He claps his hands and Walter and Elizabeth and Rachel reluctantly stand. "Who are we missing?" he asks. "Marian! We are going to work in the garden. If it weren't for the treacherous sunshine, there would be no garden at all."

"The carrots are a divine miracle," Elizabeth notes gravely.

"But who's to say they are real?" asks Walter.

"Walter," Nurse Anne says. "Must you?"

"Are you saying they *are* real?"

"Everyone, outside." the Director says. "We will find Lady Sunshine, and then we'll see for ourselves."

"Come," Nurse Anne says to the Doctor in that gentle yet persuasive voice of hers and takes him by the arm and begins to steer him down the hall. He imagines her practicing solace in the mirror at home: *I am here. You are better now.* The woman's finger tracing a circle on his thigh lingers from last night. *There, there.* And then the girl's voice returns. *Mother, I am frightened.*

He is distracted and tired and grateful for the way Nurse Anne leads him. As they float down the hall, the seashells she always carries in her pocket rattle and the Doctor's pocket watch tick-tocks, all the way to the billiard room.

"It is best not to think, for example, *What am I thinking?*" the veteran is saying when they arrive in the doorway. He rolls another billiard ball across the felt table. "What am I thinking? The way it is best not to think about certain bodily functions." He counts on his fingers. "Blinking. Breathing. Fuuu—" He pauses when he sees Nurse Anne. "... arting."

"Over there." Nurse Anne turns the Doctor so he faces the corner of the room where a man stands with his back to them, neck craned for a better view of the window with Jesus walking the sparkling stained-glass road to Calvary, oblivious as people weep and rend their clothes all around him.

"You might be thinking a million things or you might be thinking nothing," the veteran says.

"Fascinating," the man whispers, but he is not speaking to the veteran.

"If he is to be believed," Nurse Anne says, "he has been traveling on foot for years, or months. Maybe weeks. It is entirely possible he set out the day before yesterday. There is the problem of his memory."

"Magnificent," whispers the man.

The veteran rolls a billiard ball violently and it hops over the edge, crashes to the floor, and rolls to the feet of the man, who picks it up, considers it, and then returns it to the billiard table.

"Yes, that's right. There will be none of that," the veteran says as if the man were trying to steal the ball. Though the veteran professes disdain for most of the other patients, he prides himself on keeping order; he has been known to lurk outside the rooms of other patients, listening in, in the name of order.

In profile, the coil of one of the man's large ears is revealed, as well as his striking nose, whose distinctive arch begins above his large, deep-set eyes. His shoulders are slumped, but that is the only sloppy thing about him. His mustache is finely combed, and not a single button is missing from his spotless vest and waist-coat, and he has a neatly wrapped cravat.

Someone comes . . . it is the beginning of a sentence from a book the Doctor has read recently. The day he walked out of his house to join his family on the side of the road to wait for the great Léotard, he paused in the foyer to look at his reflection in the mirror. There in his own eyes was the look he recognizes now in this man's eye. It is more than just a look, it is conviction: Something is about to come whirring around the bend.

Someone comes. His father's pocket watch ticks in his hand with his pulse, ticking the blood through his veins. "There is time enough," his father said. But a few days after his father gave him the watch, it stopped. His mother took him with her to a jeweler, who, over the boy's protests, took the back off of the watch. "What are you afraid of?" his mother asked, scolding him out of embarrassment. How could he explain that he was worried the jeweler would steal the watch's magic? The jeweler was very kind and, seeing his fear, explained each step—"and now I'm unscrew-ing the screws, and here's the pinion and the pallet and the mainspring, see, there's dirt gummed up in there. It will only take a little cleaning"—and the jeweler had the watch ticking again. And those intricate tiny mechanisms inside the watch!

"Beautiful," the jeweler said. "Look how beautiful that is!" And it was. The same as with every new patient—inside, somewhere, waiting to be discovered: beautiful, intricate mechanisms.

Someone comes . . . The Doctor can't remember the rest. There is salt on his tongue from the gust of wind blowing through an open window into the long hall. Outside, Marian's red flower, its knot waiting to be undone, sways in the garden.

"His name," Nurse Anne says, "is Albert."

At the sound of his name this man, Albert, turns. His face sags with the familiar exhaustion of all of the other patients, but there is something else too. Something of his own, waiting to be discovered.

Someone comes.

"It's not a happy story," Albert says, looking at the Doctor.

It never is. Still, in this man's eyes, the Doctor sees it: an invitation.

PART TWO

Albert Observed

*M*USS ES SEIN? *MUSS es sein?*
Es muss sein!

For years, the man walking along the Weisse Elster River was a secret in the violinist's heart. He told no one as he obsessively pursued Beethoven's notoriously difficult sixteenth string quartet, completed only months before the composer's death. If he could, the violinist would play it all day and all night; he would never stop. It is all he thinks about and all he ever wants to think about. It is not mere mastery he is after. He wants to play the way that man walked; even as he was walking, it was as if he had arrived.

"Do you think I worry about your lousy fiddle when the spirit moves me?" Beethoven once said to a violinist who complained of the difficulty of the final movement, the one he titled "The Difficult Decision." *Res severa est verum.* True pleasure is serious business. Seneca's words engraved in the Gewandhaus, the first concert hall in Leipzig. True pleasure has made the violinist's fingers bleed; it has given him a permanent ache in his back; it has marked him with a raw spot under his chin that will never heal. What the violinist has learned is that true pleasure is always just up ahead on the horizon. He will never achieve his desire. The truth about true pleasure is that it's not all that pleasurable. He doesn't care. There is something in the effort—like the walking man, not quite there and yet still arriving—and so the violinist will keep trying.

Must it be? Must it be?

It must be!

7

"BUT YOU WERE *THERE*," Marian says, holding the metal watering can to her chest like a shield. "In the billiard room, *with* him. You have nothing to offer?"

It's true, the veteran *was* there in the billiard room with the new patient, but now he is here, digging and digging and digging. He would prefer to be left alone where he is, in the present. He doesn't like to live backward. He is trying to break that habit altogether; it leads him into deep holes, as deep as the one he is digging. He is a terrific digger. *I am a terrific digger.* He says this to himself, in his head, to fend off other thoughts. Digging is the task the Director has assigned him in this vegetable garden planted in the corner of the courtyard where it will get the proper sun, and digging is the task the veteran is keeping at the forefront of his mind. Since the Director entrusted him with the trowel, the veteran has not had one violent thought, not one moment of wanting to point the trowel at Marian, to poke at her watering can, to slip the trowel behind the watering can and cut her just a little because she will not stop asking him to think in the wrong direction. *I am a terrific digger. I am a terrific digger. I am digging, I am digging. I am digging. Terrifically.*

Thick clouds obliterate the sun, and Marian sheds her hat and veil. She feels not just optimistic but *triumphant* in the security of her organs, which, this morning at least, are all accounted for. "Mist," Marian declares, "is my favorite weather."

"Make sure to water evenly," the Director calls over from where he squats to examine a carrot, sniffing the dirt-clumped roots. "Very good!" he calls to the veteran. "Very good."

The veteran digs and digs and digs. It causes a steady ache in his arm that matches the one in his back as he bends. The aching helps him not to think about the fact that he is thinking. *I am not thinking. I am digging.* He is not thinking, for example: *If I dug a hole deep enough I could crawl inside. I could tunnel into the earth.* If only he could disappear along with the image that surges up in him when he is *not* not thinking hard enough of his brother's chest rising and falling behind him on the battlefield as he ran until his brother's chest didn't rise and fall anymore, until his brother was swallowed by the earth. The veteran is not thinking, for example, *Why am I here now and my brother is not?* He is not thinking, *My brother is in the ground where I am digging and digging.* Three yellow birds hop along a nearby bench, chirping, *Brother, brother,* and he would like to shoot them with a gun that isn't fucking imaginary.

"Step gently," the Director cautions Marian as she weaves through the rows of kale and lettuce, dribbling water here and there as she approaches the veteran on his knees next to a row of triumphant beans. Even the beans are triumphant this morning!

The small vegetable garden has been a success this year. "Amazing," the Director says, "that it dies and then comes alive again. Over and over." He said this last year too, and last year it hadn't come alive at all. But this year the garden pushes up out of the rich horse manure delivered by the owner of a nearby stable, a man whose brother was once a patient at the asylum.

"Well?" says Marian, standing next to the veteran. With her toe she nudges dirt back into the hole he has made.

"Marian," the Director says sternly, "leave it alone." Thinking the Director means him, Walter stops squeezing a not-quite-ripe tomato on the trellis.

The veteran looks up at Marian but—*Brother, brother*, chirp the demon birds done up in bright yellow as if nothing is wrong. He must return to his digging.

Marian is only trying to get the veteran to help the expectant shimmer, in the air since the new patient's arrival last night, to take shape. Nurse Anne claims the man is sleeping, that he needs his rest, but this morning Marian saw it. A phantom figure out of the corner of her eye as she sat on her bench underneath the stained-glass Jesus glittering red, blue, and yellow. She has lived for too long surrounded by the unknown—room after room of it; there is no more room for it in her world. There is such a thing as too much unknown. That someone is here among them, unknown to her, makes her restless.

Since the arrival of the new patient, the universe has shifted slightly. The simple vase of the asylum is not so simple after all. The arrival of someone new, and suddenly everyone is sloshing over its edges.

Even his footfall is unfamiliar. It is not Walter's shuffle, or Rachel's skitter-step. It is certainly not the whoosh of Nurse Anne. This strange new footfall—deliberate, even—walking through the world of their familiar asylum is a reminder of another faraway life, a life whose loss at first was an unbearable sadness—how were they expected to survive such sadness?—but which they have not only managed but had succeeded in forgetting until the unfamiliar came along to remind them of that other world. The new patient's footsteps cause an excruciating loneliness; as if someone is walking across a wound they forgot was ever there. Elizabeth swore she heard the new patient's voice in the night though the common room separates the women's ward from the men's ward. Marian is so desperate for information she even let Elizabeth get to the end of her sentence before interrupting. "His voice is like your *brother's?* How would any of us know your brother's voice?"

In fact, Elizabeth's brother has been dead for years but maybe this new patient is the divine miracle of him, maybe her brother has been returned to her the way her mother said would happen when they all went to heaven. But Elizabeth doesn't want to wait that long. Besides, her mother was a wretched liar who left Elizabeth here all alone, who went to be with her brother in heaven, so who cares about her anyway? She plucks all the feathers she's just finished pasting onto the wing the Director allowed her to bring back from the creek path; when she looks up, she is surrounded by forlorn feathers.

These feathers, in combination with the earlier event—Rachel taking off her shoes and promptly stepping on a bee—and the veteran understands he has willed some dark thing up from the bowels of the earth with all his digging. He realizes it is his fault and that the dark thing might claim him too. *I am only digging*, he thinks, so as not to think about the impending disaster he has surely caused.

Rachel went inside after she was stung by the bee and now Brahms's—*The buzz of the bee is in his name, darling*, the frog explains—G minor rhapsody swirls out into the courtyard, the restless motion of the music making Marian dizzy, even dizzier than when the sun scrapes away her insides, even dizzier than the prospect of a stranger somewhere inside the asylum, plotting with the sun to steal her sense of triumph.

Watching Marian begin to sway, the veteran worries that the dark thing he has dug up from the earth has set its sights on her too, so he sits back on his heels and stops digging. This is his battle. No one else should be sacrificed. *I am not digging.* The demon birds have flown away—*Brother, brother*—with the sound of Samuel's humming. *I am not thinking of my brother's rising and falling chest*, and he resolves to be vigilant because the darkness is surely on its way to him. "He is a peculiar fellow," he says to distract the darkness. *I am not thinking of myself; I am answering Marian's question.* "The new man."

"Peculiar?" Marian stops swaying.

"Where is Nurse Anne?" Samuel asks. He has been lurking behind the Director, who is examining the frayed edges of the lettuce—whatever it was that wrecked the garden of last year has been nibbling again.

"Shh," Marian says. "She is probably looking in on the new man who does nothing but sleep. The veteran is going to finally tell us one thing about him." She stamps her foot at the veteran's vagueness. Peculiar how? Peculiar what? But he has gone silent again.

"I'd like to give her some of the vegetables to take home to where she lives," Samuel says. He likes to imagine Nurse Anne, who frightens him with her stern floating. He likes to imagine her on her way home, floating sternly down the street, but that's as far as he gets in his imaginings because he is afraid. He dares only look through the window, where he sees a blurry man and the blurry children he once heard Nurse Anne speak of to the Doctor when Samuel was standing so quietly nearby he feared it had finally come true, he had vanished from the earth. He imagines the blurry man and the blurry children wait for her with a pot of hot tea. "How nice!" he says, remembering the tea.

"What is nice?" Elizabeth says, looking up from where she squats over her wing, which is now a bone wishing for feathers.

"Nothing," Marian says. "Go on," she says to the veteran.

"He has an enormous fucking head," the veteran says. It is not working. It doesn't matter how much he digs. *Brother, brother, oh, my brother.*

The Director looks over.

"He *does*," says the veteran.

"I cannot allow such language," the Director says apologetically. Discipline is not his strong suit; it is not his suit at all. "Once more, and . . ."

"An enormous head and what else?" Marian asks. She doesn't like the shape the shimmer is taking and now the sun is poking through the clouds. She retrieves her hat and veil from the bench, securing them once again to her head. She pulls the watering can close, exhausted by her own fear. "Never mind. I'm going inside."

"He is a man like any other," the veteran says, trying to concentrate on the hole. *Come here,* he thinks. *I will lure the darkness back into the hole.* He never wanted it to hurt anyone else. "What else do you need to know? He is a man like any other, thinking things he wishes he weren't thinking."

The whistle of a train in the distance collides with the notes of the piano; it whistles Marian right out of the courtyard. Samuel gathers his coat around him to keep from dissolving into the sound; it whistles through Elizabeth, who hears in it her brother's whistle and so digs her hands more deeply into the earth to take hold of the sound and keep it near. It whistles through Walter, dislodging from the sedimentary layer of that faraway life a fragment he had been grateful to forget but there it is, a trip, touring with his wife who no longer visits. He stands at the edge of the garden, helpless and rearranged. Flung into the past, he is in a museum with his wife looking at a portrait she loves by a Dutch artist. They have searched the museum and they have found it at last. The woman in the painting looks suspiciously like Walter's wife and he begins to wonder if this is why his wife likes the painting and then he begins to suspect, looking from the woman in the painting to his wife and then back again, that both of these women are seeing inside him to his confusion. Each set of eyes looks with such intensity, filling him with something like immortality, and yet he is confused. Is the painting more real than the woman standing beside him?

And then his wife takes his hand and leads him back into the world and he cannot explain though the feeling lingers of a world wholly concocted; it has lingered ever since. And then the train is whistling his wife away, his wife who has not visited in a year, who told the Director she would not be returning, but how could that be true?

"I am ready to go inside," he says. *Please*, he thinks, *someone say my name. Someone say my name before I am whistled away.*

"A fine idea, Walter," says the Director, in the nick of time.

"He has great enthusiasms," says the veteran, meaning the peculiar man, though Marian has already gone inside. But it is not working. He cannot distract the darkness any longer. It wants what it wants. *Okay*, he thinks. *Fine, then. Come in.*

8

L ISTEN.
Had he dreamed it? He has been in and out of dreams. It
hovers in the background, a possibility rather than a sound,
coming closer, on the verge of taking shape.

"Come here, darling."

A woman's voice drifts through the window.

"Darling, darling ..." Pat-pat-pat, a child's running footsteps.
"And which of us ... ?" Two men whisper, biding their time as
they wait for the theater of night. The clip-clop, clip-clop of
horses and the rattling of a fire brigade's light carriage.

Every sound is a jewel to be weighed and considered. A
pocket of space unfolded inside of Albert; a hole through which
he fell and fell, but then he woke up in this bed, *his* bed, so he
was told, and he is still here. He lies very still (that he is still!),
listening.

A door opens somewhere down the hallway and heavy footsteps interrupt the plaintive notes of a piano.

"Such wit," a man's voice says.

"It is not my wit," a woman replies. "It is a divine miracle ..."

Hiccups become a wave of weeping.

The wave becomes part of the wave of voices breaking gently on this strange beach where Albert has washed ashore.

"How is your bee sting, Rachel? I've never been stung. What is it like to be stung? Does it hurt?"

"Must you?" says another woman's voice.

The piano stops altogether. "I am so nearly finished. Why must you bother me for no reason at all?"

"But you are never finished. Where is that peculiar fellow?" says the voice of the man Albert met in the billiard room where the glittering Jesus walked, astonished but adored.

"Leave her," says a different man's voice.

"I mean you. *You.*"

"Would you like a puzzle of your own?" It is the same voice that took Albert by the hand when he arrived. *Nurse Anne. I am Nurse Anne*, it said, as if it were that simple to be someone. "Or would you like to go to your room?" Nurse Anne says to the other voices. That each voice has a room of its own!

"I am going outside."

"I will come too."

"I'd rather you didn't."

"You are tired, Rachel," says Nurse Anne. *You are tired*, she said when she took Albert's arm, leading him from the billiard room. *The Doctor will see you after you've rested. This room*, she explained to Albert, leading him to the room where he lies now. *This room is yours.* He could not believe it was his. How long has it been since he slept in a bed? *You are here. You've come home and you are here.* He could not believe he was here, and though he understands he is in the city he is forever leaving, the city that was once his home, this place is entirely unfamiliar.

The look on the lamplighter's face as he let go of Albert's arm at the iron gate returns to him, the pitying look of all of the other faces that could not bear him. He tries to forget as he has managed to forget everything else, but the shadow of guilt darkens his feelings; it will not leave him. Still, the lamplighter brought him here, to this bed, to this room, to this place where there are voices just down the hall. The shadow of guilt is long, but the sound of other voices helps to push it back.

"Listen, you," says a voice inside the courtyard.

Bells and then shadow bells sing in Albert's ear: *Does this ring a bell?* There is the sharp, quick sound of love: *Listen.*

He listens. He hears nothing more, but the hovering thing comes closer. Even now that he is still, there is the feeling he had when he was on the road, of something up ahead, always up ahead, if he could only get there faster. But it was always disappearing. It is still disappearing. Just around the bend. Just out of reach.

When he stretches his arms, he nearly pushes the pitcher of water off the edge of the bedside table and he leaps to his feet to catch it.

The room is beautiful in its simplicity—a table and a bed and a chair, and laid over the chair a fresh set of trousers, a shirt, and a waistcoat. Underneath the chair: a new pair of shoes. Nurse Anne's laugh, soft as the blue moss he puts in his shoes to keep his feet from blistering. *Here is your room, here you are, yes, right here.* Time does not hide here. It doesn't vanish into the woods or splash into the deep black water or flitter away into the sky. It doesn't duck behind this monument to such-and-such a general or that one. Time is all around him and he is moving through it, sliding through it and it through him as he slips cautiously out of bed. He will ask someone here, *What day?* And that will be the day he is in. He walks carefully, softly, fearing he might—why should he believe any differently?—suddenly wake up to find himself somewhere else altogether. Until that happens he will pretend he is a man like any other, waking up and dressing himself for the day. He picks up one of the shoes and brings it to his face, inhaling the rich smell of the oil; he rubs its soft leather against his cheek. The shoes are so new and clean he is afraid to put them on; instead he pads down the hall in his bare, callused feet, and then out to the courtyard, in search of the voice he heard earlier.

Ring (shadow ring). Bells and then a shadow bell.

A woman wearing a hat and a veil is perched on a bench. Even folded into herself as she is, Albert can tell she is tall, with lovely curves. "The church bells, the asylum bells, more church bells, more asylum bells," she is saying. "I am talking to you," and she looks straight at Albert. "There's no end to these bells."

Inside her suspicious face is a younger face, sweet and inviting—a dimple revealing itself before a tightness around her eyes grabs it away. She reminds Albert of a frantic woman who grabbed his arm when he discovered himself admiring the tomb of a general at Andernach. "You were nearly crushed by an avalanche," the woman said, offering him a glass of wine, which she drank herself. She wanted to lie down with him but then he walked from April into May and discovered himself in a hotel room in Le Buisson with an empty envelope from the French consul in his pocket.

"You," the woman in front of him says, brushing strands of hair from her face and the face inside her face. "I won't pretend to guess. You are Albert."

The black sky has a mineral smell, threatening rain, and the wind rattles the branches of the birch trees and shivers the fir trees. The way this woman looks him over, that she knows his name—what might he have done while time was hiding? The problem with oblivion, Albert has learned, is that your life goes on without you, making a fool of you. "Have we met before?" Albert asks, though, really, he would rather not know.

"Come sit, silly man," the woman says. "Nurse Anne told me who you are." She pats the empty slab of bench next to her. "You have been sleeping forever. I was beginning to think you would never wake up."

"I . . ." he begins. He wants to argue with her, but he is too tired. "For how long?"

"You slept through all of yesterday," she says indignantly.

"Was I supposed to meet you?"

"No," she says sternly. "I was just eager to make your acquaintance. Now, please, sit."

There were rare moments on the road when Albert stood still for so long that deer gathered in the shadows around him, when he stood still for so long a wildflower bloomed in front of him. In those rare, still moments he dared to imagine he was not the only one; that there were others like him walking astonished too, just around the next corner. For this reason—because she is here instead of just up ahead—he does as he is told. He sits and he is grateful.

"There have been too many substitutions," she says. "I am exhausted."

"Yes." He isn't sure what she's talking about, but it doesn't matter; he knows what it is to be exhausted.

When he sits, the woman nods, and the tightness of her older face relaxes; there again is the face inside her face. Its dimple returns.

Ring (shadow ring).

"Those bells will ring you into next year if you let them," the woman says. "I'm not going anywhere. Sit with me a while longer."

"I'd like that." A drop of rain falls on Albert's cheek; so clear and bright on his skin it hurts. "I don't mind the rain."

A man as old as the lamplighter but not so grizzled appears in the doorway and walks toward them cautiously, as if they were on fire. "There you are, Marian, my dearest one," he says to the woman. He puts a tentative hand that smells like pudding on Albert's shoulder. "I wanted to see for myself. It's hard to tell. The concocted ones are very lifelike."

"We're enjoying the weather, Walter," the woman says.

"It's starting to rain," Walter says.

"We *were* sitting peacefully." She sighs, her eyes gray as the sky.

Those eyes are strangely familiar to Albert, like the clean, bright rain on his tongue—but then everything is strangely familiar. Once, when he stopped, he curled up in a hollow log rotting from the inside out. He had hoped to rot away too, but instead he woke to lightning splitting a tree nearby. Why had he not chosen to sleep near that tree? He huddled with sheep and a lone cow in a pasture, hoping to wake up transformed into a sheep or a cow, as dumb as that. When he heard laughter he thought, *Maybe they are not so dumb, these sheep and this cow, maybe they're laughing at me,* but it was a group of men and women huddled together farther down the field, whispering and laughing around a fire. His heart beat faster, hoping these were his people.

"Join us," one of them said.

"We'll teach you all the tricks," another said.

"No one needs to learn *your* dirty tricks," said a third.

These whispering, laughing men and women moved only when they had to, they told him, only to avoid arrest. They spoke to one another the same way this woman and Walter did, confident the other wouldn't disappear; it wasn't even a question, and Albert thought for a moment he could join their group. Then one of the men huddled around the fire touched Albert's shoulder with a hand as cold as glass and Albert felt himself on the verge of shattering so he walked away into the night.

Though Walter's hand is warm, his touch is like the rain, painful in its clarity. Still, Albert lets Walter squeeze his shoulder as he looks up at the dark sky, considering. "Masterful," he says. "Masterful."

"At what?" Albert asks. Though the man's touch on his

shoulder hurts, he doesn't feel afraid. This seems less like a trick than like a secret language.

Walter squeezes Albert's other arm—"Quite real, I believe"—then one leg. He is about to squeeze the other leg when an enormous potato-faced man appears and takes him gently by the arm.

"Walter," the large man says.

"Yes, Claude?" Walter says to the man. "Not one of the real," he whispers to Albert.

"It is nearly time to come to the table," Claude says, giving Walter a stern look.

"May I squeeze you, darling Marian?" Walter asks when Claude and his stern look leave.

Marian laughs.

Ring (*shadow ring*). "It is time for breakfast," she says, pulling her shawl around her as she stands. It has started to rain in earnest.

Ring (*shadow ring*). *Is it time for breakfast? Is it time for lunch? Is it time for dinner?* Entering into time is like squeezing through a too-small door. Still, Albert wants these to be his questions now.

"Just one arm?" Walter asks. "I'll squeeze it quickly so you won't even notice."

"What is wrong with you?" Marian says.

"You are crueler than you know," Walter says.

"I know precisely how cruel I am," Marian says.

It is a murmur with no words at first, and then a windy whisper. *Il revient, il revient.* It calls Albert back—he returns, he returns—but he doesn't want to return. He wants to follow Marian and Walter inside as they argue their way toward breakfast.

But the whisper insists. This is not what Albert has been listening for. This is the same old life calling him back. He was a

fool to think it had gone away. Perhaps if he goes to his room—
Here is your room, here you are, yes, right here—and lies down he
can make it go away. "Please excuse me," he says to Marian and
Walter as they walk back inside and begin down the hallway. He
will take care of this in private and then he will return to become ·
a normal man tick-tocking his way through the day. Why can't
he be? "Please excuse me," he says again, and Walter and Marian
turn. "I will be there soon."

"You are excused," Marian says.

"I'll be there soon," Albert says.

"Well, go, then," Marian says sharply. "No one's keeping you."

"Breakfast will expect you," Walter calls over his shoulder.
"And so will we."

Albert wants nothing more than to keep an appointment
with these people rather than to, for example, wake up on an
unfamiliar narrow street, with an ache in his bones, surrounded
by sheep.

Il revient, il revient, sing the River Garonne, the Tarn, the
Aude, the Orb, the Têt, the Rhône, the Nive, the Adour, the
Weisse Elster, the Meuse, but he will not. He will deafen himself
to their call. *He returns. He returns.* What rivers? What *il
revient*?

He will not. He is not. He is not. *Il ne revient pas.*

In his room, he lies on his bed. He unzips his trousers and
cradles his beautiful instrument, holding its velvety wrinkles
until the wrinkles disappear and grow smooth in his hand. There
is no urgency, he thinks, stroking it. There is no trembling in the
arch of his foot. Here is his soft bed. Here is his room. His beautiful instrument nods in agreement. It nods and nods, rising as it
crescendos, but its song does not leave him somewhere else altogether. It sings to him, and then lies still, sleeping in the sticky
puddle of his palm. He washes himself in the basin by the bed,
and then tucks his beautiful instrument away.

There are bells and then shadow bells singing in Albert's ear: *Does this ring a bell?* Outside, the rain has cleared completely and the sky is pink where the sun shines through.

There again, the sharp, quick sound of love: *Listen.*

The hovering thing is a voice and the voice takes shape. The voice that Albert thought had gone forever silent. The voice he thought was lost to him. And there, the face he thought was lost too, illuminated—the waxy swirl of scars on the left cheek and the ropy cords of skin edging the collar of his shirt and coat sleeves. *Il revient. Il revient.* His father's beloved face, the story of which his father told only once.

Listen. Il revient. Il revient. The story returns. His father had been working underneath the opera house, mending the connection between the flaking pipes of the old building and a main pipe in the street. As the matinee performance of *Zampa* began and the theater filled with two hundred theatergoers, he and another gas fitter continued working silently underground. When his father first noticed the crack in the pipe, he instinctively wrapped it with his coat. He nodded to his partner to light a match to make sure the invisible gas was contained; he was sure it was.

Even when the fire peeled the skin from his hands and neck and face, even when it burned the hair from his head, he continued to hold his jacket there. He didn't let go. "The opera was never interrupted," he told Albert, "and only those theatergoers who read the article in the back section of the newspaper the next day ever knew their lives had been in danger."

"A miracle!" Albert said, sharing his father's pride.

"The chaos of gas needs to be contained in a perfectly fitted pipe," his father corrected him.

That his father's familiar scars have returned to Albert *is* a miracle. Their colors changing with the lamplight's flicker: a sky infused with red dusk, then sun-bright again, as constant and beautiful as the sun moving through the sky each day. How Albert had longed to run his hand over the waxy swirls. How he longs to run his hands over them now.

Where had he been? Why had he left him alone for so long? It didn't matter. He was here.

Shhh. Lie still. I will tell you a story.

Listen, his father began as he had each night. Each night, his father untwisting him with a story.

Listen, and Albert was stilled.

His father spun a world into existence and Albert would think, *I'm still here.* His body hadn't been consumed by meningitis like his brothers', who died in infancy before their faces had even taken shape; he hadn't disappeared into pneumonia like his mother. He had lived. Puff, puff went his father's pipe; puff, puff went the cottage that contained their lives, lives that had taken a shape as familiar as the tobacco packed into the pipe. Puff, puff went the cottage and the little lives of a man and his son alone in the world—gas fitting, meals, sleep, gas fitting, meals, sleep—disappeared.

His father's voice has returned and with it the story of a magic ball of yarn, an evil stepmother, a good king, and his six children, five sons and one daughter. *One day the evil stepmother transformed the boys into swans, but the girl, being quite clever, escaped. In order to break the curse, the girl had to remain silent for six years; if she wanted to save her brothers, she could not make one sound. She couldn't even laugh. For six years. A king from a neighboring land asked her to marry him. How could she refuse? If she spoke, her brothers would remain swans forever. She literally couldn't say no. She spent her days using the ball of magic yarn to sew magic shirts for her brothers. She sewed in a hurry because she wanted them back so badly. Still, these magic shirts were complicated; they took a long time. Six years passed, and though she hadn't quite finished the fifth shirt, she had grown unbearably lonely after so many years. So, without having*

*finished the last shirt—she would finish it on the way, she thought—
she escaped the king's castle in order to track her swan brothers down.
Sisters have a way of finding their brothers, even brothers who have
been turned into birds.*

*When she found them, she gave each of them a magic shirt. Four of
the brothers put on the magic shirts and became men (six years later
they were no longer boys)—their feathers turned back into skin, their
wings back into arms. But when the fifth brother put on the half-
finished shirt—still missing one arm—one swan wing remained, its
beautiful feathers rippling uselessly.*

Oh, darling boy, don't cry.

*That brother with one swan wing? He made a life for himself.
More than that, he was the only one of the brothers who remembered
that he had once been a bird. For the rest of his life, he was the only one
who remembered what it was like to be something else entirely.*

A great cloud of damselflies hovers just outside Albert's
window, on the cusp of movement, and Albert hovers with them.
And then the cloud of damselflies is in motion. They fly back and
forth, back and forth. They go nowhere, and yet what an exquisite show of spindly legs and blurred wings!

What will you do? Stay.

Where is relief? Here.

What is the question?

Ring (shadow ring).

What time is it? *That* is the question.

It is time for breakfast.

9

"**B**UT HOW DID CHOPIN'S sister travel all that way without dropping it?" Rachel asks. "Carrying his heart all the way to the cathedral in Warsaw?"

The Doctor—at Marian's request ("Unrelenting sadness is not good for us," she said, and he had to admit she had a point)—has been trying to convince Rachel to play something other than Chopin's Funeral March, which she has been playing all morning in honor of the dead bee. "Very carefully, I'm sure," the Doctor says, "but even Chopin's sister would surely have liked a break now and then from thinking about death." He pulls Rachel's hair off of her face and reaches in his pocket for some string with which to tie it back. It is then he rediscovers the worn scrap of paper Nurse Anne gave him yesterday.

In neat, careful handwriting, someone has written: *He is off his rocker.*

"Everyone's a doctor," Nurse Anne said. "It was pinned to Albert's waistcoat when he arrived."

"But how? She had to travel so *far*," Rachel is saying.

"It is a question for another time," the Doctor says. All morning he has been meaning to speak to the new patient. Since he first met him yesterday morning, but then the man nearly fell onto the billiard table with exhaustion and Nurse Anne very rightly suggested he should go immediately to bed where he slept right through until this morning. He had caught a glimpse of him, sitting contentedly at breakfast with Marian and Walter, but then he'd had to convince the veteran to tuck his imaginary gun back into his trousers. "I can't tell if I'm thinking a million things or if I'm thinking nothing," the veteran said, and the Doctor futilely suggested to him, "How about no more thinking for now?" before he'd had to give Walter a bromide once breakfast was done, then walk him to the window to show him the people buzzing around the square and up and down the stairs of the Palace of Justice, assuring him the people were as real as Walter and himself, until the stern statues on the roof of the palace glaring down at the Doctor from their perch—*And? So?*—reminded him of the new patient and he asked Claude to take over. The predictable unpredictability of life in the asylum has caused the great doctor's fierce girl to fade, and forced the Doctor's mind to shrink to the problems immediately in front of him.

But now he will leave Rachel to think of Chopin's poor sister bringing a small piece of her brother home, his life over and done too soon, before he was through, before he had achieved all he could. He doesn't want to think about all of the cemeteries full of the hearts of people not yet finished with their lives. *It is not a happy story*. But he has a different unhappy story to attend to, so he heads out into the courtyard, carefully avoiding the bench Marian has declared hers, in order to clear his head to make room for the new patient.

There is a slight chill in the air and he feels the cold stone through his pants. Good, he thinks, the chill will wake him up. When Nurse Anne put the man to bed yesterday, she learned that he had come from a long journey on foot and was exhausted, but that that was not the cause of his tears. He wept because he could not prevent himself from departing on a trip when the need overtook him. Provins, Vitry-le-François. Châlons-sur-Marne, Chaumont, Vesoul, Mâcon, Budweis, Prague, Leipzig, Berlin, Tournai, Bruges, Ostend, Ghent, Liège, Nuremberg, Stuttgart . . . It was here Nurse Anne stopped him.

"We both would have been up all night if I hadn't," she said.

Nurse Anne told him that the man is not a vagrant. "He is insistent on that fact," she said. He grew up in this city, in his father's cottage by the river, but often wandered away for long stretches of time and—she learned this from the man who dropped him off ("He couldn't get away fast enough. I was lucky he told me anything at all")—the cottage had been destroyed in a fire in his most recent absence.

The Doctor's leg has gone numb from the cold stone and he stands to shake it, then brushes the dirt from the seat of his pants. "Not there," a voice beyond the walls of the asylum cries. "No, here. *Here.*" There are deliveries not far from the asylum gates at this hour. Something thuds against the cobblestones and two men curse at once. Otherwise, the noise of regular life in the city is faint. He barely hears it when he is here, the patients aren't the only ones who find protection from the noise of life in here. In his pocket, his father's watch ticks into his palm. He never knew the precise moment of his father's death and it has always bothered him. The hands of the watch moving so fluently through the minutes: Was this it? The hour of his father's death? Was this? But the hands never stopped to tell him. Tick. Now? Tick. Now? Tick.

"Oh, for God's sake, where are you now?" A woman's voice rises up out of the murmur on the other side of the wall.

Where am I? the Doctor's father asked, batting away the incompetent doctor's flapping cuffs. *You are right here,* said the incompetent doctor, in a rare moment of competence, and his father became still again. The only sound was the leeches doing their work. *You are right here.* On the mat on the floor beside the bed where he slept each night, the boy Doctor listened to the ticking of his father's watch until they both fell asleep.

Mother, I am frightened. There isn't time for this, for everyone's unhappy story all at once, and so the Doctor heads back inside to focus on just the one, heading toward the new patient's room. The man does not remember arriving; he does not remember leaving. He is an exception to the generations born after the last humiliating war, the Doctor thinks; the trauma suffered by the mothers of the French Revolution and the First Empire has resulted in generations that were born tired, but this man may be something altogether different.

When he walks in to the room, the man whose name is Albert is sitting with his back to the door, looking out the window at the park in front of the Palace of Justice. He appears to be listening to something. Did he hear the fierce statues on top of the palace who glared at the Doctor: *And? So?* He is dressed in fresh clothes, but his long, callused feet are bare. They are *huge*, these feet that have traveled—if the man's story is true—all over Europe. They are as big as the feet of the Doctor's father. One summer, he studied those feet as they walked along the beach. The footprints in the sand were twice the size of his boy feet. His mother showed him how she could fit her hand three times in just one print. As the three of them walked, the moment seemed as though it would last forever, and it has, hasn't it?

The man's slumped shoulders shake slightly. At first he appears to be laughing, but when he turns from the window he is not laughing at all. He coughs, choking on tears that come too fast. Leaning forward, he spits up a tumbler's worth of vermilion blood into his hands.

"Oh, dear," he says.

The Doctor is relieved to be given something to do.

"Here." He offers the man his arm, helps him to his feet. "Here." He walks him to the bed where he lays him down and applies a plaster to his chest near the top of his right lung and another underneath his shoulder blade. There is no reason to believe he is tubercular, but what does it matter? The answer to the wrong question is still an answer. Not *the* answer, but *an* answer. The plaster does its work, drawing blisters, but the man closes his eyes as though he is wrapped in the softest blanket, and when the Doctor gives him the hemostatic mixture of cod-liver oil, he swallows it as if it were a bite of the first ripe peach of summer. He pushes gently on the man's shoulder, coaxing him to lie back.

"Are you well enough to talk?" the Doctor asks after the man has lain quietly for several minutes.

"Yes," he says. "Yes."

"You've had a good, long sleep. Exactly what you need." He puts his hand on the man's shoulder. *And, so, you are better now.* These practiced small gestures—the steady, unwavering touch, the certain tone that gives the ethereal *if* a solid spine: *You are.*

"I have never slept so well," the man says, his eyes still closed, holding himself stiff and still.

"So perhaps I may ask you a few questions?"

"I will do my best to discover the answers."

"How old are you?"

"I am not sure," he says. "Inquiries could be made."

The ghostly murmurs of the other patients drift down the hall. Beethoven's Sonata No. 8 in C minor finds them too, fitful, melancholy, then finding its way, full, and urgent. Rachel and her frog have decided to give death a break for now.

"There is no need for inquiries," the Doctor says. "I would guess your age is twenty. "

"What a useful thing, to know one's age," the man says, as if the Doctor has restored his whole life. "I am delighted to know that. Thank you."

Suddenly the man sits up. "I am not able to say how I got

here," he says. "I am always leaving. I cannot prevent myself from leaving. I go straight ahead, and then I discover myself, not knowing how I got there, far away. I discover myself in this public square and then suddenly I am in another. I wake up somewhere else entirely."

"Why do you cry?" the Doctor asks, gently coaxing him to lie down again. "We have only just started." He hopes to speak to the man just a little longer. It is true what Nurse Anne said. He does not appear to be a vagrant, but he doesn't appear to be a tourist either. He is not, for example, the man the Doctor met on the train for whom travel is a souvenir, a lovely vase to be lifted from the mantelpiece and admired and then returned. Maybe he would go; maybe he wouldn't. For this man, it appears travel is a broken shard that has lodged inside of him, causing him not to be so much consumed by an obsession to pursue travel as consumed by travel itself. *Travel*, from *travail*, bodily or mental labor or toil of a painful, oppressive nature. From the Old French *travail*, suffering or trouble. In German, "tearing free." *Travel*, from the Latin word for a three-pronged stake.

"Please don't send me away," the man says. "I am so tired."

"We won't send you away," the Doctor says, closing the shutters to block out the sun's glare, as well as that of the statues on the Palace of Justice. "You need to rest. You can rest here." *And? So?* He carefully removes the plaster and then covers the man with the sheet. *And, so, you are better now.*

"The leaves of the trees in the public garden were gold that time," the man says. "From the gas lamps, I believe." He props himself up on his elbows, leaning his head against the wall. "I once discovered myself in Aix pitching hay. And once I woke to find myself in Brussels. There was work in a ceruse factory there. There may have been an avalanche. In Andernach."

"That is very helpful," the Doctor says. "When were you in Aix, and Brussels, and Andernach?"

The man looks at him miserably and closes his eyes. "I do not want to disappear anymore," he says.

"You will remember," the Doctor says. "Your life, it will come back. There is plenty of time to talk."

"What day is today?"

"Friday."

"And tomorrow is Saturday?"

"Tomorrow is Saturday," says the Doctor, taking the man's hand in his.

In the man's large eyes, the Doctor sees it again, the same look he recognized when he first saw him in the billiard room. *What will happen next?* it says. That invitation. But to where? "I will see you tomorrow," the Doctor says. "Rest." He touches the man's forehead to distract himself from his unsettlement, but the man's warm forehead sends him back to the Niger where he is once again a teenager on a ship wondering what will become of him, orphaned and alone, so seasick he thinks he will die, looking out over the vast and endless ocean insurmountable as his life.

"I fear I will walk far, very far, with no one to watch over me," the man says, startling the Doctor off the treacherous, indifferent sea and back into the narrower corridor of his life here in this room. It is as though the man is hauling the words up from the bottom of the ocean, as though he were on the ship too, all those years ago with the Doctor.

"There is time," the Doctor says, to steady himself as much as the patient. "We will help you to remember. Do not worry. There is time."

As the bell of St. Eloi rings, the Doctor recalls the inscription underneath the clock: I call to arms; I announce the days; I give the hours; I chase away the shadows; I sound the celebrations; I cry fire. The man smiles up at him. Is this what the ship's doctor meant when he said to the Doctor, *You have a gift*, and set him on the path that has led him to this moment? That there would be moments like this when he would treat a patient and a bell would ring in him?

"You are safe here. We will watch over you," the Doctor says. "If you walk, we will bring you back." His words drift out the window, floating up like the smoke from the factory chimneys, disappearing with the sound of the church carillons. "You are here now."

Someone comes.

What was the rest?

Since he first saw this man standing in the billiard room, since the wind blew through the room and salted his tongue, the phrase has been lodged in the Doctor's brain, unfinished: *Someone comes.*

"We will talk more tomorrow," the Doctor says. "I will stay here while you fall asleep."

This man called Albert appears reassured. His eyelids close and his face, which has appeared wrapped in a shroud of sorrow—the hooded eyes, the long nose, the cowlick that begins at the center of his forehead—relaxes.

The Doctor pulls a chair up next to the bed and watches as the man falls more deeply into sleep. His leg moves—maybe he is dreaming of walking?—and his pants leg rides up to reveal a naked calf. It is exquisitely shaped. That calf, its smooth curve against the rough blanket, stirs something in the Doctor. How strange it is to move through the world, through the depths of one's own solitude. Details that would normally pass unnoticed rise up, offering themselves to him—the far away smell of wild-flowers; the bob and tug, tug and bob of boats anchored on the river; the iron rings of bed curtains rattling down the hall.

Someone comes . . . someone to whom one wants to give . . . something. Something something, something, and another part of a phrase arrives . . . *there's no need for words—people just find one another—they have glimpsed each other in dreams.* A line from a novel he read months ago? A line spoken by a wicked man to lure a restless woman into an affair. There was a word the wicked man used to describe how he felt as he looked at the woman's face. In the quiet of the room, there is only the tick, tick, tick of his father's pocket watch. Tick, tick, tick, and the forgotten word returns: *dazzled.*

The man's mind is a dark street and the Doctor will light the lamps, one by one.

10

ODAY, WHICH IS SATURDAY; tomorrow, which is Sunday;
then Monday and then Tuesday, the days coming one after
the other as if that were all there was to it. It is Saturday, and as he
lies in this bed, his bed, he hears mothers out on the street calling
their children. *We will talk more tomorrow*, the Doctor said, and
today is tomorrow. *If you walk, we will bring you back.* Albert wants
nothing more. *We will help you to remember.*

"Baptiste!" The sound of his friend's name, and he is offered
another glimpse. "Madeleine!" The daughter of the butcher.
"Jean-Luc!" The son of the varnisher. "Alexandre!" The son of
the wheelwright. "Marie!" the daughter of one of the fishermen. "Albert!" his mother would call right over his head as it
grew dark, the only light from the gas lamps along the quay.
Albert, too shy to play with other children, sat at her feet on
the lip of the door of the cottage, listening to the river and to
the mothers of the neighborhood calling their children inside.
She would pretend she didn't see him sitting there at her feet;
she would pretend he was somewhere out there playing with
the other children. "Albert!" she would shout into the street,
but she was never able to hide her smile, and soon she was

laughing. "Where are you, Albert?" as he squirmed and giggled. "Where am I?" he would shout into the night. "I think I hear me out there," he would say, and his mother would cup her hand to her ear. There had once been so much love. How could he have forgotten it for so long? It hadn't disappeared; it had only gone into hiding.

Ring (shadow ring). Time doesn't pummel him; it doesn't smash him like a hammer. It sings: *Today is this day. This is the music of days. This is what it is to be a citizen moving through the days; this is what it is to be a citizen moving alongside the hours and the minutes.*

The bells peal all day long, beautiful in their constancy.

What time is it now?

It is time for breakfast. He puts on the new-smelling shoes Nurse Anne had set out for him and walks down the hall, past the billiard room, where he pauses to admire the walking red, blue, and yellow glass Jesus walking without shame, no menace he, too busy walking to be bothered by such accusations. He wedges himself between Walter and his pudding smell and tall Marian with her lovely curves, all of them held by the gravitational embrace of the table anchoring one side of the large common room, the piano and the fireplace and the table with Elizabeth's puzzle.

"Good morning," Walter says, leaning behind Albert to whisper to Marian, "This way we can keep an eye on him." He gives Albert's arm a squeeze and winks at him.

It is all Albert has ever wanted. *If you walk, we will bring you back.* Underneath the long table, as Rachel slides a bowl his way, he counts the nights and the days on his fingers: Soon he will know what it is to be a citizen held by an entire week.

"There you are, Albert," says the Doctor. "I'm very glad to see you." A warm hand on the back of Albert's neck as he passes through the room, and Albert feels it, the truth of that gladness.

"Hello, hello," says Samuel.

"I have already said my hellos," says Marian.

"Doctor," calls Nurse Anne, and he is on his way again but the gladness remains, hovering over Albert's neck.

Ring (*shadow ring*). And then it is time to walk to the creek. The Director, whose mottled red face reminds Albert of a man in Berlin who saved him from a vicious dog, clap-claps his hands and everyone gathers at the door. "Off we go," he says, lifting his knees high as he marches in place. "Nature is waiting." And soon everyone is marching after him, and Albert is part of everyone marching out into the day.

"I don't like nature," Marian, walking on one side of Albert, says.

"Perhaps the veteran could shoot it for you," says Walter, walking on the other side of Albert.

"I am not thinking that," says the veteran just up ahead. "That is not something I am thinking." He points his finger at the ground. "Follow me, I dare you." He points at some invisible thing, following him already. "That's right," he says.

"It has taken too much from me," Marian says, her lovely curves shrinking as the sun comes out from behind a cloud. "Go on without me."

And they do. Walter puts his arm through Albert's, squeezing and squeezing, and they march after the Director, between the creaking birch trees along the courtyard path. Walter pushes aside the branches, leading Albert through the blackberry bushes, down the path after the veteran, after Samuel, who is an exception to all of those who the veteran would like to shoot; after Elizabeth, who would rather be doing her puzzle; and Rachel, who would rather be playing the piano. "Like this," Walter says to Albert when they arrive at the creek bank, taking off his own shoes and wading into the ankle-deep water.

The veteran bends down to help Samuel with his shoes,

concentrating on the laces. "These are his laces. I am undoing his laces."

For once, Albert discovers himself in the midst of water and he knows why his shoes are left behind on the shore. He knows how he arrived here in the bracing cold water.

The Director, his face red with the excitement of nature, asks them to close their eyes, as he tells them about the Koine Greek word for "beauty" that contains the word for "hour."

"Close your eyes and listen," says the Director.

"Yes," Elizabeth says, "how interested I was the first time you told us this story."

"Shhh," the Director says. "*Beauty* means 'being of one's hour,' and you can't be of your hour if you are talking to me."

Albert is of this hour, his hour, with that bird and that bird and the smell of the muddy earth and the roots of the trees and the sound of the water pushing its way around the rocks. He stands there in his new pants, in the pocket of which is no train ticket to somewhere else, no train ticket he doesn't remember purchasing. In his pockets are his hands and that's all. He is of his hour and beauty is the rope pulling him out of the mud where he has been sinking for so long he doesn't even know how long. *It is better not to thrash.* He does not thrash. He does not move at all.

"Reverence is a ringing in the soul," the Director says. "Quiet, you will hear it."

Albert isn't sure if the ringing deep inside him is reverence or not. It doesn't matter; it is as if someone has dropped a stone down into the well of him and there, after all these years, is the faint splash of water.

Ring (*shadow ring*). And then it is time for lunch. At the long table that anchors them all, Walter's warm thigh against Albert's on one side, Marian's warm thigh against Albert's on the other. Nurse Anne hovers around the table, encouraging Samuel to at least roll up the sleeves of that ridiculous coat if he refuses to take it off. "Now you've got today's soup on top of this morning's porridge," she says. "Congratulations, you are a meal."

"Stop fiddling with Albert's soup spoon," Nurse Anne says to Elizabeth, who wants to show Albert her puzzle of the funicular in Lyon. A fleeting illumination along a pitch-black road: He has been there. Has he been there?

"Lyon," Albert says. "It seems . . . it appears . . . I once . . ." Hadn't he walked past the funicular in Lyon and wished that he were the sort of person who might stop and ride it?

"Yes, yes," Elizabeth says, as though he has completed his sentence. "That's wonderful. I have a beautiful something to show you later."

"Samuel, you are fading," Nurse Anne says.

"*Faded*," Marian says, as Samuel slumps over his plate.

"I will be done soon. It is a simple test I'm conducting," says Walter, tapping Albert's elbow with his spoon. "The evidence is not complete."

"I cannot hear you," says Marian, putting her hands over her ears. "I am not hearing you."

"A soul murder," Walter says. "This is undoubtedly what you fear."

"You are not listening at all," says Marian.

Listen. All day long: the beautiful constancy of the bells. *Ring (shadow ring). Is it time for exercises?* Yes, it is. After they have returned from the creek and those who needed to have changed out of their muddy clothes—"Every one of you," according to Nurse Anne—after it is time for lunch, they go out into the asylum courtyard, even Marian, who has decided to be brave.

"I will let the sun have its way with me," she says.

"That means she likes you," Walter whispers to Albert.

They line up in two rows: Elizabeth, Rachel, and Marian in

the front, Albert and Walter in the back with the veteran. The Director leads and they follow, except for the veteran, who marches behind them, back and forth, back and forth, keeping an eye on the deep hole he dug in the garden until the Doctor comes out, takes him by the elbow, and escorts him inside.

Miraculously, Albert's body obeys him as he lifts his arms, squats, stands, squats, windmills his arms.

"Not all of you are soldiers," the Director says. "Pace yourself. You are not all soldiers like the veteran, but fitness is still the key to good citizenship." Albert feels the muscles in his arms and his legs and his back, good citizens moving through the minutes and the hours.

Ring (*shadow, ring*). And then it is time to dig in the garden, to gently pull without tearing the kale and the lettuce they will eat later for dinner, to put it in the basket, to smell the tomatoes on the vine for ripeness, to not step on the beans, to spread the manure someone has brought for fertilizer. "This is how it's done," says the Director, using his rake, while the veteran, who has returned, digs in his hole. "That is not for eating, Samuel," as Samuel puts manure on his tongue.

Elizabeth holds up her hands, dirt caking her nails. "Divine," she says.

"Certainly," Albert says. He wants to be friendly to this woman who is being friendly to him, but it is also true—her dirt-caked nails, they *are* divine. That he pulls a head of lettuce up from the rich, moist earth and smells its roots; that he does not disappear; that he is here.

"Here," Elizabeth says. "Look here. This is it. The beautiful thing I wanted to show you." She points to a bone with feathers pasted on it, lying on a bench. "My wing."

Sisters have a way of finding their brothers, even brothers who have been turned into birds, his father said when Albert asked him how the sister found the swan brothers in his father's story. But even after his father comforted him, *Darling boy, the prince with one swan arm made a life for himself*, Albert felt them. He feels them now, underneath the tick-tock of the day, his beautiful feathers rippling uselessly.

"I will not cry," he tells Elizabeth, because suddenly he feels certain he will. Looking at the wing, its feathers plucked, suddenly he is afraid again.

"Why would you? I've fixed it. I've put all the feathers back on," Elizabeth says, looking as though she might cry too. "It is beautiful."

"It is," Albert says. *Darling boy, don't cry.* "It is beautiful," he says, but didn't she see that was the problem? The beauty of one's hour made the pain of leaving it that much worse. "It is, but . . ."

"Come with me," Nurse Anne says, though the basket Marian is carrying is not yet filled. She takes Albert by the arm, her voice soft as the moss he put in his shoes. *Here is your room, yes, right here, here you are, right here.* "They can finish without us."

"Let's wash your feet," Nurse Anne whispers, leading him inside, leading him down the hall to his room. She sits him in the chair, then picks up his old mended shoes from the corner, letting them dangle from the tips of her fingers. She reaches inside one of them and pulls out the moss stuffed into the toes. "Very clever," she says.

"My feet are always clean," he says, because they are and because he doesn't want her to think they're not.

"I would hope so," she says. "Still, the Director believes in warm baths and your blisters need soaking. Sit. I'll be right back." He sits in the chair and she is, as she says she would be, right back. She pours a pail of steaming water into a washbasin. "Ready?" she asks, but doesn't wait for an answer, and the touch of her knowing hands as she places his feet, his beautiful feet, in the silky soft water and begins to scrubs his toes, brings another glimpse of his forgotten life, a similarly kind woman in a

Friedrichsdorf boardinghouse with a hairpin shaped like a sword who once gave him walnuts and cheese.

With her touch, his white-webbed calluses and his cracked heels begin to soften; with her touch too comes the memory of disbelief. The people he encountered on the road never believed that he was clean even when he said he was. Even the kindest people doubted him. A tailor's wife who offered him a straw pallet in the back of the tailor's shop inspected his hands for dirt only to discover immaculate fingernails; a farmer who, though he had eight children, offered him shoes, was shocked to discover the splendid state of Albert's impeccable feet; a wool merchant who gave him the scraps from his dinner was startled when Albert pulled back his large ears to reveal shining, clean skin. How could he explain to them that even when the roofs were laced with icicles, in the name of cleanliness he would take off his mud-caked pants to wash in a river? That even so he was never immodest. If there were people walking, even far away, even if they were only specks on the horizon, he would hide himself behind a copse of trees. He was clean as often as he could be; if he was not, there was a twitch in his right eye. Too much dirt, and the blood rushed to a place just above that eye and protested, beating there as if his heart had taken up residence in the wrong place.

"It appears I have misspoken," Albert says. He wants her to know he is grateful. *We will help you to remember.* She is helping him. "What I meant to say was thank you."

"No need to thank me," she says. "But you are welcome."

There is a scraping and a shuffling at the door.

"What is that?" he asks.

"Only the veteran, eavesdropping," Nurse Anne says. "Go away, brave man, this is not your room."

"I was not thinking it was," a voice says, and then the scraping and shuffling disappear down the hall.

But Albert does not hear. He is as silky as the water. The

cleaning of his willing feet he always saved for last; for them he reserved the most special care. He would wait, fighting off the urge to walk as he waited for his shoes to dry by a river or a pond. Only one, or perhaps three, times he discovered himself suddenly in another town without shoes. The first thing he did was run a finger between each toe as if each toe were a tiny loaf of bread, like the ones Albert sometimes discovered left outside behind a bakery to cool; each toe delicious.

The silky water and the caress of Nurse Anne's hands make him sleepy. But he doesn't want to wake up in such-and-such a public square or in the cold rubble of the cemetery, so he grips the edges of the chair until his hands ache so he won't fall asleep and wake up somewhere else entirely. He wants this new life where love isn't always somewhere else. He wants this new life where he is not merely a man who has appeared out of thin air but a man with a history.

"I am not a vagrant," he says. Though he had stopped bothering to tell people, it seems necessary to explain to her.

"I never said you were." The way she doesn't even look up suggests it was the furthest thing from her mind and then, as if she were a magician, out of her apron pocket she pulls seashells! She places them carefully into his hand. They are still warm from her body and smell of her clean apron and—Albert holds them to his nose—the sea.

"Where did these come from?" he asks.

"My father brought them back to me when I was a child," she says. "From the Red Sea. He wanted me to see the world." She leaves out the rest—the way, after he'd shown her all of its wonders, her father had wanted her to leave the world alone; the way he'd insisted she marry her flatulent cousin, shouting, "Who else will have you?" when she refused. How could this be the same father who would joke that she would make a wonderful *flâneur*, her heart ticking like a

clock as she wandered Egypt or Algeria? She keeps herself
to herself now, always having considered modesty a virtue,
always having believed it to be the secret of one's own truest
love for oneself. She never said to her father, for example, *I
always thought I would make a fine flâneur*, the same way she
never said to the Doctor when he once said to her, "You look
like my sister," that she knew he did not mean a woman with
a face more beautiful than his. He meant a woman with his
face; he meant his unfortunate sister. This unfortunate
sister's face was the last face a handful of dying soldiers ever
saw when she ran away from the flatulent cousin to join the
front; to them, she was no unfortunate sister. To them, she
was *mother, darling, my heart. My heart* is what the man who
shares her bed now calls her. "We will make a new life," he
said, but when they drank a toast to their new lives she
understood the moment was a pair of scissors, cutting her
life in two. Half of it left behind in England, the other half
yet to come. Once, she met her mother secretly in Budapest
and they rode the funicular up into the Buda Hills, the
Danube disappearing below them. They strolled arm in arm,
making their way tentatively in their high-heeled boots on
the cobbled streets. "Come back home," her mother said, but
it was too late. She was already on the other side of the river,
far away, looking back on the moment as it happened.

"That was a long time ago," is all she says.

"The smell of the sea has traveled a long way," Albert says.

Layers of callused skin drift on the surface of the water in the
basin. When she tosses the water into the sewer the river will
carry the skin all the way to the ocean. "It's true," she says. "The
shells carry their past with them."

How could she know that Albert has wanted nothing more
than exactly that, to carry his past with him? She wraps his feet
in a towel, holding them against her chest as if they were her

babies, patting them dry. "You should rest for a while," and he hears how tired she is.

"Thank you," he says again as she leaves, shutting the door behind her. He is so grateful for the tender way she bathed his beloved feet and for letting him hold her Red Sea seashells, a gift from her father whom she clearly misses as dearly as he misses his own.

The scratch of hay he pitched in Aix, the stink of the ceruse factory in Brussels, the not-distant-enough roar of an avalanche somewhere, he cannot remember where, but it doesn't matter that he can't remember where because if Albert listens, *he returns*; his own father's voice returns. His father's face with its sunset scars returns to him. It keeps him still. It keeps him here when he falls asleep in the same bed to the sound of boots on cobblestones just outside his window. In his dreams he wanders off along the tight streets winding past the ancient amphitheater where the gladiators fought, through the ancient gate to the city, the arch underneath the giant clock of the church of St. Eloi as it tolls the hour—*les armes, les jours, les heures, l'orage, les fêtes, l'incendie*—but then wakes to find he is not somewhere else at all. Instead his mind shrinks from the expansiveness of dreams to fit inside his body as the ordinary world reveals itself to him again—footsteps in the hall; the cry of a young girl—"There are so many . . ."—and what there are so many of is swallowed as the girl walks farther and farther away, the bells and then the bells, the sweet, sweet song of bells. And love? It returns to him in glimpses.

He discovered himself once, not knowing how he got there, on a bridge not far from home, and in the water lit by gas jets was the reflection of a strange man, and he knew the strange man was him. "Hello," he said to himself, who said hello right back. He was no longer the child being scolded by his father for wandering away. Now he was a man whose large eyes were tugged down at the corners by sadness. He broke his own heart. "Help me," he said, but the sad man only beckoned from the water, *Come join me.*

Fire floated through his reflection. A tiny boat set aflame. Sometimes children set their dead animals on fire and sent them down the river; he and his friend Baptiste once tied a dead mouse to a raft of sticks and lit it on fire. Their dead mouse raft burned as brightly as the little bundle floating downriver in front of him; turning to ash, it floated up into the air. He threw one heavy leg up onto the parapet.

"And love?" a voice asked. He thought it was his reflection speaking. He leaned over the parapet to listen closer and was nearly startled into the water by the laughter behind him.

"You're not talking to yourself. Turn around." He pulled his leg down and turned to find a real live woman. She was dressed as though she had just come from a party—her face freshly rouged, her lips painted a luscious red. She erupted again with laughter.

"I'm a mess," she said, catching her breath. Her hair was tousled, strands of it escaping its loose braid.

"No, no," Albert stammered. "You're not a mess at all." Above him, another cool sliver of moon disappeared into another morning sky. "You are quite . . ." She looked so solid, so thoroughly *there.*

"High praise," she said, laughing still. Had she ever stopped? It was as though she had spent her life laughing.

"Quite lovely," he said.

"Enough of *lovely*," she said, smiling as she put her hand on Albert's shoulder and stepped closer. Her breath smelled sweetly of cabbage and wine. "What about *love*?" She put her other hand on his other shoulder, swaying. "I'm a little drunk," the woman said, still swaying, causing Albert to sway too.

He looked over the side of the bridge to check on his reflection. *Hello, myself.*

"Oh, I've looked there," the woman said. When she laughed, Albert wished he could stay there, inside that laugh.

She stepped forward, balancing on his shoes; it was then he noticed she wasn't wearing any herself.

"Your feet," he said, "are splendidly arched."

"Would you like to marry me?" she asked. She told him to meet her at her family's house at four o'clock the next day.

"I am drunk but I'm honest," the woman said. "I'm honestly drunk." She laughed and touched her luscious red lips to his, and he dared to dream that he was capable of keeping such an appointment.

Was it an hour or a day later?

He discovered himself in Verdun, walking a narrow street filled with bleating sheep, their bells clanking. Why had he ever thought he was capable of love? He should have a sheep's bell fastened around his neck. When he discovered himself later, the sound of a cart carrying pine trees for firewood rattling by cracked his heart into jagged, useless pieces.

"Fuck," the veteran yells from the billiard room, and there is the sound of billiard balls crashing to the floor and then the gruffness of Claude telling him to stop. "It is not me," the veteran says. "It is not my doing. It is not my doing at all."

Love was something from long ago. Love required staying in one place. Love required knowing where you were last night and last week and last year, where you would be tomorrow.

What about love?

Here is love: his father tapping the dying embers of his pipe into his hand and throwing them into the fireplace.

It is time for bed, as if Albert were a normal boy who never disappeared at all.

For a moment, it is as if he never did.

There was the lamplighter and his father standing in the doorway, deep in a conversation about the need for more gas lamps in the neighborhood, or the most recent advancements in house drainage. Some nights, the lamplighter would let him accompany him on his rounds; he'd even let him hold his ladder when a ladder was necessary. Albert watched with fascination as the lamplighter used his rod with its metal U at one end to open the switch that turned the gas on. As the lamplighter lit the taper with a match, suddenly the dark street: *illuminated.* Later, back home, the sunset swirl on his father's cheek: *illuminated.* His father settled into the chair in the living room that received him like a lap and lit his pipe, filling the cottage with the delicious bitter smell.

His father struck a match, touching the flame to the gas-soaked taper, and the lamp's light pushed back the night. "So," he said, "you'd like a story." Then his father waited, on the verge of the story. That moment before the story was as sweet as the moment the flame of the lamplighter's match touched the gas-soaked taper in the lamps and lit up the dark street to reveal a rat scurrying under a shop; the cracked sidewalk; a cracked pile of dried horse manure.

Albert's body hadn't been consumed by meningitis to become the sound of a body in agony like his brothers'; he hadn't disappeared into pneumonia like his mother. He had lived.

I'm still here, Albert thought.

His father's voice spun a cocoon around him and held him with its silky thread.

Here, Albert, a story just for you.

Listen.

Always as if his father had pulled the story out of a hat—magic!

For years, the prince with one swan wing lamented his lot. He wondered why he'd ever wanted to see the world in the first place; if this was the more *of the world, he wanted to go home.*

What came next?

You know what comes next.

There was a magic dove. "Do you hear me?" she sang. "Does this ring a bell?"

It did! He remembered why he set out. Walking over hill, over dale, the prince's eyes filled with the whole wide world before him. There was so much of it! His legs were strong and solid; his heart brimmed with something he came to think of as the future.

Ring (shadow ring).

Does this ring a bell? The quick, sharp sound of love in Albert's ears carries him forward. It carries him up and out of his bed; it helps him put on his shoes; it walks him down the hall to join Marian and Walter in the common room. He wants to explain to Marian about the face inside her face, in part because he would like to ask her whether there is one inside his face too, but he is still a little afraid of her and he isn't sure he wants to know about his other faces.

"You are doing very well this evening, Marian," Walter says. "Perhaps Albert's arrival has cheered you?"

"We'll see about that," says Marian, but Albert can tell she means *yes.*

"Hey, hey," says Claude, the pouches of his face alert, opening up like a purse, as the veteran stands, pointing his finger in Albert's face. It is clear he is not shooting love out of that finger. "And fuck you, too," the veteran says.

Albert doesn't care. Point a finger at him. Curse him. It doesn't matter. He is staying. And besides, how Albert has longed to be a *too.*

"That man is an outrage to the nation," Marian whispers.

"He doesn't bother me," Albert says. "He is no bother."

"As if you cared about the nation," the veteran says over his shoulder as Claude escorts him out.

"Everyone," says Nurse Anne, snapping her fingers, "settle down."

"I'd like to sit in the big chair by the fire now," Elizabeth says as Henri snaps twigs for kindling.

"Her blue feet are no divine miracle," Marian whispers to Albert. "She wears no shoes and holds her feet out the window at night."

Albert has no idea what she is talking about, but it doesn't matter. From where he sits, he can look out the window to the sky over the courtyard filling with those charcoal clouds that darken the whole world though it is not evening yet. They used to darken Albert too, those harbingers of nothing, but as Elizabeth protests—"That is not true except for the one time . . ."—and Nurse Anne touches him on the shoulder and reminds him he is to see the Doctor soon, the sky does not swallow the whole world, and Albert goes to sit by the fire.

11

THE MAN SPEAKS HUNDREDS of kilometers in a breath: from Montpellier to Narbonne, from Pézenas to Geneva, from Cette to Berlin, from Castelnaudary to Charleroi. From Verviers to Vienna! The place names trip off his tongue, an incantation of bemusement and bafflement, as if he is speaking about the adventures of another man entirely. There is something oddly innocent about his befuddlement, as if he were astonished at his own debilitating condition.

The Doctor finds himself imagining this man as a part of the throngs of pilgrims during the Middle Ages who sought refuge in the asylum when it was on the pilgrimage route of Saint James. If the man had lived then, he might very well have been considered a spiritual pilgrim, but he didn't, and so he is a patient.

"Where else have you traveled, Albert?"

"Maastricht. Düsseldorf, Cologne, Bonn ... Kassel, Frankfurt ... Hanau, Aschaffenburg, Darmstadt ... Würzburg, Nuremberg. Linz ... Amstetten! Salzburg, Schaffhausen, Basel, and Delle. Interlaken ... the canton of Vaud. Bonsecours? Yes, Bonsecours!"

He was here and then he was there. There is nothing in between.

"I found myself in Tours," Albert says, "but first I was sleeping on a bench in the Orléans station in Paris." But then he is somewhere else. "Once the Dutch police, because I had no money, sent me to the Belgian frontier." Then, somewhere else entirely. "In Prague, a group of French students took up a collection for me. Eight florins and a shirt, they gave me."

As far as the when and where, the *if*, of his eating or drinking or his sleeping, the Doctor notes, the man has not a clue. If he ate or drank, he doesn't remember it; if he slept, he cannot recall. In this town, the consul would have nothing to do with him; in that one, he was given a travel warrant to return home on foot. He wakes up and wakes up and wakes up here and here and here, but the journey remains a mystery.

"Arles, or was it Nîmes? I left it abruptly."

His life is an endless sentence with more ellipses than words, with intermittent and puzzling punctuation.

The smell of burned mushrooms drifts down the hall.

"All of them burned?" the Doctor hears Nurse Anne ask.

"Most," Henri says.

"Would you like me to go on?" Albert asks. He sits in a chair across from the Doctor. Out the window above Albert's head, the Doctor watches as the public officials spill onto the steps of the Palace of Justice. The bell of St. Eloi rings, followed by the asylum bell.

"It is time for dinner," Albert says.

"It is time for dinner," the Doctor says, "but from the smell of things, dinner will be a little late today. Would you mind if we spoke for a while longer? I'd like to make a map of your travels."

"Of course," Albert says. "Whatever you like. I want to do whatever you like."

"But why?" Elizabeth cries. "I only want to fix the wing."

"No more glue." It is the Director. "Not after the mess from last time . . ."

"Beauty. Lies," Elizabeth says. "Lies. Beauty lies. There lies beauty."

"It is useless," Albert says.

"What?"

"That wing."

"Well, perhaps," the Doctor says, interested to discover Albert has been listening as keenly as he has to the noise from down the hall. "But Elizabeth is very fond of it."

"Yes," Albert says. "It is useless but beautiful."

"Let's make something useful," the Doctor says. He pats Albert's knee and his knee jumps. "I'll be right back."

When he returns with a thick black pencil and a map of Europe torn from a newspaper, the Doctor traces Albert's peregrinations. The thick black line meanders through much of the German Empire and some of Austria-Hungary; it passes through Serbia, Bulgaria, and Eastern Rumelia.

"And Constantinople," Albert says.

"Constantinople?" the Doctor asks.

"Yes." Albert nods. "It's a longer story, I'm sure, but I only remember leaving."

And always home to Bordeaux.

The Doctor connects the dots and there is the map of Albert's life.

"Does this look familiar?" the Doctor asks, holding up the map.

Albert tilts his head. "How curious," he says, as if the Doctor is showing him a magic trick instead of the shape of his life.

"These are your journeys," the Doctor says.

"How delightful," Albert says.

It is not a happy story. Still, the Doctor thinks, there are so many different unhappy stories. *Happy families are all alike; every unhappy family is unhappy in its own way*, but this is not a novel. The stories—happy and unhappy; these are the invisible lesions.

This is what the great doctor has missed. In the women hysterics, the great doctor believes the cause of hysteria is always moral but the origin is neurological. What the Doctor wants to describe goes beyond an invisible lesion. It has more to do with the story the patient tells as a means of achieving peace. The problem is not that Albert's story of his life is happy or unhappy; it is that it is invisible to him.

"Stay away from me!" the veteran cries from the billiard room, and then there is the sound of billiard balls crashing to the floor and the murmur of Henri's voice trying to soothe him and then Claude's voice demanding that the veteran come with him to his room.

"Let's start again from the beginning, Albert. How old are you?"

"Inquiries would have to be made."

"Do you remember that we have already discussed the likelihood that you are twenty?"

"If you made such inquiries . . . well, then . . . you must know."

"Do you know how long you have been traveling, Albert?"

"Years? Years and years? I was not a vagrant."

"How many years?"

"I cannot say. I first walked when I was a child, but then again, I am not sure . . . it is gone as soon as I think of it. The leaves of the trees in the public garden were gold, and so tempting, though I did not mean to leave, but that was another time altogether."

"How old were you?"

"I'm sorry, time does not present itself to me. In Mont-de-Marsan, I think I enlisted there . . . but then it is gone. The 127th Infantry Regiment at Valenciennes. But later I left. I could not stay. I can't remember. It is gone again. There is sometimes a feeling before I walk. Headaches . . . I have headaches. A ringing in my ears? I am sometimes very thirsty. I sometimes fall down. There are times . . ." Albert's face goes red to the tips of his ears.

"Yes?"

Albert points to his lap, and the Doctor notes a possible proclivity for self-abuse.

"I will tell you more tomorrow."

"There is no rush," the Doctor says, though all he wants is for Albert to tell him more right now.

"When I stop walking . . ." Albert says, "everything begins to go dark. It's as though I'm disappearing. It is too painful to contemplate. I'm afraid I will walk again. I don't want to leave."

"We will not let you walk. We will keep you here. Do not worry for now. Do you have a family, Albert?"

"No longer."

"Do you remember the last time you saw your family?"

"Inquiries could be made. I do remember this: a night when the gas lamps were lit, and the world had started to disappear. It was as if all of the doors of a house were closed and then suddenly thrown open all at once. 'The spirit of coal,' my father would say. He was a gas fitter by trade. 'Gas turning night into day,' he would say."

"So you remember your father?"

"Please let me stay."

"We will keep you here. We won't let you leave. Tell me, do you remember your father? There is no need to cry." Albert takes the handkerchief the Doctor offers. "There is time. You will remember. You are not to worry. This is enough for today. There is plenty of time."

It is clear Albert doesn't like to speak of his father, and the Doctor knows not to rush him. *There will be time enough*, the Doctor's own father said once. But the incompetent country doctor—his unbuttoned cuffs flapping frantically as he leeched his father until there was no more blood left to take—forbade him to enter the room. That he was sixteen and not a child made no difference to the country doctor, who thought of him only as a nuisance, a thing underfoot. Still, he snuck into his father's room where he lay ill and alone, in a rare moment of stillness. He reached out to touch his father's face, and into the stillness came a great flapping, a hundred little birds descending, the incompetent country doctor's flailing cuffs, driving him from the room. With the foolish indignance of youth he fled his home, abandoning his father to death and a lonely grave. Later he would vow to become a doctor better than the one who ran him out of his home forever. He is certain he could have saved them both—his mother and father—if only they'd waited to become ill until he became a doctor, until he could save them. *What did he know of medicine?* Not enough, but this man's anguish is familiar.

"Albert, let's go out into the courtyard. Let's get some air."

"There, there, there." The song of Nurse Anne's voice comforting someone cuts through the shadows of the hall as they make their way out to the courtyard.

"I think I have met her before," Albert says. "Nurse Anne."

"We all feel that way," the Doctor says. But then he realizes: If you can't remember your life, to find someone familiar is fraught. Who knows what may have happened—what you might have done or said—when you encountered them before? It is the problem of a life in pieces.

"You met her here, Albert," the Doctor says definitively. "For the first time." And he sees Albert's body relax.

The clouds are gone and the remnants of late afternoon light fill the courtyard as Walter explains something to Marian through her veil and Nurse Anne whispers something to the veteran, who circles the hole in the garden. He stops when he sees Albert. "There he is with his clean feet," he says. "Why do you wash his feet and not mine?"

"Why do you listen at doors when you should be minding your own business?" Nurse Anne says.

"Then there is nothing to be done here," the veteran says, peering into the hole as if it went straight to the center of the earth. "It is too late."

"What I am wondering . . ." Walter says to Marian. "What I'm wondering is if the woman who claimed to be my so-called wife was the representation and the woman in the painting was real. That's all I'm asking. It's not so much. I'm sorry the nerves of morally deprived men such as myself are blackened and you have to smell them burning."

"Those are the mushrooms burning," Marian says. "Walter, I have other concerns. Hello, Albert."

"Hello, Marian," Albert says cautiously.

"A friend?" the Doctor asks.

"I wouldn't be so bold as to say that," Albert says.

"Well, she didn't say hello to me. She doesn't say hello to just anyone," says the Doctor, putting an arm through Albert's and leading him down the path, the birch trees looming over them.

"The clouds are gone," Albert says.

It's true. The air is clear, and full of the possibility of spring. Each of Albert's journeys must have seemed full of possibility, the Doctor thinks. What must it have been like to set off again and again and again? To disappear and then reappear—into what? He looks over to see if that look in Albert's eyes is still there—the suggestion that something might come whirring around the bend at any moment.

"What was it like, Albert? To walk? To walk so far?"

"Everything was . . . funny," Albert says, ducking to avoid a low-hanging branch. "The trees took fantastic shapes."

"It sounds . . ." But the Doctor isn't sure how to finish the sentence, and he is a man accustomed to finishing his sentences. There is something curious about this man, his funny big ears, and his lost life. It is difficult to know the truth when someone professes oblivion.

"We don't have to talk," says the Doctor. There is a train in the distance and the memory of his recent train ride rumbles through his body.

"It was astonishing," Albert says, and for a moment, standing there in the courtyard with the train's whistle fading into the distance, the truth is beside the point.

On his way home, the Doctor decides to go for a short ride around the lake of the public garden. "Supraorbital foramen." There is this. "Foramen, foramen, foramen." There is that, and in goes another gnat, down his throat. Click: He is his skeleton. Click: He is his muscle. Click: He is his blood circulating. Click goes the crank on the magnificent bicycle as it propels him through the world. This sort of movement *is* astonishing. He may not know exactly how Albert felt when he walked and walked and walked, but he knows the wonder of this.

"Lacrimal," he whispers. "Lacrimal, lacrimal, lacrimal." He rides past the fir trees—as it grows dark, they *are* rather fantastically shaped—around the lake, where the geese are battling with the ducks—everything *is* a little funny—concentrating on the rhythm of the bicycle, moving his ankles to the machine's music. *Always pedal vigorously*, instructed the book he bought to teach himself how to ride properly. *The cyclist is a man made half of flesh and half of steel that only our century of science and iron could have spawned.*

The rag merchant packing up his cart waves: "You're out late, aren't you?" The bicycle quivers—*Look ten meters in front of you and never look at the road*, and what does he do? He looks directly at the road and nearly runs into a tree. When he manages to right himself, he shuts his eyes, erasing the difference between the dark outside and the dark inside, feeling the same excitement as when he held his parents' hands as they waited for the great Léotard to come whirring into town. It's as though he is on the verge of knowing the correct time of his father's death; as though it is about to reveal itself to him, falling into place like a tumbler lock.

So fierce is his certainty, he almost expects to see the great Léotard when he opens his eyes. Instead, out of the evening mist steps a man who— How could it be? The same strange face, those expectant, sad eyes, oblivious to everything except putting one foot in front of the other; he looks just like Albert. *Someone comes.* The man is so fixated he doesn't notice the Doctor bearing down on him and the Doctor is forced to veer off the path, squealing to a halt just before a hedge of prickly gorse bushes, somersaulting over the handlebars, not at all in the style of the great Léotard.

As he flies through the air, his father's watch slips from his pants pocket and a voice—*his* voice!—cries out, "Papa!" But he doesn't have time to be embarrassed at having cried out like a child; his only concern is finding the watch that has marked the minutes of his life. As soon as he hits the ground, he is scrambling to his feet again, diving headfirst back into the same prickly bush he spends every morning so carefully avoiding. Though he searches and searches, the watch is nowhere to be found until, in despair, he looks once more and there it is, shining up at him through the thick brambles. There are long scratches on his arms, his waistcoat is torn, and his cravat is in an unruly state, but he does not care.

Ignoring his dishevelment, he looks for Albert on the path, but he is nowhere to be found. The man is not Albert at all; instead he is a shadow on the other side of the path, waving his fist. "Are you blind?" the man shouts as the Doctor jumps on his bicycle and pedals quickly away into the night. It is his greatest fear: That he won't see past the familiar, that his eyes won't become new. That he won't see Albert at all.

12

"THIS IS FOR YOU," the Doctor said yesterday (which was Sunday, and now there is today, which is Monday), leaving the map of Albert's journeys on the bedside table. "This is where you have been. I will leave it here for you to study. Perhaps you will remember something else." His father once looked at Albert the way the Doctor looked at him then, his face a question. Albert wants now what he wanted then, to smooth the lines of that face the way he smooths the wrinkles out of the map that makes a shape out of his mysterious life, out of those places that returned miraculously to Albert from somewhere far off so that he could recite them, offering them up to the Doctor: *Montauban, Moissac, Agen, La Réole, Castel-Sarrazin, Puyoô! Posen, Posen, Posen* . . . The shape is as beautiful as the large silvery fish that swam between his bare feet one day when he discovered himself, not knowing how he got there, sitting on a log fallen across the cold swirl of a river, his shoes somehow back on shore. He felt the pressure of it against his feet dangling in the bracing water, moving with such certainty, a glimmer and there it went: going, going, gone.

The places too swam through Albert's mind, so clear and then they were going, going, gone. He runs his hand over the thick black pencil marks from here to there, from there to here, hoping that the movement of his hand will ignite movement in his mind. But it is as if it never was.

He is twenty. He is twenty. He is twenty.

"We will watch over you." In the Doctor's voice when he is with him, he hears the watching; he hears it enough to rest. "We won't send you away," the Doctor says, his watch ticking Albert back into time. The Doctor said they would talk more tomorrow (tomorrow, which is Tuesday). *We'll give you time to remember and then we will talk more again?* Tick, tick, tick, he will bring him back.

But there are so many questions Albert can't answer. What if there isn't enough time in the world for him to remember? *How long have you been traveling? When was the last time you saw your family? Where have you been? Why do you go? Why can't you stop? What causes you to stop when you do stop?* Albert cannot smooth the lines on the Doctor's face if he cannot answer the questions. *Who are you, Albert?* This is the question that swims beneath the other questions. *Who are you?*

Ring (shadow ring). It is time for dinner. In the park outside the Palace of Justice, the trees are on fire with the brilliant colors of the setting sun. Albert wishes they would light his mind on fire so he could see from here to there and there to here.

"You need to eat your beautiful dinner in order to continue to make your beautiful music," Albert hears Claude say to Rachel, trying to entice her away from the piano as he does every night. "You can leave the coat on but roll up the sleeves," Henri says to Samuel, who is lurking in a corner. "Look what a mess . . ." It is time for dinner, but what if the fleeting illuminations continue to be fleeting, if the setting sun doesn't light his mind on fire long enough for him to see his life? It is right in front of him, some-where in the shadows of this map, if he could only see.

His finger moves over Mont-de-Marsan and there is the flicker he offered to the Doctor: discovering himself there and not knowing what else to do, he enlisted voluntarily in the 127th Infantry Regiment at Valenciennes, though there was a letter at home declaring him unfit for service by the review board.

What was the rest of the story? Something terrible happened. On the road in Mont-de-Marsan, marching with the other conscripts. And then, there he was, his friend Baptiste! Albert discovered himself and then he discovered Baptiste. *Here is love*, this shrunken man who was once a boy who smelled of apples and dirt. Together, they deserted the infantry and crossed the Belgian frontier, trading weapons and uniforms for laborers' clothes and three francs each. Baptiste marched with him through Tournai, Ostend, Bruges, Ghent, Brussels. He was thinner than a rail. Unable to find work, they begged until they were run out of every town. Albert tries to catch the memory by the tail before it trails off into darkness. He touches Angoulême on the map and out of the darkness comes the grape harvest; he touches Aix, and there is a hayfield; he traces the Rhine, and there is the sound of the thin lightning-bolt crack that chased him across the surface to the other bank. As much as Albert yearns for the crack to split him open, to split him open and send him crashing into the water, it never happens.

"In Saint-Étienne, I remember lying in a hospital with a cold compress on my head, given quinine sulfate to cure a toothache," Albert offered yesterday as it rose up into the light of his memory—the cold compress, the quinine, the toothache, and Saint-Étienne disappeared. Through Lyon he walked, past the funicular railroad, through Grenoble, on the promenades along the Isère River; through a town whose name he never learned, filled with the delicate fragrance of the rosewater manufactured there, walking until the earth's tremor rumbled through his feet and up his shins, until his bones expanded, until his blood circulated astonishment, until, finally, there it was, the urge to walk, and he was lifted into oblivion.

"The leaves of the trees in the public garden were gold that time," he said yesterday, but the memory escaped him before he was able to speak it. Now he looks at his home, Bordeaux, on the map, and remembers the leaves of the trees in the public garden sparkling gold through the green from the lights of the gas lamps his father had helped install and Albert, a boy, walking past them; the lights glittered and filled his eyes. The chestnuts rained down when he looked up at the tree's spindly arms, and he imagined that if he settled on a sturdy branch he could see out over the slated rooftops of the city and the church steeples. From that perch, he could see the flickering lights of hundreds of gas lamps illuminate the city—the giant clock of St. Eloi, and the church of Saint-Paul, and Saint-Michel, and Sainte-Croix; the Pont de Pierre, the grand theater, the ancient gate to the city, the ancient amphitheater where the gladiators once fought. He might reach up like the arches and buttresses of the nearby cathedral, up and up and up all the way to the heavens, but then the memory went up and up all the way to the heavens. It too was gone, back into darkness.

"There is time," the Doctor reassured him today. "You will remember. You are not to worry." He smiled and nodded, but Albert is sure the Doctor smells it on him—the stench of not remembering. How could he not? It fills the room; it smells of wet, dead leaves, of dying and rot. It lingers even after the Doctor is gone; it fills Albert's nostrils now. It has driven people away, causing them to leave him by the side of the road, as if he were contagious. To be a man is to be forged out of days, adding up to something with weight and heft; to be able to look back and say, *I was here and then here and then there and then there and then here.* He has heard people say, *I've lost these days.* They might be gone but the people do not mean they are lost entirely. It was the difference between growing older and oblivion. "There is time," the Doctor has said, and Albert wants more than anything for this to be true, but he is not so sure.

When there is a knock at the door, Albert thinks it is the Doctor, come to say they will try again today after all. Or perhaps he is making sure that Albert is all right, that he is coming to dinner. Dinner cannot go on without him. But when he opens the door, it is the veteran with his fuck-you-too face.

"I have found you out," the veteran says. "I know who you are." He is a much taller man than Albert realized; the only other time he has been this close to him was when he first arrived and the veteran had been busy throwing billiard balls and retrieving them. He shoulders his way in to the room, pushing Albert so he stumbles backward. "Going from town to town. Claiming not to remember. And then I heard you say it to the Doctor. I listen in for places where the darkness might get in. I listened in, and I heard it. At first I told myself not to think at all. Not to think about the fact that MaryfuckingMagdalene washes your feet. Let her, I said. I am not thinking of her."

The veteran is looming over Albert, but large men have loomed over him before. They have dragged him off to jail; they have caught him playing his beautiful instrument behind their stables and run him off their property with pitchforks; they have accused him of vagrancy, of theft, of not being a man. The only thing he ever feared was that he would disappear again. The veteran looms over him, on the verge of an accusation but this is not the first time Albert has been accused of something—

"I thought you were the Doctor," he says. More than anything, he is disappointed. Unless the veteran can really tell him who he is—and Albert is fairly certain that isn't what the veteran is here for—he doesn't care to hear the rest.

But the veteran is determined to tell him. "You enlisted at Mont-de-Marsan. I heard you. I heard you tell the Doctor. You are a deserter. I knew there was something peculiar. You were peculiar from the beginning."

"I am not sure what you want," Albert manages to say, sitting down on his bed as the veteran pushes him forward with his chest. *Let the man loom if he wants.* They always did.

"You are an outrage to our nation, but I'm not thinking that, I'm just trying to prevent further outrage," the veteran is saying.

A fleeting illumination, and there is Albert's childhood friend Baptiste, no longer boyishly round but sickly thin, his army clothes in tatters, staggering along a road behind Albert, but he can't remember why this is his fault. He can't remember why this causes him such pain.

"Why are you smelling me?" the veteran asks. "Back away."

"I am not," Albert says, though he is, inhaling deeply the glorious smell of the veteran in order to bring himself back to the room. It is the smell of remembering—dirt, sweat, and a loyal body that is not a deserter; it is the very opposite of dying and rot. It is the smell of a life. This man, with his hand on Albert's collar, remembers all his days all day long.

"I would like to put you in a hole and cover you up until your chirping mouth is full of dirt," the veteran is saying, but Albert isn't listening. All he can think is, *Teach me then. Teach me how to remember. Teach me how to be a man.*

Claude's body fills the doorway and then the veteran is being dragged out, protesting—"This man should be arrested"—and Nurse Anne is scolding Claude—"You should have your eye on him. Always"—and then she is telling Albert it is time for dinner. "We've been waiting for you," she says, and when he begins to cry, she thinks it is because the veteran scared him, but how could Albert explain to her that these are tears of joy at being expected at dinner?

"Why don't you lie down for a little while and then come to dinner?" she says. "We will save you a plate. The veteran will not bother you again. It is not you he is angry with."

Albert waits for her to close the door. Instead of lying down, he moves around the room, touching the chair and his shoes and the basin and the bedside table and the pitcher with the cracking ice and the bed. He is here. He is here. He is here.

Only after he has touched every object—here, here, here—in the room does he lie down on the bed. For so long, it has seemed to Albert that the surface of the earth would never be unfrozen again, not even in spring. But when the Doctor said today at lunch, "You look well, Albert," it created gaseous ejections in Albert's deepest heart. How can he explain to Nurse Anne that, for years, his greatest fear was that he would disappear, and now he wonders what will happen if he doesn't? Before, he expected nothing; now he is poised for *more*. All those years of yearning to be still and now that he is still, what is he expected to do? He pictures the still, frozen surface, the way the gas is invisible but the aqueous vapors from the geysers hang silently in the air, the gas cultivating the vegetation and slowly the forests rising up to provide the animals and humans, when they arrive, with great sources of minerals. Underneath the earth, the collision of the gas and fissures forms volcanoes that spew hot mud and throw fragments of rock that form mountains. *There were flames that blazed for as far as the eye could see*, said his father when he told him the story of gas. *Fires that burned and burned. Fires that burn still.*

How could Albert possibly explain that there are geysers taking shape inside of him? How can he explain that this moment, this exquisite *now*, will soon become something glimpsed only occasionally in fleeting illuminations from the pitch-dark road of an unhappy story?

Thousands of centuries ago, his father said, *there were gaseous ejections in the deepest heart of the world. There were geysers formed by gas colliding with fissures and crevices. In the very veins of the earth there were explosions. The surface of the earth was still. For so long, it was frozen. It seemed it would never be unfrozen again, not even in spring.*

He is twenty. He is twenty. He is twenty.

Albert's surface has started to thaw in the spring of the Doctor's attentions. The gentle growth of scrubby vegetation might someday give rise to forests.

Here, Albert, a story just for you.

For him and no one else, the sound of this voice he thought had been lost forever. which wasn't lost at all.

Listen.

The prince with one swan wing who wanted to see the world woke to discover himself in the midst of a family of geese.

"You look strangely familiar," said the father goose, eyeing the prince's swan wing. "Anyway, we need your help. We are fewer than we were. You see, each night, a fox comes around and takes another of us off for his dinner. Some nights he takes two: one for dinner, one for dessert."

The rest of the geese gathered around. In one voice they told the prince: "Each night for a week, the fox has come; each night, there is one, sometimes two, fewer geese." The goose family was dwindling. "We used to be many," the father goose said, and he began to weep.

"I have an idea!" the prince said. He whispered his idea to the father goose, who whispered it to the rest of the goose family. As night fell, the prince began to disappear limb by limb into the dark and he found a tree and clung to it, hoping that, finally, he might stay up long enough to watch night turn into day. Meanwhile, the geese prepared for the fox's arrival.

When night covered the land, the fox arrived, his red face like a demon's.

"Wait!" the father goose shouted as the fox prepared to pounce on the

mother goose. "If we poor geese are to yield up our lives," he said, according to the prince's instructions, "grant us one favor. Let us pray so that we may not die in sin."

The fox sat back, eyeing the prince clinging to the tree doing his best to remain invisible. "Oh, why not?" the fox said. "Go ahead. Have your prayer."

And so the geese began.

"Ga! Ga!" said the father goose. Then the mother goose chimed in, "Ga! Ga! Ga!" And then a third goose. And then a fourth. "Ga! Ga! Ga!" And a fifth. And then the sixth and final goose. "Ga! Ga! Ga! Ga! Ga! Ga!" This was their prayer, and they prayed and prayed and prayed until their prayer was a song.

"When they are done praying," Albert's father would say, "the story will end."

"Why?" Albert always asked, though he had heard the story before and knew what his father's answer would be.

"Because when they are done praying, the fox will eat them."

"But instead . . ." Albert prompted his father.

"Instead, they pray unceasingly and the story continues."

"Ga! Ga! Ga!" his father would say to him, instead of good night, keeping the prayer of the story alive. *We will always be together, you and I,* is what Albert heard. In the flickering light, his father's face took this shape and then that—a goose, a fox, a king waiting for his son to return home. His father's face could take any shape it wanted, Albert knew; it could be things that it wasn't, not only the things that it was.

There is his father about to blow out the gas lamp, the story still shimmering all around them. *Ring (shadow ring),* the sharp, quick sound of love in Albert's ears.

What time is it? It is time to lie still.

He lies in his bed and time doesn't pound him into nothing as he listens to the rain wash clean the piss-drenched streets. He listens as a soaking wet horse clop-clops its way along the slick cobblestones. It is beautiful: the sound of something washed clean; the sound of the horse's efforts as it makes its way from here to there. There is the clanking of the dinner dishes being cleared; Rachel playing Chopin's C sharp minor prelude, *"Not the Funeral March,"* she tells Marian, "the ghostly one," to which Marian responds, "What a relief, a ghost galloping away from death," before returning to the sweet murmur of Walter. "Good night!" says the Director. "Listen to Nurse Anne. Tomorrow will bring a new day."

Ga! Ga! Ga! Never mind tomorrow. Albert wants nothing more than to keep this moment—there it went—alive.

13

I T IS THE TIME of the year when the sulfurous smell from the gasworks rides the wind up the hill from the river and hangs heavy in the air. Despite the smell, despite the dust his bicycle spins up that sticks to his face, the Doctor is eager to go to work each day. Ever since Albert's arrival, the Doctor has looked forward to the moment he slides off his bicycle and walks through the iron gates under the gentle arch of the asylum entrance. Every day our traveler, as Nurse Anne has taken to calling him, offers a new detail, a gift—his dear childhood friend Baptiste, the woman he met on the bridge who asked him to marry her, the story his father told him of the ancient magic of gas, that his father was a pipe fitter for the gas company; every day, there he is at meals with his large, funny ears, sitting contentedly between Marian and Walter at meals—"My pet," Marian calls him, and Walter no longer squeezes him because he believes in his reality completely; every day, Albert's large sad eyes glisten with gratitude when he sees the Doctor.

Since Albert arrived, only a small corner of the Doctor's mind has remained tethered to the daily life to which he had grown accustomed—cutting the ends off the mouse-nibbled bread to eat the softer center for his breakfast, waving to the bartender down-stairs as he calls out, "Don't be a stranger," remaining a stranger. He still spends time with the other patients—walking Walter to the window to remind him the people are not invented each day only to be invented all over again tomorrow, pulling Rachel's hair from her face and consoling her when she cries over Chopin's sister walking her brother's heart to Warsaw, reminding Marian that she has all of her organs even when she tells him he is a know-nothing wretch. Still, the *before* is fading. A small corner of the Doctor's mind remains tethered to his daily life *before*, but here in the *after*, the rest has been given over to the question of our trav-eler, *his* traveler. *Someone comes.* And you are changed.

This morning, the Doctor must perform his usual navigation as he pedals through the tangle of schoolchildren, government officials, the occasional drunk staggering over from the café in front of the cathedral to collide with a government official. There was a time when officials used to drop the drunks off at the asylum; this was before the Director made it clear that his asylum wasn't a catchall. The Director has worked hard to distinguish the asylum as a place where people might not be treated as criminals, where they might be treated without the presence of criminals. "This is not a prison," he would say when people arrived with the drunks, and then he would provide directions to the jail.

The Doctor swerves to avoid the end of a government official's walking stick as he uses it to nudge a drunk man away before returning to his conversation. "They. Must. Do," punctuating each word with a tap of his stick against the ground, "Something. About. That. Smell."

"Aren't you *they?*" the drunk man says, suddenly suspiciously lucid, but the official chooses not to hear him.

The Doctor hopes never to grow so deaf. Click-clickety-click—he delights in the rhythm of the bicycle propelling the great weight of his body. His teeth gritty with dust, there is still pleasure in *his* system, still system in *his* pleasure. Despite the sulfurous smell, people are sitting at the outside tables at the café on the corner of the square where just last night the Doctor found himself dining, tempted out of his usual routine of eating at home alone by the thought that sometimes the answer to complicated questions such as Albert's are to be found in unlikely places. Sitting next to him was a man reading *Journey to the Center of the Earth*. How would someone who hadn't read the book, as the Doctor has, have any idea that it involved, say, volcanic tubes? And yet, how alluring, how inviting, that title.

A life exceeds our ability to describe it, he found himself thinking; names alone do not suffice. *Hysteria*, for example. The word should not be expected to carry the entire life of that fierce girl in the great doctor's amphitheater on its back—how could it? A name becomes fixed, but the story underneath a name is ever shifting. And still, there is something in a name, akin to the title of a book.

The dignified trees, the hornbeams that line the public square outside the Palace of Justice, shiver in the wind. *Hornbeams.* Before they were called hornbeams, they were only *trees*; before they were *trees*, before they were given a name, weren't they still noble, still beautiful, as they sought the sun? They existed though they had no name, but then someone called them *trees* and their silhouettes grew sharper, and when someone called them *hornbeams*, their silhouettes grew sharper still. There are lavender bushes between each of the hornbeams; delicate and lovely even before they were called *lavender*, but then someone called them *lavender* and the soft outline of their purple spray became visible to men who cannot see things that have no name. For the same reason, the Doctor realizes, Albert's condition needs a name.

He is almost to the gentle arch of the asylum when the sky thickens with dark clouds and the rain starts to fall. People squeal and scatter, tenting newspapers over their heads, huddling under the umbrellas of those lucky enough to remember theirs during this season of unexpected showers. The Doctor gets off his bicycle, hopping from one cobblestone to the next to avoid the water rushing between them. All around him, rain batters the roofs, its roar an enormous waterfall threatening to drown the city. The answers often lurk in unlikely places and so he turns left instead of right, into the small stone church across from the asylum.

Cavelike, the cool darkness inside of the church is like being inside a mind, and that is where the Doctor wants to be, inside Albert's mind, inside the mysterious realm of his experience. He trails his fingers through the holy water in the cold marble font, then shakes the water from his hand and wipes it on his trousers.

Tsk–tsk.

Thick incense burns on the altar as he reads the tiles covering the walls: *Merci à Saint Jacques, merci à Jésus, merci à Dieu.* Placing his hand on each cool tile, he wishes fleetingly he were a man of the church and not a man of medicine so that the answer to Albert would simply be God.

"*Tsk–tsk.* You are disturbing our prayers," a familiar voice says, and there is the witchy woman, emerging from the shadows.

"There is no one else in here."

"Do you think I pray only for myself?" The witchy woman is less witchy in the shadow of the prayer candles' guttering flames. In the near dark, there is evidence of a more malleable creature, soft and fluid as the wax dripping from the candles. The Doctor thinks he almost detects sweetness. Almost.

"Is this where I put money for a candle?" he asks her.

She nods suspiciously as his coins clink against the other coins already in the box and he retrieves a thin white stick of tallow.

"All right, then," she says.

He lights the candle with another candle already lit, then

waits for the wax to pool, tilting it so the wax falls into the empty metal cup in the candelabra. He fixes his candle there and holds it steady while the blinking eyes of the woman float in the dark, watching him.

"Amen," she says.

"For a friend," he says. He has never lit a candle in a church in his life, but the answers often lurk in unlikely places.

"We all need the light of God. No need to run from it. We can all use more light." She holds out her hand.

He puts a few coins in her palm, but when he turns to go, she follows him down the aisle.

"You can't hide," she says. "There is no fleeing . . ."

"I have no more change," he says, putting his hand in his pocket to show how empty it is.

"We can all say no," she says. "It means nothing. No, no, no."

When he pushes the door open to go, a river runs over the cobblestones. The rain pummels him as he tries to step outside.

"You will be washed away if you go out there," she says. There is a question underneath her words: *Will you stay?*

He takes a seat in a pew near the back and the woman takes a seat a few rows away.

"There is no escape," she says. "Why do you flee?"

"I'm not fleeing," he says. "I'm right here." He lays an arm across the cool wood of the pew, resting his head for a moment there, and closes his eyes. Behind his eyelids, the word remains: *flee*. One usually flees *from* something, but might one also, contemporaneously, flee *toward* something? Astonishment? *Flee*, the word, echoes in the cave of his own mind: flight from and toward. *Fugue* means flight. Originally from the Latin *fuga*, an odd combination of *fugere*, to flee, and *fugare*, to chase. Or maybe not so odd. *Fugueur*.

And? So? Albert might be the first of his kind, similar to a musical fugue, a contrapuntal counterpoint, a style rather than a fixed structure. Together, the sounds Albert's story makes create a new sound. Different than the recent case of the great doctor's, in a journal the Director showed him just yesterday. The case involved a deliveryman, a collector of bills for clients to whom he delivered bronze artworks and chandeliers. The Doctor could imagine the deliveryman, blinking and blinking as the hairy bear led him into the amphitheater, coaxed by the great doctor into telling his story, which began with a headache as he took the Rue Amelot to Avenue de Villiers, where he stopped in front of number 178 Avenue de Villiers, the address to which he was meant to make a delivery. But he did not go in. When he woke up, fourteen hours later, he had no memory of where he'd been or how he'd gotten there. He said, *I discovered myself in the Place de la Concorde. I was famished.* Though it appears the delicate, blinking man wandered only once and never again, the great doctor chalked it up to a male form of the Great Neurosis probably caused by some kind of physical trauma, favoring a neurological explanation. "There may be something to this," the great doctor is quoted as saying. The Doctor heard a claim being staked in the *this* that was the question of Albert. "This is not so rare," the great doctor went on to say in the article. It was clear to the Doctor then—the great doctor would take Albert's questions, as he had taken everything else, for his own. *Why do you walk? Why can't you stop?* But there is more yet to find out about this man who escapes and escapes and escapes without success from a world he cannot seem to bear. The Doctor would draw his own conclusions about his patient, and besides, Albert does not belong to the Doctor. What he is after is a new diagnosis, and diagnoses are stories, and this would be Albert's.

"It is still raining," the woman says. *Stay a little while longer in the dark with me.*

She is lonely, and though he is eager to return to Albert, he is no stranger to the desire for company and he stays a little while longer in the dark with this woman who has helped him, though she will never know why.

The answers often lurk in unlikely places.

"I'll stay a little while longer," he says. "Thank you."

When the rain lets up, the Doctor crosses the slick street, rolling his bicycle carefully through the asylum arch. There is Marian, perched on her bench, and Walter next to her, leaning in to whisper conspiratorially, something the Doctor can't quite hear about a *soul murder.* "I can't pay attention to you," Marian says, grabbing Walter's hand as though they were on one more sinking ship. Rachel huddles around the Director, examining something. "These worms help the soil. They are not disgusting," he says, putting a worm in Rachel's outstretched palm as she winces but not without fascination. Claude and Henri keep an eye on the veteran as he digs and digs, while Samuel trembles in his giant coat, looking on. "I'm not thinking about him," the veteran is saying, "I'm not thinking about that deserter, his running away, running away. Fuck those chirping birds . . ."

"And all is right with the world," Nurse Anne says from the doorway as the Doctor approaches.

"Amen," he says.

"The veteran is making trouble," Nurse Anne whispers so that anyone paying attention—the Director is not—might hear, "He should be separated. The Director is too kind."

But the Doctor isn't paying attention either. He is anticipating Albert's glistening, eager eyes. *Here you are at last,* they say. *Yes,* the Doctor thinks, *here I am at last.*

In the common room, Elizabeth is bent over her puzzle. "It is the funicular that requires my attention," she says to no one in particular.

"Those people won't wait for that funicular forever," the Doctor says, trying for lightness. He only means to joke with her the way he sometimes does, but he hears the prickle in his voice at that eternally unfinished puzzle and Elizabeth's insistence that it will be finished tomorrow. *There is time*, his father said. But impatience with waiting for tomorrow is causing him to itch. "They'll grow tired and they'll walk up the hill," he says.

As Elizabeth tucks a strand of hair behind her ear to reveal her pointed chin, he already regrets his words. Her thin, thin face and the dark circles under her quick eyes that never fade no matter how much she sleeps; that puzzle that is her whole world for days on end. How could he be so callous?

"Well," she says. "That would be terribly disappointing."

"And what is your smart answer for that?" Nurse Anne says, appearing out of nowhere, as she so often does. She is right to scold him.

"It will be all right," he says, putting a hand on Elizabeth's back and looking apologetically at Nurse Anne, but his mind is already with Albert.

The bells of St. Eloi ring, and then the asylum bell.

How can the Doctor not believe that his own ringing will ring Albert open too?

"How are you this morning?" he asks as he walks into Albert's room to find him waiting eagerly, as he does each day. The Doctor sits in the extra chair he had Nurse Anne bring in so that he and Albert can sit together, eye to eye. "You look well."

He *does* look well. Each day, there have been visible improvements. Because of Nurse Anne's ministrations, Albert's calluses have healed; the raw blisters, gone. Each day, he follows the bells to breakfast, to exercises, to lunch, to dinner; he follows the Director down to the creek; he pulls enthusiastically at the lettuce in the garden and tosses the manure until he is covered in it. (The Director asked him yesterday to toss "less vigorously.") The Doctor has never seen a patient who has followed the regimen of the bells quite so strictly or with such apparent pleasure.

"There is pleasure in a schedule," the Director has said. "It calms the mind."

Certainly this is true, but it seems to the Doctor that Albert is less calmed by the bells than he is delighted. "I am delighted to hear that," Albert says when the Doctor reminds him of his age. And the bells? The bells delight him endlessly. He anticipates them, listening into the silence just before they ring.

"I am very well," Albert says. "I feel sure I will remember more today."

Here in the *nearly*, the *almost* of Albert's story, the Doctor feels himself sharpen to a point. *Fugueur.* There is a name for this man, and very soon there will be a story. "Let's look once again at the map. You've studied it, I know." He traces Albert's route with a finger. "These are the towns from which you've disappeared; these are the towns in which you've appeared. This is where you've been, and now we need to learn more about what happened in between"—he points at the dots on the map—"here and here. Here. Here. Why you began to walk. Why you stopped."

So far Albert's memory has been like a photographic plate of which some parts are blurred. It is not one episode of oblivion that has invaded his life but a series of episodes. "Give it time," the Director has said to the Doctor. "It takes time. He has walked across most of Europe. The man is exhausted. He is not a toy to be shaken upside down until his soul falls out of his ears." He is right; still, Albert's answers to the Doctor's questions are pebbles at the bottom of a vast and mysterious ocean.

"I will remember more tomorrow," Albert says, and the next day there will be another pebble: *I was thrown in jail for vagrancy.* Or, *I had a childhood friend named Baptiste.* Or, *I had headaches before I walked and sometimes I fell down.* Or, *when I stopped everything became dark, as though I was disappearing.*

At first Albert offers answers, and then slowly he grows sleepy, promising he will remember more tomorrow. Something is happening in his effort to tell, the Doctor is sure. He is trying to make a life out of words, but perhaps there is something the Doctor might do to hasten the process.

According to a recent article, the great doctor has been hypnotizing his hysterics. He believes that the ability to be hypnotized in and of itself is a sign of hysteria, that it can be used to create an artificial world in which hysterical symptoms can be reproduced and transformed, but surely it is a more malleable treatment than that, a purely psychological means of finding hidden truth. It is this invisible truth, or near approximation of truth, that intrigues the Doctor, that makes him think another trip to the amphitheater to watch the great doctor might be fruitful. Isn't it enough if the mechanism unlocks a story? If it is a life that undoes a person, maybe it is a story forged from that unruly life that can do a person back up? *What is your unhappy story?* It begins with a question.

"Are you ready to begin, Albert?"

"I will remember more today," Albert says. "I am certain."

How bright and shiny he looks this morning, as if the rain has washed him clean. The alertness in his eyes gives the Doctor hope that he may not need to subject himself again so soon to the amphitheater full of high foreheads and aristocratic noses, that the answer may be right here, with Albert.

"You will write down what I say?" Albert asks.

"Yes, yes," says the Doctor. "What you have to say is very important."

How easy, how simple the dance is today! "Let's return to your travels."

"Yes," Albert says. "Yes."

The wind spins around the bell tower, shivering the bell from the inside out, and there is that weird, muted ringing. Albert's large, sad eyes glisten and, for a moment, it seems as though he might cry. But there are no tears. There is no bemusement, either, at learning he has walked across great swaths of Europe. No *How curious it is, this map of my travels.* Instead, Albert pulls his knobby shoulders back and sits up straighter in the chair. He smooths his pants legs with his hands. He might be a man at a dinner party.

"I remember a trip from Warsaw to Moscow," Albert says.

And for a moment the Doctor believes that the sparkle of the dust motes in the air is the sparkle of the future after all, that today will be the day he will look back on as the turning point.

"One fine day I woke to discover myself in a cattle car."

The Doctor's desire for this to be Albert's story is a veil, which transforms the shadows into whatever he wants them to be, but then—

"The police wore strange pointed helmets," Albert says, his voice gaining confidence. "They mistook me for a nihilist. For the assassin."

"Whose assassin?" The Doctor wants to be the very opposite of the people who pinned Albert with a note—*He is off his rocker*—and told him to go home or threw him in jail, but the velvet in his voice is slipping away. The rough, impatient texture that lies beneath is, he imagines, what these people felt.

"'Where are your papers?' they demanded," Albert is saying. "Being always without papers, I had none. 'Finally we have got him,' they said. 'To prison with the nihilist!'"

"Albert." The story is familiar, too familiar.

Shaved heads, he is saying, freezing cold that turns your fingers blue, bedbug-ridden blankets, fifty people called up to be sent to Siberia. The story is familiar, the Doctor realizes, because it is the story of the assassin of czar Alexander II, an event from some years back that has moved beyond story into history.

"When I was not among them," Albert is saying, "I thought, *I will be hanged.* But the Russian government must have learned of my taste for voyages! They decided to send me on a trip to Siberia after all! I thought to myself, *Siberia, let's go!*"

Later the Doctor will be able to admire this detail, the dash of truth in the midst of the lie.

"The Russian government marched us to the Turkish border. *This* is how I arrived in Constantinople. Cossacks galloped alongside of us. If we didn't move quickly enough, they would smack us on the legs with the flat side of their swords."

The Doctor stops writing as Albert uses his hand against his thigh to illustrate the Cossacks thwacking the prisoners with the flat of their swords.

"That is enough, Albert."

The Doctor fiddles with the pin in his cravat. He cannot wait for *tomorrow*. He has been patient. They were moving in the right direction; piece by piece, they were recovering Albert's life, and now this? Every day, he has been patient. He pulls the pin from his cravat and taps his wrist with it to calm himself. He imagines tapping the pin along the inside of Albert's right arm. Tap, tap, tap along the bridge of his nose. He imagines plunging the pin through one of Albert's ridiculous ears.

Each prick along the Doctor's arm produces a pimple the size of a grain of millet.

"This is not your story, Albert, is it?"

Albert closes his eyes, mumbling something the Doctor can't make out. "Careless." Is that the word he whispers? The Doctor isn't sure, but that's what he thinks he hears. Each day, expecting answers to questions that have plagued this man his whole life. Why wouldn't Albert try anything to please him? He is only trying to give the Doctor what he thinks the Doctor wants: the gift of an answer, any answer. He has been careless.

"What have I done?" Albert asks as the Doctor stands to go.

"I will be right back," he says, leaving Albert there. And he planned to be right back. He did. He planned to go outside only for a moment. He planned to take some air to relieve his shame. He planned to ride his bicycle once around the loop of the lake and then return refreshed. But then there is the Director in the common room, a small rake in one hand, squatting next to Elizabeth, who is in tears over her puzzle.

"My dear, my dear," he is saying, "a funicular is a complex piece of technology."

"But," she says, "what if they walk up the hill before I am done?"

"There is no rush," he says, stroking her back. "No rush at all."

"How could you know?" she wails. "You are not inside their minds. How could you know?"

He has caused this too. The Doctor planned to return, but then: *What do you know? What do you know?* It seems he knows nothing, nothing at all.

The answer lurks in unlikely places. It is not to be found, for example, on the well-pedaled loop around the lake. It doesn't matter. The Doctor mounts his bicycle and pedals to the lake path, not marveling at the connection between his own skeleton and the metal of this wondrous machine—*the communion of man and metal,* as his beloved book on bicycle riding calls it—not finding the system in the pleasure or the pleasure in the system. He will take that trip to Paris after all. He will leave tomorrow. Perhaps the great doctor has something to offer; perhaps the Doctor will learn something.

Click-clickety-click. The Doctor completes another pass around the lake. *I fear I will walk very far away, with no one to watch over me.* Wrapped inside this sentence like a poorly kept secret is another question: *Will you help me?* More often than not, we rely on what has worked before. What to do until we see beyond the familiar? Until our eyes become new? *I am in pieces.* The Doctor pedals faster to feel the wind, to feel anything other than the fear that the vague *something* of Albert will never take shape. This was certainly not what Michaux felt before he invented the clever pedal.

The geese float in the center of the lake, their heads tucked beneath their wings, while on shore the ducks waddle and squawk. Click-clickety-click. This wonderful, gravity-defying machine, so carefully constructed, so solid, so *there*, is nothing like the mysterious gray matter tucked inside the shell of the skull. It is nothing at all like the nebulous mind; nothing at all like the nebulous mind gone awry. Click-clickety-click. He pedals until he is no longer aware of pedaling, until he becomes the pedaling, until he is movement itself; the wind tickles the hairs in the coil of his ears. He rides too close to the fir tree to test his balance, and though the bicycle trembles, he will not fall again. He will not. The tree sprays his face with dew.

Honk! A goose floating in the middle of the lake suddenly lifts its head from its wing. Honk, making fun of the Doctor. Honk: You are ridiculous. Honk: so young, so serious, so full of big honking thoughts.

But the goose isn't concerned with the Doctor's big honking thoughts, not at all. A little boy and his mother have wandered into the park. The boy's delight has startled the geese awake and now they honk and float in anxious circles. He points and waves, points and waves. He is waving at the Doctor. It is still exciting to see a bicycle. To spot one is to see time and space forever transformed. Cycling telegraphists bringing news from the cities to the countryside and back again; infantrymen on wheels; and on certain saint days, it is rumored that a parson in a village dresses up as the patron saint of the local parish and rides his bicycle from house to house to house, taking confessions. The bicycle is a vehicle of forgiveness in addition to being a cure for gout, rheumatism, hernia, curvature of the spine, anemia, tuberculosis! Sterility too, though as the Doctor hits another bump in the path he thinks maybe not. A stimulator of appetite, an expander of the thoracic cage, a creator of better posture, improved fibrous tissues!

He pedals faster and the boy jumps up and down, pointing and laughing on the opposite side of the lake as his mother brushes the hair from his eyes. He pedals past his bones, past his muscles, until he and the machine are one and his ambulatory powers are multiplied, until he is half steel, half flesh. One moment the pebble-shaped end of his fibula is awhirl, and the next his heart is being tugged like a balloon. He is so close to grasping the *something* of Albert; he would give anything to grasp it. Take his vertebrae. Take his clavicle. Take his lacrimal bone. *Lacrimal, lacrimal, lacrimal!*

He rushes ahead, through space and time to the moment when he will give Albert an answer to his question: *This is who you are.* The wind on his face slices through the feeling of *almost* and then his bicycle lifts off; it flies above the lake, over the city. It flies until there are his mother and father. They are alive again and he is their jumping-up-and-down boy. When they take him up in their arms, the answer is: *You are forgiven.* When he puts his face in the warm crook of their necks, they are healed.

A great swoosh, an enormous flutter and splash, and the geese rise up: over the park, over the cathedral, up and up and up. The Doctor yearns to go with them, to show the jumping-up-and-down boy just how magic this new machine is. He feels the possibility of flight in the beautiful coral of his bones.

But the jumping-up-and-down boy has lost interest in the Doctor and his magical machine. He pulls at his mother's skirts, pointing at the sky, his finger tracing the path of the geese as they fly away.

14

I T WAS MEANT AS an offering. He only wanted to smooth the lines on the Doctor's face. Yesterday as he was waiting for him to arrive, he studied the map, trying to remember what came between *here* and *here*, and *here* and *here*, but he could not. When he heard the veteran saying, "Deserter, deserter," desperation shone its anxious light on the story of the man who was mistaken for the czar. It was a story his father told him, one of the many of the prince who wanted to see the world. This story with a beginning, a middle, and an end seemed like the solution to the problem of the cracked pieces of Albert's own life with their cutting edges.

But then, *I will be right back*, and like everything else in Albert's life, the Doctor disappeared.

Prick. Prick. Prick.

Prick. Prick. Prick.

Prick. Prick. Prick.

The *prick, prick, prick* of the pin against the Doctor's wrist. and Albert found himself once again in the foothills where the old women searched for healing herbs so rare they only have names in Catalan. *Prick, prick, prick*, and he discovered himself, not knowing how he got there, in a public square in Pau.

"Here, my friend," said a well-scrubbed man with large, kind ears, and he gave Albert a kilogram of bread and twenty sous.

"Thank you, my friend," replied Albert, though he wasn't sure if he had ever met the man before. Better *my friend* than to be impolite. He wiggled his toes through the leaves stuffed into his battered shoes—*there you are, there you are*—and the well-scrubbed man told him about the centuries-old ancient cure the old women made from the nectar of the flowers that grew on the hill.

Ancient cure was all he needed to hear; it was all he had ever wanted.

He walked until he found himself in the foothills of the Pyrénées; on the honey pots was written *les petits pharmiciens*. Little doctors! The Pyrénées were *truly* magnificent! He stuck his fingers into the honey, plunged his hand up to the wrist, his arm coated in the thick amber drawn by the industrious bees from the nectar of the mysterious flowers. Sucking his honeyed fingers until they pruned, he sucked the ancient cure until he had sucked away all traces of the magic sweetness.

On that stony hill with the little doctors, his own sweet fingers in his mouth, it seemed, it appeared . . . here he was, he was here. The ghost of sweetness in his mouth was an ache in his teeth. *Here I am.* No trembling. *Here I am.* No want in his bones.

When the first bee fastened itself to his lip, he thought, *The little doctors have arrived.* He was so ready for the ancient cure. But then the swarm began to prick him. *Prick*, up his arms. *Prick*, his face. *Prick*, along his jaw. *Prick*, inside his mouth where their furry legs found their footing, and *prick, prick, prick.*

He ran down the hill, stung and stung and stung. When the old women searching among the rocks looked up, what they saw was an exuberant man, arms waving, trampling their precious flowers. "Hey! Hey! Stop!" the women called after him, mistaking his shouts of terror for the recklessness of a honey thief.

"Careless man!" they shouted.

Albert *was* a deserter, the veteran was right, but Albert was not merely a deserter from the army. He deserted everything and everyone. Careless man, and he found himself once again walking in formation. Out of a morning mist, his friend's familiar face marching next to him. So thin, as though Baptiste had just squeezed himself between the bars of a banister, his pinched body one enormous held breath. When he saw Albert, he let the breath out as though he had only been waiting for Albert to appear. Winter was brutal and cutting as they walked without good coats, the only sound their shoes wearing away on the road. Still, *Here is my friend*, he thought, but it didn't matter because there was the tremble in the arch of his foot. The urge to walk returned, and he woke up into another day, not knowing how he got there, and Baptiste was gone. As quickly as he could he retraced his steps through the snow, his toes burning with cold even wrapped in the strips of wool he tore from his jacket. One kilometer and then two and then three, and there was his friend limping along, his face and his pinched body, that enormous held breath, turning blue. *Here is love*, he thought, but it didn't matter. The urge returned, and again he woke, not knowing how he got there, somewhere else entirely. He was in Maastricht and his friend had disappeared. Have you seen a man? Thin? He sucked in his face until he thought he might swallow himself and a woman said, "Oh, *him*," and pointed down the road.

When he arrived at the home of the doctor who took Baptiste in, it was too late. He had already died of exhaustion.

The fragile thread from the past to the present snapped.

What was the question?

Through nameless towns Albert walked until his tears became the weather itself, raining down on him.

This was the curse for which there was no ancient cure.

Ring (shadow ring). I will be right back. Lying on his bed, *ring (shadow ring), ring (shadow ring), ring (shadow ring)*, he watches through the window the sun moving across the sky without realizing he is watching it. It is as if he is being drawn up into the sky until there is only sky and the Doctor isn't back and he isn't and he isn't.

He is a deserter, and now the Doctor has deserted him—isn't this what he deserved?

It is only when Nurse Anne appears in his room, swiping the dust off his bedside table with her hand, that Albert realizes hours have passed.

"This isn't Versailles. Lunch will not be brought to you on a platter."

He is afraid to ask her where the Doctor has gone. If he doesn't ask and if no answer is spoken maybe it won't be real, like one of Walter's fleetingly improvised concoctions.

"Coming?"

"Yes, yes," and he is grateful for the arm she offers.

At the table, secure between the warmth of Marian and Walter, he arranges his food in such a way as to make it appear eaten.

"I will have that," Elizabeth says.

"Here," Albert offers.

"You *are* just like my brother," she says. "So generous."

For a moment Albert wonders if he has woken up into another life in which he is simply someone's brother.

"No, Elizabeth," Nurse Anne says. "One dinner is plenty." She nods at Rachel's plate, where usually half of the meal remains. "One and a *half*."

"Help me with my puzzle?" Elizabeth asks when the plates are cleared and lunch is done.

"He is not your brother," says Marian.

"You think I am nobody," Elizabeth says. "I've had shocking dreams, you know. Even you would be afraid."

But Albert wants to wait in his room while the smell of the Doctor's pomade still hangs in the air. *He will be right back.*

"He has divine urgencies of his own," Marian says to Elizabeth.

"I am feeling a bit dizzy," Albert says.

He walks as quickly as one can who has claimed to be dizzy. In his room, the smell of the Doctor's pomade is beginning to fade and the stench of his own forgetting has returned. Before he shuts the door, he hears the rumble of an argument down the hall, and then the veteran's voice grows loud enough to be audible. "I don't know what you're talking about."

"You know what you said." It is Walter. "You know what you said to him. You've upset him. You have frightened the hunger out of him."

"Walter," says Marian. "We are wasting an opportunity for me to go outside."

"Why would I be thinking of someone who isn't worthy of my thoughts?" the veteran says. "I am not thinking of anything but what is in front of me. And I'm not even thinking of that because that would be you."

"I will join you, Marian," Walter says.

"Listen, you," the veteran says.

Listen.

And into the room comes Albert's father's voice. *Il revient. Il revient.*

Here, Albert, a story just for you.

The prince with one swan wing woke to discover a young woman standing over him, carrying an armful of chopped wood and a concerned look on her face.

"Perhaps you should see a doctor?" she said. "You don't look very well."

"*It's the swan wing, isn't it?*"

"*Oh, no,*" *she said.* "*The wing is quite beautiful. You just look a little tired.*" *The prince sat up in the hopes of looking less tired.*

"*Do you know a doctor?*" *he asked, in as casual a tone as he could muster.*

"*I only know Dr. Knowall,*" *the young woman said, putting down her armful of wood in order to take a seat on the knoll of soft blue moss beside him. The girl was very lovely. She smelled deliciously of pine needles.*

"*He is my father.*" *And with that, she began to cry. The prince offered her his sleeve but she waved it away.* "*It will pass,*" *she said.* "*It always does. It's just . . .*" *and she began to cry harder, but eventually it did pass and she was able to tell the prince the story in its entirety.*

Her father, after many exhausting, ill-paid years as a woodcutter, had grown tired of it. Around this time, a stranger passed through their village. One night, the girl returned home to discover that her father had invited this stranger to dinner. The stranger said he was a doctor and over several nights—and several hearty dinners cooked by the girl at her father's insistence ("She is a wonderful cook," he told the stranger, which was true, the girl assured the prince) the stranger regaled them with stories of his rich doctor's life.

"*Doctors,*" *he exclaimed loudly, his mouth full of beef stew,* "*live well.*" *He took another swig of wine.* "*They drink well too. There's never a day they go without. Never a day they are bored.*"

"*How do I become a doctor?*" *the girl's father asked eagerly. All his life he had worked and worked, with little to show for it except piles of wood.*

"*Funny you should ask,*" *said the stranger, raising a finger. The girl had learned over the course of several dinners that when the man raised his finger it meant he was about to embark on a lecture. He used his hands quite a bit when he spoke. The girl had also learned to serve him from across the table to avoid those quick hands.*

"First," he declared, wagging that finger, "you must buy yourself an ABC book with a cock as a frontispiece."

"Where do I get such a book?" the girl's father asked.

"Funny you should ask." The man rummaged through his bag and pulled out an ABC book with a cock as a frontispiece.

Her father, the girl explained, though she loved him dearly, was easily duped. Amazed by the coincidence of the stranger having just the book he needed in his bag, the father sold his wood-hauling cart and the donkey that pulled the cart for the money to purchase the ABC book from the stranger. As soon as the transaction was complete, the stranger left under cover of the night.

The girl's father did everything the book instructed: he purchased a smock and other clothes that pertained to medicine; he got a sign that read DOCTOR KNOWALL and hung it outside his home.

"This was several weeks ago," the lovely girl said, beginning to cry again, "and there's not been a single patient. I am the new wood-hauling cart."

The girl was very lovely. "Perhaps," said the prince, "perhaps I could be your father's first patient. I am trying to stay awake long enough to watch night turn into day. Perhaps he could help me."

"I doubt it," the young woman said. "He isn't a very good doctor. Still, all my father wants is to cure someone. You could help me by making him believe he cured you."

And so Dr. Knowall gave the prince a potion and the prince gave Dr. Knowall some money and the young woman was able to buy a new wood-hauling cart and a new donkey so she no longer had to serve as both cart and donkey. And though the potion didn't help the prince stay awake long enough to see night turn into day—in fact, it only seemed to make him sleepier—it did make him feel better.

Puff, puff went Albert's father's pipe. Puff, puff went the story on their little lives.

"Why did the potion make the prince feel better when it didn't help him stay awake?" Albert asked his father. The waxy swirl of his father's scarred cheek spun like a pinwheel in the flickering light.

Puff, puff went his father's pipe, smoke drifting up to where the story still hung around them like a cloak.

"Does it matter?"

No, Albert thinks now, wrapped in his father's voice. From where he lies on his bed, he can see a piece of the sky. It is the same sky that shelters the Doctor too, wherever he is. No, it doesn't matter. All that matters is his return. If his father's voice could return after all those lost years, the Doctor will return too, and if he returns, Albert will show him how much better he is.

Ring (*shadow ring*). The fringe of dawn appears over the trees lining the square outside the Palace of Justice and there is the clatter of merchants' carts as night turns into day again. A sliver of moon still shines faintly in the sky as the sun comes up, evidence of the night before, and Albert remembers the Doctor has gone, that he hasn't come right back. The warm touch of Nurse Anne's hand on his arm startles him.

"You can't sleep your life away."

"The Doctor said he would be right back," Albert says. He cannot keep it to himself any longer.

"The Doctor has gone to Paris," she says. "He will be back. Oh, now, it's not the end of the world. Hold out your hand."

She places her seashells in his outstretched palm.

"Keep them for a little while," she says, and then glides out the door and down the hall.

He sits up, brushing the wrinkles out of his slept-in clothes. He is *here*, he reminds himself, smelling the seashells until he has smelled the sea right out of them. But his head aches and his ears are ringing. He has started to sweat. He is so thirsty. He slides out of bed, leaving the seashells on the bedside table. There is dirt on the bedcovers from sleeping in his shoes but he cannot stay to brush it off. He cannot stay still. Trembling, he walks down the hall in search of the warmth of Marian and Walter.

"I cannot hear another word about your blackened nerves," Marian is saying to Walter in the courtyard. "I cannot be distracted. I must be vigilant. My lack of vigilance is exactly why I'm breathing with only one lung today."

"A morning constitutional?" Walter says when he sees Albert, taking his arm. "Why are you trembling?"

"It always begins like this," Albert says, but he can't explain the rest. He can't explain what comes next. If he doesn't explain it, maybe the urgency won't arrive.

"Come," and Walter takes Albert's arm gently, not squeezing.

"Albert, you *are* trembling," Marian says, taking his other arm.

"I am terribly thirsty," he says.

"You are sweating," Walter says, wiping his hand on Albert's pants leg.

"Stop exaggerating, Walter," Marian says.

"I wish I were," says Walter.

"Let's stroll."

"Thank you. Yes, a stroll," Albert says, as if such a thing were possible.

And that is how it comes to be that he, Marian on one arm and Walter on the other, walks around and around the asylum courtyard, past the vegetable garden, underneath the birch trees, past the stained-glass window where Jesus walks and walks and walks on the road to Cavalry.

"This is quite a pace you keep, Albert," Walter says, his breathing quickening.

"It's good to be quick," Marian says, patting Albert's arm, looking out of the corners of her eyes, wincing at the light around the edges of the clouds.

"Thank you," Albert says.

"Oh, don't be a fool," Marian says.

Marian and Walter are still here, and so is Albert. The urgency has not come upon him; it has not obliterated him. They are all here together, walking and walking under the same sky whose ominous smears do not mean the end of him. In fact, the sun is creeping out from behind the clouds; though she is afraid, Marian stays.

He has not disappeared. Their feet are walking him back, back into *here*, into *now*. A fleeting illumination through the pitch-dark of his mind: while he was still on the road, those horse's eyes staring at him—*It is better not to thrash*—sinking and sinking into the mud. He hears the horse still, squealing until the mud fills its nostrils and its mouth, until the horse is only those eyes above the surface, staring. Albert is not thrashing; he doesn't need to thrash. Marian and Walter are walking him out of the mud.

"You are making me dizzy," Nurse Anne calls from the doorway. "Breakfast is getting cold. And what have you done with my seashells, Albert?"

"We won't stop just yet," Walter says. "Though perhaps we could slow down."

"They are on my bedside table," Albert calls over.

"Well, don't worry yourself," Nurse Anne says in a voice that says: *Worry.* "Don't worry. *I'll* get them. I wouldn't want to *interrupt* you."

Ring (*shadow ring*).

"Never mind her," Marian says. "Pay attention."

And Albert does.

Walter whispers something to Marian that Albert cannot quite make out.

"Of course he is," Marian says, reaching across Albert to thwap Walter on the chest with the back of her hand. "Of course he is. I never doubted it."

Albert's waistcoat is damp with sweat, but underneath the hands of Walter and Marian his arms have stopped trembling.

The three of them move through the minutes as if the minutes were nothing; their beautiful feet move forward together, having a conversation of their own. Albert's astonishment fills him until it is spilling over, into Marian, into Walter, until they are walking, astonished, together.

15

THE AIR IN THE amphitheater is already electric, but this time the girl is not small or weak or fading. This time, there is no girl at all. All the Doctor can make out from where he sits waiting for the great doctor to appear is a lump of something on a platter. It might be lunch. The Doctor doesn't want to think about lunch; he doesn't want to think about food at all. He is not feeling well. Even the murmuring in the amphitheater—a thousand tiny hammers in his head. How could he possibly think about lunch? In the corner, the tall, skinny photographer has appeared, once again magically transported, glasses perched on his pointed head as he unwraps the plates from their cotton swathing, the clunk-clunking a larger pounding hammer that joins the tap, tap, tap of the amphitheater conversation inside the Doctor's skull. Behind the platter is a large chalkboard on which is scribbled: *To force the womb to descend: bitumen, sulfur, and petroleum oils, woodcock feathers, billy goat hairs, gunpowder, old sheets.* He doesn't want to think about billy goat hairs, or old sheets either. What was he thinking when he accepted the bartender's invitation the night before last—*Don't be a stranger*—? He should have remained a stranger.

When he woke up yesterday morning, fully clothed, on top of the covers of his lumpy bed, he had only a vague recollection of making his way up the stairs from the bar underneath his apartment. *I'll be at the top by the end of the week.* This is the part he remembers, a hand on either wall for balance. *One day for each step.* Had one of the men huddled at the bar—the one whose face up close was as lined as the map of Albert's travels—put a hand on either side of his face? "The good doctor," the man's breath thick on the Doctor's cheek. "You'll be fine." The men's laughter, a streak of sound through the sky of his dreams all night long and again, still, last night in the hotel.

When he walked into the bar the night before last, the bartender cried out gleefully, "A stranger no more!" The Doctor was no longer a stranger, but after several drinks he wasn't entirely sure what it was he had become. He had only wanted to escape the feeling of riding his bicycle up into his parents' arms, their forgiveness so sweet he was better off erasing it completely.

"Tell us that story again, sir doctor," the man with the map-lined face said. "The one about the Greeks and the electric eels." Had he told them a story? Had he told them he was a doctor?

"I've got an electric eel for you," said the map-lined-face man's companion, always one drink ahead.

"Come, now," the man with the map-lined face said, nudging the Doctor with his shoulder. And when the Doctor couldn't remember the story he wasn't sure he'd told the first time, the men returned to their banter, the easy hop from one subject to the next—their work at the docks (which drove them to drink), their wives (who drove them to drink), the relentless wind off the river (which drove them to drink).

It was then that *they* slithered through his mind—the electric eels. *Zzzzzz.* "The Greeks," he said, remembering, "treated gout by having the patient stand on an electric eel."

The men laughed and laughed and the laughter surrounded him. It *was* funny. Standing on eels to cure gout, but also to be sitting here, with these men whose laughter had always been in another room. This is what his life might be if his ethereal *if* ever developed a solid spine—a life full of nights in which laughter was in the same room.

"No one cares about *your* eel," the man with the map-lined face said, shoving his companion playfully.

"But it is *enormous.*"

The bartender had retreated to the other end of the bar to rummage through clinking bottles, the novelty of the Doctor's presence having worn off.

"To the eels!" the drunker man said, clinking glasses first with the map-faced man and then the Doctor.

"To the eels!" Why not?

But he didn't really care about the eels. *Soul murder.* Walter's strange phrase had been stuck in his head and he wanted to chase it out. *Soul murderer. Careless man.* Those words Albert spoke at the end of his story that wasn't actually his about being mistaken for the czar's assassin. Why wouldn't the man weave himself into history? The Doctor had driven him to it. The drinking had helped for a little while and then he had collapsed into his lumpy bed, dreaming of the amphitheater. He was wearing a new suit and the great doctor was whispering in his ear. What was he whispering? The laughter of the men downstairs became the murmur of the high foreheads and aristocratic noses. *Aaaah. Ooooh.* "A toast!" the great doctor cried. To what? The Doctor was not yet finished with his case study. He had not even begun. "To Albert!" cried the hairy bear. When the morning finally came, it felt like years later, and the Doctor was drenched in the sweat of envy and failure. Shivering naked over his pail of water he tried to sponge it away, but it clung to his skin in persistent beads.

Careless man. He didn't want to be one, so he put himself on a train to Paris in order to be less careless, resolving as the train hurtled through the countryside to take more care. And here he is once again, foggy still even after drinking the awful concoction the bartender offered him yesterday morning. Myrrh, rhubarb, chamomile, aloe, cardamom, peppermint oil and a number of other ingredients the Doctor was afraid to ask about, including a grape-infused spirit. And on top of it all, here he is once again, enduring this amphitheater full of pointy knees and aristocratic noses and high foreheads, all these waiting bodies, hot and lemony with sweat.

"There's been an incident with the monkey," the high forehead in front of the Doctor is saying to the aristocratic nose next to him. "It got loose," the high forehead says with evident delight. "Crashed through the door and bounded around, climbed on top of peoples' heads. The doctor finally pulled a banana out of his coat and that was the end of it."

The Doctor's not sure he believes it, but there's a certain pleasure in imagining the stout oak door banging open and the monkey, shrieking, bursting free, taunting the hairy bear, the hairy bear taking a swipe at the monkey, the monkey going faster and faster, just out of reach, the hairy bear stumbling and falling facedown into the sawdust.

"This is what happens when wild animals are turned into pets," sniffs the aristocratic nose.

"This circus could use a monkey," the high forehead says. "It's gotten a bit dull."

The Doctor realizes now he too has been missing the *thump thump* of the monkey. It would be better than the *zzzzzz* of the eels that lingers still. He tries to focus on what is about to unfold—a demonstration of the great doctor's new treatment that isn't new at all. It is in fact quite ancient. Not even its resurrection is new. The Doctor tracked down an article that gave the lie to the great doctor's reinvention of it. A Danish entertainer had finessed that trick on a tour through Central Europe. *Clench your jaw muscles*, the Danish entertainer instructed volunteers he plucked from the audience and quickly put into a trance. He asked politely. *Please*—and they did. *Here's a delicious apple*, he said, and offered them a potato from which each took a big bite. Every last one of them cooed over its crisp sweetness. *You will go rigid and stiff. You will lie down between two chairs, your feet on one chair, your head on the other, your body a stiff board suspended in between.* And they did and they did and they had. An outraged doctor in Breslau wrote an article declaring the entertainer a fraud (*Sir, you are not who you appear to be*); in response, the entertainer invited *all* of the local doctors to come see for themselves. The entertainer called them to the stage one by one. The outraged doctor who had written the article was the first to fall under the spell. *Clench your jaw.* He clenched. *Eat this apple.* He ate and cooed. "Delicious," he said. *Lie stiff as a board between two chairs* and, having always been the sort of student who excelled in his studies, he became even stiffer than a board.

Near the end of the Danish entertainer's Central European tour someone in the audience raised his hand and asked, *What really happened that evening you hypnotized the doctors?* Before the entertainer had a chance to answer, another audience member, a doctor, reportedly raised his hand. "What does it matter if we do not understand the exact mechanism of the phenomenon?" he asked.

Not much is required: one chair, one lamp, and a peaceful effect. An amulet, a letter, a telegram. These were said to be the best devices. The most effective method is the use of two fingers to make circles on the top of the patient's head.

The Doctor has heard rumors, of course, of doctors using the treatment for their own entertainment—putting a man in a trance and asking him to drink a glass of ink and telling him it is beer; inducing a man into sleep, a man whose beard has been carefully cultivated for many years, and then giving him a pair of scissors in the midst of his dreaming and instructing him to cut it off . . .

Aaaah, says the audience. And there he is, with his Napoleonic profile and his spectacular nose, walking slowly into the center of the amphitheater like a bullfighter. The Doctor wishes for a bull as the great doctor gestures to the platter.

"In the past," the great doctor says in that voice that falls like a fantastic cloak over them all, "I have performed with you an anatomical-pathological study of the encephalon . . ."

And the Doctor realizes that the something on the platter is not lunch after all. It is a brain.

" . . . notice the attractive exterior . . ."

The monkey, punished? Was this the brain of his beloved pet?

". . . the white matter, the flattened portion of the crura . . . the gray layers of the island of Reil . . ."

The Doctor's mind skips like a stone over logic into the frigid depths of panic. It is much worse than he had thought. It is not the monkey's brain at all. He wiggles his knee into the back of the high forehead in front of him. "Where is the girl?" he whispers.

Shhh, the forehead says. *Shhh*, says the audience. *Zzzzzz*. The Doctor finds himself wishing Monsieur Eager were here. *He* would know, or he would claim to know, what has happened to the girl. What has the great doctor done with the rest of her? Chopped her into pieces? The tall, skinny photographer lurking in the corner, adjusting his tripod, preparing his plates for the first photograph—he must know something. There is something about the man's thin face that makes him seem as though he knows useful things, or maybe it is just his displeasure at the entrance of the great doctor that catches the Doctor's attention.

The great doctor hoists the platter onto his shoulder and carries it around the room.

"...I wish to isolate the Great Neurosis as a purely nosological object," the great doctor is saying, returning the platter to the table. "The etiological theory is clear. A pathophysiological alteration in the nervous system. But this alteration is of an unknown nature, in an unknown location." He gestures to the brain. "A physiological phenomena, beginning in an elusive lesion."

"Where is the girl?" the Doctor whispers.

"Quiet!" the high forehead hisses.

"The lesion itself?" the great doctor says. "Invisible."

Invisible, and yet they were meant to believe it was there. Where is the girl? What has happened to her?

"Today, we will witness a treatment that is not blind to the invisible lesion. It sees it. It speaks to it."

Aaaah, says the audience, and the hairy bear appears from the wings with the girl. The Doctor's mind skips back, an obedient stone, from panic to logic, and it is only then he realizes he has been on the verge of tears. It is not the girl's brain on the platter. He needs more sleep; he will go to bed early, he will sleep on the train. But as the hairy bear coaxes the girl gently down into the wooden chair, as he pulls the straitjacket slung across his shoulder and lays it across the table next to the platter, the Doctor waits for whatever comes next. At least she is here; at least she is not in pieces. The silence in the amphitheater is thick; an enormous held breath. The pressure of the silence builds, rumbling through the benches, through the Doctor, connecting him and his low forehead, his close-together eyes, his lumpy nose, to the men all around him: something is about to happen. They all perch on the edge of the benches: *Make it happen.* Had the Danish entertainer called the Doctor to the stage right now, he thinks, he would have eaten the potato and tasted its secret apple sweetness.

The girl does not look at the brain on the platter on the table, though it is close enough that she could reach out from the chair where she sits and touch it; instead, she opens her mouth. She puts her hand to her wide-open mouth; it looks as though she is pulling something from deep in her throat.

The girl eyes whatever imaginary thing she has pulled from the depths of herself with scorn. "I don't have the time," she says.

Flash goes the camera from the photographer's corner, where his rail-thin legs stick out of the bottom of the camera's tent: an image of the girl and whatever it is she's dangling from her fingertips is illuminated, etched eternally onto a plate.

At the sound of the clunk, clunk of the plates, the great doctor turns, fixing the photographer with his owly stare. "*Everything* I'm about to do is worth recording," he says.

"I do not have the time," the girl says again.

"She is capricious," says the great doctor.

The Doctor recognizes the sour look that crosses the great doctor's face; he felt it in his own face as Albert told his story of being arrested as a nihilist assassin in Moscow, and shame burns through him.

Out of his coat pocket the great doctor pulls an amulet on a string. "There will be three distinct stages."

Dangling the amulet before the girl's eyes, he swings it back and forth, back and forth, back and forth. "You are tired. So tired. You are sleeping and you are nothing." The hairy bear steps back, arms folded, watching the amulet until his chin falls to his chest and he snaps to attention, looking out into the audience like a guilty child.

It seems impossible to the Doctor that this same fierce girl could be tired, or sleeping, or nothing, but her eyes move back and forth, back and forth, and her lids grow heavy. Soon her head is nodding; soon it falls to her chest.

"Here we have the lethargic state," the great doctor says. "The appearance of a deep sleep. Suggestion is impossible. But a certain muscular hyperexcitability ... pressure upon the facial nerve, for example ..." He nods to the hairy bear, who presses a thick finger into the girl's left cheek.

Flash: an image of a spasm in the left side of her face, distorting itself into a grimace, while the right side remains utterly still.

"The cataleptic condition," the great doctor says. He lifts the girl's face in his hand, almost tenderly, prying open one closed eyelid. Simultaneously, the hairy bear lifts the girl's left arm, spreads her fingers, and puts them to her lips as if she is about to throw a kiss.

Flash: an image of the girl smiling broadly, throwing a kiss to the audience.

There is a smattering of polite applause.

Shhhh!

There is something missing, the Doctor thinks. What was he listening for? The *thump thump* of the monkey? No, it is the girl's anguished keening he is waiting for.

"You are very tired," the great doctor says. "You are so tired. You are sleeping." She begins to slide down the back of her chair as though she is being poured. "And now, somnambulism." She is sinking to her knees, pressing her hands together in the semblance of prayer, when suddenly there is a great crash and the shattering of glass.

The great doctor turns in the direction of the noise, slow and steady as the swing of the amulet, and the eyes of the entire amphitheater follow. The jagged pieces of a plate, slipped from his bony fingers, lie at the feet of the photographer.

The Doctor's stomach drops; he recalls his sneeze and the heat of the great doctor's gaze. The photographer is no longer floating; he is no longer invisible. It is as if he had crashed to the floor along with the plate. It is hard to tell from here, but the Doctor swears he sees a tiny smile of satisfaction on the man's face.

"Did I hire an orchestra to take photographs?" the great doctor says as the photographer frantically picks up the shards of glass.

"A stampeding herd of elephants?"

The photographer's thin legs become tangled until one of his feet slips out from underneath him and a poof of sawdust rises all around him. He puts his hand out to protect his face as he falls, and when he stands, blood runs down his long arm. *There* is their blood, the Doctor thinks.

The great doctor is silent now. In the photographer's hurry to get to his feet, he falls again. When the photographer drops the second plate, the shattering glass echoes through the quiet.

This time he rises slowly to his feet. "No," he says into the silence of the amphitheater. "No," he says again. The word hangs in the air as he walks slowly, proudly, out of the amphitheater. But once the hairy bear sweeps away the glass and the blood-flecked sawdust, it is as if the photographer had never existed at all. What photographer?

The great doctor turns back to the girl. "Our statue of living pain," he says in the same steady, unwavering voice as before, and the Doctor feels it pulling the audience's attention with it—*Come into the great house of my voice, look into all the secret rooms*—and his too.

The statue of living pain is not where the great doctor had left her.

When the glass shattered, the girl rose from her knees and began walking slowly toward the table with the platter. At first she appears to be reaching for the brain itself, and the Doctor thinks, *She will eat it.* But it isn't the brain she wants. She picks up the straitjacket instead, slipping her arms expertly through the sleeves.

"Please," she says, turning her back to the hairy bear, lifting the hair from her neck. "Buckle me in."

It is not a happy story, Albert has said again and again. But an unhappy story doesn't always begin unhappily. The Doctor imagines the girl as a child at the dinner table. Maybe there are two gangly older brothers who wrestle unless they are told not to, one writhing body with many limbs. Maybe there is a mother. *She is not eating enough*, the mother says, eyeing the stew her daughter has barely touched. Maybe there is a father. *She never eats enough*, the mother says to him. He recently moved his family to the city so he and his sons could work in the textile factory that has dyed their fingers an indelible blue. *She is fine*, he says, without looking up. The same conversation every night. He could speak any words as long as he uses the same reassuring tone: *Rats ate mine. What a vine. There is time.* The fact is the girl *is* fine, rosy and plump. She has always been this way. She is one of those children who brim with love. What does it matter if she eats less than her brothers, who eat and eat with their blue fingers unless reminded to use a fork? If she is healthy, if she shines with life, what does it matter? The Doctor will never know it, but he is partly right. There has been happiness for the girl; there has even been happiness for her here in the great doctor's hospital. It is only once she is retired, only when she is no longer the great doctor's best girl, that happiness disappears altogether. It is then she will lose track of the days, which seemed for a while to be adding up to something—those moments when the audience *oooed* and *aaahed*, all of those eyes on her as she moaned or dreamed up something lodged in her throat (let them use their imaginations), those moments when she was the doctor's best girl. She was the doctor's best girl even, perhaps especially, when she did something to cause a look of concern on his face. It is when she is removed from her private room to make room for the next best girl that she will understand he is done with her, and when she is returned to the general population of women in the large room, her strength will leave her altogether. Some of the women in the large room will look like her mother—that woman in the corner there, when she turns a certain way and remains enough in the shadows—but they are not her mother who died some months ago. The girl will grow smaller still. Eventually, she will lose track of herself altogether; there will be days when she can't distinguish herself from the woman in the corner there or that one there or that one there. She will sleep as often as she can; in her dreams it isn't dark. In the sunlight of her dreams, her mother's face returns to her, a face that expected nothing of her, that was satisfied to watch her knead dough, content even to watch her shirk her duties and gaze out the window on to a view the girl always complained about—why did they have to live in such a shabby place? In those dreams, her mother's face says, you are my own girl. In the dark room though the girl will continue to fade until one day, when no one is watching, her light will go out completely.

"Buckle me," the girl says again, her back to the hairy bear, the pieces of her life that added up to this moment hovering all around her. What if things had gone differently? the Doctor wonders. What if the father the Doctor has imagined for her hadn't died in a factory accident, if her brothers hadn't run off to create trouble with their blue hands, if their mother hadn't fallen into such despair that the asylum seemed like a place to rest and to find a meal? What if the rosy, plump girl hadn't followed her mother, and there been discovered by the great doctor? What if instead she lived the kind of life in which she might be asking to be buttoned into a lovely dress? *Button me.*

In the slow shuffle out of the amphitheater, the Doctor is surrounded by the cluck-clucking of the high foreheads and the aristocratic noses.

"The girls will be running the place soon."

"I wouldn't mind seeing that."

"You just did."

"What about the photographer?"

"What about him? He's through."

What about the photographer? Those long thin legs, the outraged look on his face as though it were the great doctor who had interrupted *him*, as though it were he, the photographer, who held the secrets. When the Doctor stops in the shabby bar next door to his shabby hotel to escape the cluck-clucking of the high foreheads and aristocratic noses, the photographer is so present in the Doctor's thoughts that when he sees him in the corner nursing a drink with his bandaged hand, it is as though the Doctor has caused him to appear.

"May I join you?" the Doctor says.

"Plenty of other seats," the photographer says, gesturing to the rest of the bar, which is empty except for the bartender, a man reading at the bar, and two men playing cards in the corner. "But do whatever you like."

"I was just there," says the Doctor, taking a seat. "At the amphitheater."

"So you're a doctor, then?" The photographer slides the glasses perched on the top of his pointy dome down onto his nose and looks the Doctor up and down. "A man of mental medicine?"

"I've seen your portraits in the journals." The Doctor knows the way flattery can work on a man and he sees the way his words work on the photographer. He wants to win the man over, but he means it. In each of the portraits, there is a question on the girl's face similar to the question on the girl's face tonight, not unlike the question he has seen on Albert's face. The look of a feral child subdued, as if someone has turned a crank at the back of the girl's head one more notch and there it is, a different kind of smile. Not the smile of recognition—there *I* am in the mirror—so much as there *someone* is. Before one could mind manners, there had to be a lesson in what manners were. Here, try them on, like clothes. The smile is an offering and a question. *Is this her, the girl you want?* Careless man. The Doctor *was* a careless man. Albert's story of being mistaken for a nihilist assassin of the czar? *Is this him, the man you want?*

"Why take pictures of these people? Why not let them be? That's what my wife says," the photographer says. "It takes three seconds for me to switch the plates. What anyone might discover if they were paying attention is those girls hold their poses long enough for me to photograph them. They perform in sync with the speed of the shutter. They wait for me to press the bulb. It's not proof of any invisible lesion I'm capturing. But you don't want to know. Or you don't care."

"They are not my theories," the Doctor says. He hears his defensive tone and tries to soften his voice. "I do want to know. You cannot claim to have really seen something until you have photographed it, he said. I'm interested to know what you think that means."

The photographer finishes his beer before he speaks. "I recently went to a demonstration," he says finally. "A scientist used a volta-faradaic apparatus to isolate muscles in the woman's face. The muscle for fear, the muscle for sadness, and so on."

"Yes," the Doctor says, "I've seen that demonstration. The woman's spirit, enacted in her anatomy, that's how the scientist described it."

"*That's* what photography can do," the photographer says.

"Yes," the Doctor says. He thinks he understands. Isn't this what he hopes to capture with Albert? Something elusive and ephemeral—call it his soul, or its approximation in words. Something whose essence is, *This is me.*

The photographer rustles around in his bag and, clunk, clunk, pulls out one of his plates wrapped in cotton and puts it on the table between them. "When I have a girl in the studio, I some-times put a mirror on the wall to catch her attention. She is like a child seeing himself for the first time. 'Is that me?' the girl asks when I show her the photographs. *A statue of living pain?* That fat little man. As if it were possible to make any less noise while changing plates the size of his head. *Cough, cough, the photograph is the scientist's true retina.* He is right about that but only that." Carefully, the photographer unwraps the plate from its cotton cocoon. "Even before it took shape, I knew this one was different."

He holds the plate up to the Doctor. There is the fierce girl standing in the sawdust of the amphitheater, looking as though she is about to wrestle the great doctor. Above her head, a shimmering black cloud. There are other explanations for it, the Doctor knows—a smudge, a blur—but the shimmering black cloud looks like time's signature, a vibration in the girl that exceeds her body.

"It is beautiful," the Doctor says.

"Yes," the photographer says. "It eludes you, as art should." He wraps it back into its layers of cotton, puts it in his bag, and slips on his coat, wanting suddenly only to get home to his wife where he can shake off the cloud of the day. It always takes him a little while to become real again, as though, over the course of a day's work, he has become the person in the picture.

"Is there something wrong with your cabbage?" his wife will ask.

The photographer hates cabbage. For years, so how to explain it now? This too he'll keep to himself.

"Nothing's wrong with it," he will say, and he will eat his cabbage. "You've never liked cabbage, have you?" his wife might say tonight. "Tell me the truth, you never have," and she'll push him and his grasshopper-thin limbs onto the bed. He'll watch her unpin her hair, marveling yet again at the way the very same things that cause him to grind his teeth—with a different lens, a tighter focus, better lighting—look like love. The photographer would shed his cloud entirely for this glimpse. "I never, ever have," he will say as she lies down beside him.

On the train home the next day, the Doctor wakes from dreams— the fierce girl buckled into her straitjacket, swallowing fire—to the rustling of a young woman's skirts as she enters his compartment.

"Let me help you," and he and a porter lift her battered trunk onto the overhead rack. "Thank you," the woman says. She looks anxiously out the window at an older woman being jostled by the crowd on the platform.

"Is that your mother?" the Doctor asks as the train begins to move and the older woman and the jostling crowd grow smaller and smaller.

"No."

"I'm sorry. I didn't mean to make you cry."

"I don't want to trouble you," the girl says, her eyes brimming.

"No trouble," he says.

It is not a very happy story.

Outside, the trees reach up and up into the sky streaked purple with evening. *Look up*, they say.

The Doctor's eyes make shapes and patterns out of the stars that appear in the sky. There is so much he will never know. Is that Orion? It frustrates his eyes, trying to make sense in the vastness of the sky, but he is intrigued too by the simple, human way his eyes try to discern the shapes and the patterns automatically, to identify a few of the constellations.

"She is my aunt," the girl says, and she begins to tell him how her father ran off when she was young, how her mother died of cholera, how she went to live with this aunt whom she loves dearly, but then her aunt could no longer afford to keep her and now she is going to live with a wealthy distant relative who needs a house servant. "A fairy tale in reverse," she says.

And? So?

She looks out the window. "Is that Orion?" she asks.

"I think so," the Doctor says. Then, wanting to give the *if* a more solid spine, "Yes, it is."

Buckle me.

That's all anyone ever wants, really, the Doctor thinks as the girl nods off to sleep. To be contained. To be given shape by the constraints of a narrative.

Not much is required: one chair, one lamp, and a peaceful effect.

An amulet like the great doctor's, a letter, a telegram, but the Doctor doesn't want to use props. There will be no need for props.

It will be like dreaming. He will start simply.

With two fingers he will make circles on the top of Albert's large head. This is said to be one of the most effective methods. He will pause only to brush Albert's eyes closed.

It will be like dreaming together.

Your eyelids are warm. They are getting warmer.

Those rumors—this will not be that. It won't be turning ink into beer or asking a man to cut off his own ten-year-old beard. It will not be slipping a tube filled with brandy down the neck of a lady's dress and whispering into her ear, "*Eau de vie*," causing the lady to shout, "I am drunk!" and then to stagger and fall on the floor. This will not be that. And it won't be telling a man that when he wakes, he will be a little dog in a hospital full of big dogs, a big dog hospital, and then inviting his friends to watch as the man wakes yapping.

It would be nothing like the competition he'd heard about in which two doctors challenged each other to see whose trance lasted the longest. One of them induced sleep in a former army sergeant and when the doctor snapped his fingers sixty days later, the sergeant believed the president of the republic was giving him a pension and a medal. The other doctor beat him—by three hundred and five days! He told a patient he would see him on the next New Year's Day, that he would wish him a happy new year; on the New Year's Day he watched from behind a tree as the patient hallucinated the doctor wishing him a happy new year. And it wouldn't be the doctor who lulled a man with a gangrenous leg into a somnambulant state, first telling him he would be grateful for whatever was done while he slept, and when the man woke up, the doctor had sawed off his leg.

This will not be the debacle in the great doctor's amphitheater. This will be something else entirely.

The Doctor is not entirely sure what it will be. The girl across from him snores gently as the train rattles along.

Shh, Albert, shh. You are sleeping. You are a good sleeper. The Doctor's voice sounds foolish, unrecognizable, as he rehearses, whispering into the compartment. *You don't see anything. Your arms and legs are motionless.* Someone else's foolish voice. *And now you are asleep,* he will say, and it will give the ethereal *if* a solid spine. *And, so, you are better now.*

Outside, the darkness is thick—uniform and endless, except for the smattering of stars. The Doctor's eyes continue their poignant effort to seek shapes. There, Albert's silhouette. There, sharper than ever, walking astonished through the night sky.

He will blow on Albert's eyelids to wake him. It is said to be the gentlest way.

And. So. We are better now.

PART THREE

Dreaming Together

THE VIOLINIST FROM LEIPZIG, the coal miner from Liège, the hotel maid in Mulhouse, the baker in Coblenz, they all came forward to say they had seen him. This was years after the Doctor published a paper on his *fugueur*, after people had started referring to the walking man as *le voyageur de Docteur*, this was after the small epidemic of *fugueurs*. Workingmen with homes and families who walked away, who traveled extraordinary distances with no memory of how they got there—the fisherman from Marseille who woke up in Bougie; the wheelwright in Nérac who woke up in Budweis; the blacksmith from Brive, say, who woke up in Danzig. Men who wandered away for reasons mysterious even—perhaps especially—to them.

When those others came forward, the woman in the lowlands, washing the limestone grit out of her brothers' clothes, she came forward as well. *I saw him too.* It was the first time she spoke of him, but not the first time he had crossed her mind. Each year, she and her husband gathered with everyone else in their village to watch the storks fly away. For months the storks nested in the villagers' chimneys, the clack-clacking of their bills as much a part of their lives as the weather. And then one day the storks unfurled themselves from their enormous nests. Awkward at first on their red stick-legs, they rose up with enormous black-tipped wings. Just when it seemed they might fall out of the sky, an air current lifted them up. It was at that moment that the woman remembered the walking man, his strange grace. How could the storks move her to tears every year? her husband always asked. It became a joke between them. Though she loved her husband dearly, she never explained. It was her secret, too delicate for translation.

16

"As long as Henri accompanies you," Nurse Anne says to Marian over the veteran's shouting.

"Your secret is no secret. Deserter!" He has been shouting all morning. Even as Claude hauls him down the hall, his voice reaches them. "Shame. Shame."

"It is your eavesdropping that is shameful," Nurse Anne says. She knows he doesn't hear her. Still, it must be said.

"Come," Marian says to Albert and Walter, leading them in the direction of the rough-hewn path to the creek. That suggestion. *Follow me!* She will!

"Look," Henri says, pointing a slender finger in the direction of the blackberry bushes. "I think I see a fox."

"Henri," Marian says, "tell us what you know about—"

"Marian," Walter interrupts, "let's not speak of the veteran and his vibrating, blackened nerves. It significantly decreases the voluptuousness of everything."

Albert agrees. He might be a deserter—but what is he supposed to do about it? Anyway, Marian and Walter don't care. They have not deserted him. The Doctor may be gone—yesterday, which was Friday; the day before, which was Thursday; the day before the day before, which was Wednesday—but Marian and Walter are not. This morning Albert only cares about the breeze, the faint, familiar pudding smell of Walter, the warmth of Walter's arm and Marian's arm on his as they keep a steady pace.

"There is no fox," Marian says.

Henri holds back the tree branch that marks the entrance to the creek path, and though they are forced to walk single file now, though Nurse Anne has forbidden anymore walking around and around the courtyard together, the astonishment of walking with Marian and Walter lingers in Albert still. Maybe love didn't have to be something from long ago. Love requires staying in one place. Love requires knowing where you were last night and last week and last year, where you would be tomorrow. And so far, Albert is; so far, he does.

When they reach the creek, they take off their boots—"Socks," Henri says to Walter—and stand in the cool water under the shadow of the trees.

"This is quite pleasant," says Walter. "Masterful, really."

"Yes," says Marian. "Don't you think so, Albert?"

"Very," Albert says.

"Very of our hour," says Walter.

It is as if Albert's whole lost life has led him here. *I am here, I am here, I am here.* He closes his eyes to make the moment—the sound of the creek, the birds, the breeze in the trees, the heavy quiet that is Walter, Marian, and Henri nearby—stay, but it is in motion even if he is not. Still, he keeps it in his mind when they walk back up the hill to where the Director demonstrates a series of exercises: windmilling his arms, marching in place, jumping up and down. "Like this!" Elizabeth watches with her vigilant green eyes on the lookout for a miracle, while nearby Rachel smooths and smooths her stomach. When Samuel sees Henri coming, he runs to embrace him.

"Oh, stop it," Henri says, though he receives Samuel with open arms.

This is a life, Albert thinks. *Here.* This is his life.

How could he know that what is about to happen would make him willing to give even this up? How could he know that what is about to happen would make him willing to give up all the things he hadn't known he'd been yearning for—Nurse Anne's hands pouring silky water over his beautiful feet, the ribbed backs of her seashells rubbed soft, the pleasure of dreams in which he walks with the earth rumbling through his heels but from which he always returns to wake in his bed, not lost at all. *His bed.*

How could Albert know that what is about to happen will make him forget both his fear that the Doctor would never be back and the flood of relief he feels now that the Doctor *is* back, not *right* back but back all the same, putting an arm over his shoulder and leading him to his room? "I would like to try something new," he says, clearly having forgiven Albert for his lies. "You will have to trust me. Will you trust me?" When they reach his room, the Doctor says, "Sit here in this chair." How could Albert know that when the lamp flickers, he will flicker too?

The noise from the courtyard peppers the quiet as he sits. The Director's voice booming, "I dare anyone to find me a lovelier day!" Nurse Anne speaking gently, persuasively to Marian, "Your stomach will return. Name me one time that it has not returned," to which Marian replies, "This time." Walter pronouncing Elizabeth "a fine specimen of a woman." Inside, click, click go the cracked billiard balls as the veteran tosses them across the worn felt of the table, reciting his promises, "I will not knock the balls over the side of the table if I like." Followed by a crash. "Fuck, fuck, fuck, it is better not to think. Better not to think at all. The thanks I get, when all I am doing is keeping peace." Rachel's frog has demanded she play anything else, but she insists on playing one of Chopin's mazurkas; defiant, it rains down on all of them.

And then the Doctor begins.

You are sleeping. You are nothing.

The Doctor's voice is a different kind of music; different than the music Albert heard when he first arrived—the blur of *my stockings have fallen down*; *bang, bang*; *Nurse Anne, Nurse Anne, come quick*; St. Eloi's giant clock; *ring (shadow ring)*—before he became a citizen held by days and then by over a week. The music of the Doctor's voice fills his body with a new sound. What sound? It doesn't matter. It sings in harmony with the people milling around the square outside the Palace of Justice. "Oh, no, not you *again*," a man says, laughter in his voice like the snort of a horse, or was that a horse? The scuffle of children's feet. "Slow down," says a woman. "I'm not sure that's fair," says a man. "Fair?" asks a different woman than the first.

You are sleeping. You are nothing.

But he does not sleep. He is not nothing. Everything except the brightness of the Doctor's voice falls away. His warm whisper is a spark in Albert's dark forgotten heart, the lit fuse of a gas lamp, illuminating blood and muscle.

When his eyes flutter open, he feels as though he will disappear into the Doctor's eyes.

Perhaps because the Doctor says, "You are disappearing."

And then the room disappears too.

Shh, Albert.

The Doctor's voice is a tabletop, its surface expanding. Albert could lay his whole body there.

Shh, Albert. The Doctor's hand strokes the top of Albert's head; it smells of pomade and sausage. *Your eyelids are warm.* He flutters them, and it's true. *They are getting warmer.* Everything is warm: the Doctor's breath on Albert's face; his swirling fingertips; this body he's carried with him over the years, or years and years and, oh, he has been so tired. His body grows warmer; it burns off all those lost years. Where did they go? It doesn't matter. When his eyes flutter open again, the Doctor's eyes say: *I know everything you have forgotten.*

There were times when, not knowing how he got there, Albert would discover himself walking at night. The clang of church bells, a trickle from a nearby stream, the texture of the road underfoot his only guides as he stumbled into woodpiles; on one occasion, he fell over the side of a bridge. The Doctor's eyes are like the sheep Albert once saw up ahead, tufts of white in the pitch-dark night, the time he discovered himself crawling out of a coal bin: *This way, this way.*

Your arms and legs are motionless.

Where *are* his arms?

He swims in a long-ago feeling, not caring where his arms have gone. *You are sleeping. Your arms and legs are motionless. You are disappearing.* He is a boy playing hide-and-seek with Baptiste and his father. He always had to tug Baptiste's sleeve because Baptiste was content to stand in the middle of the street, not hidden at all. Even as Albert pulled him into the shadows, even as he pleaded—*We must hide!*—he understood his friend's desire. Why hide when all you want is to be found? When he finally managed to drag Baptiste behind a barrel, Baptiste would shuffle his feet, as if to announce, *Here we are, over here!* When Albert's father looked over the side, Albert saw himself in his father's eyes widened in feigned surprise. How beautiful he was to his father. How delighted his father was to find him.

In the quiet room with the Doctor, Albert is a miracle. He is a beautiful boy.

Shh, Albert. Shh. You are sinking. You will not worry about anything anymore.

He is a beautiful boy found instead of lost. He is fascinating. He is magnificent. This is an escapade like no other, no *yet another, yet another, yet another.*

Shh, Albert. Shh. You are disappearing.

But he does not disappear. He does not vanish. The swirl of the Doctor's fingers spirals through Albert's scalp into his ears.

He swallows the swirl—down his throat, into his chest, his stomach, his groin, his beautiful instrument, his legs, his beloved feet. It swirls the hair on his arms and legs on end. *There you are, Albert, there you are,* it sings, singing its swirly song.

Once, on the road, he stopped and a good woman seeing his distress invited him into her house. When he refused because to be rescued again was unbearable, she walked out to him there where he stood and held a glass of sugar water to his lips. The Doctor's whisper slakes Albert's thirst. Here, your lost life. Here, your ragged memory.

You will stay in the asylum.

"I will stay in the asylum," Albert says.

You will not walk.

"I will not walk."

You will not walk. And if you leave again, we will find you. We will bring you back.

The Doctor blows gently on Albert's eyelids.

Ring (shadow ring).

Does this ring a bell? The sharp, quick sound of love in Albert's ears.

Albert, you are a good sleeper.

Somewhere in the sky, the birds and the Doctor's voice chirp together: *If you walk far away, we will bring you back.*

"Thank you. I'm so glad to hear that."

Now it is time to wake up.

The Doctor blows once more, breathing him back into the world.

He opens his eyes.

"May we do that again?" he asks.

"Tomorrow," the Doctor says. "We will do it again tomorrow."

17

"I HEARD ABOUT A DOCTOR who told a woman, 'When you wake up there will be a dog with a monkey on its back doing a dance.'" Nurse Anne dances her fingers across the Director's desk to illustrate. They are there to discuss the recent problems with the veteran, but the Doctor's new intervention has proved a distraction. "When she woke," Nurse Anne says, "There it was, a dog, and a monkey on its back! But there was a bear too. He didn't know she had that up her sleeve. Still, the woman jumped right into his arms, which is what the doctor wanted all along."

"There are a lot of stories," says the Doctor. "But this isn't that." He knows she is teasing him but he doesn't want to be teased. He wants the Director and Nurse Anne to understand exactly what has happened but he isn't sure he knows. How could he explain, for example, how surprised he was by the softness of Albert's hair? That when he was rehearsing on the train, he imagined it would be bristly but it is as soft as the dandelion flowers his mother used to string into a crown for him as a boy. That as he concentrated, making circles with his fingertips on Albert's head, speaking those words—*Shh, Albert, shh. You are sleeping. You are a good sleeper. Your arms and legs are motionless. Shh. You are sinking*—only foolish words, there was a subtle, drowsy movement as Albert's head swayed slightly underneath his fingers? *You are disappearing*, and the smell of wildflowers through the open window was the smell of disappearing.

Around and around, his fingers continued to draw circles, circling back to his own boyhood, when his village was the world. What else was there? Until the great Léotard whirred into town, bringing with him that invitation to leap over thousands of heads, there was only his village. Now, in the room with Albert, there was so much to know; so much that was unknowable. It was all so mysterious, what lay inside that skull beneath his fingers. Albert's eyes flickered underneath his closed eyelids; his neat little mustache twitched; his head tilted the same way it had when the Doctor showed him the map of his travels, as though he were listening to something far away. How could he explain that he could see something stirring beneath Albert's skin? That it was as though Albert were out on a ship on his own private ocean, a very different ship than the ship where the Doctor had served as a cargo clerk so long ago, so seasick he thought he would die out there, despairing of what would become of him. But Albert seemed neither orphaned nor alone. The sadness vanished from the corners of his big, hooded eyes; his lined forehead smoothed. His large ears were no longer absurd but somehow strangely elegant. Beneath the surface of that long face—almost handsome in the dusky light—there was a slight trembling, and then the trembling slipped beneath the Doctor's own skin. It rushed through him, and it was as if *he* were the lady and someone had slipped a tube of brandy down *his* shirt, whispering softly, *Eau de vie*. It was he who was drunk. How could he explain that until then his whole life felt as though it were an argument against itself, but in that room there was no argument?

"I heard of a patient," the Director says, laughing. "He went to sleep. The doctor had him convinced he was Caesar. *Et tu, Brute!*"

"*The hypnotized belongs to the hypnotizer as the traveler's stick belongs to the traveler,*" the Doctor says. It is something the great doctor was quoted as saying in a recent journal article. "All I know is something useful happened. That's all I know." He knows only what it is not; what it is has not yet taken shape. "This is not the great doctor pointing to a brain on a table." The Doctor hears that prickle in his voice. "This is something else entirely."

"Oh, come, now, we're only making fun," says the Director.

"Some fun must be allowed," Nurse Anne says, her hand on his arm. "Especially after you left without telling Albert where you were off to, after you left me to deal with the tribe of walkers."

"I . . ." the Doctor begins, but she's already out the door, headed to the common room. "It is a flaw in your design," Walter is saying. "I am *not* a design!" Rachel protests. "I am making the funicular first," Elizabeth announces. "So that the people won't walk up the hill before it is done."

"*That,*" Nurse Anne says, looking over her shoulder, "is your fault. You started that. If you hadn't told her to build that funicular first . . ."

"We can't all be perfect like you."

"Children," the Director says. He puts a hand on the Doctor's shoulder. "If you think this will work, continue."

And so he does.

The Doctor finds Albert waiting patiently in his room looking out the window to the square. That large head balanced on that wiry, pipe-cleaner neck sticks out from between those thin, slumped shoulders rolling forward, knobby waves.

How had the Doctor not realized it before? Every morning, he pedals through that square. Albert has surely seen him, riding past the stone justices, wincing under their glare, a man among all the others on their way somewhere. He has surely seen the Doctor pedaling eagerly on the way to him.

"What do you see out there?" the Doctor asks

"Do you see the house across the way?" Albert asks. "Upstairs the mother brushes her daughter's hair and downstairs the father sits alone reading his newspaper. See, through that window? The newspaper spread across his lap. Every day, they are never in the same room."

The Doctor pours a glass of water from the pitcher on the bedside table and offers it to Albert but he shakes his head no.

"They are like me," he says. "I am living in different rooms. But with no doors between them."

"There are doors. We will find the doors," the Doctor says, and because he wants more than anything to help Albert find a door, any door, there is something else he wants to say. "Albert, I'm sorry I left in such a hurry to go to Paris. I was in a rush. But that is no excuse. I was careless. I hope you will forgive me."

The sun's light frames Albert's head and his large, sad eyes. The Doctor is reminded of the picture the photographer showed him of the shimmering black cloud hovering over the fierce girl's head. The light framing Albert creates a similar vibration, a vibration that exceeds his body.

"You came back," Albert says simply.

Out in the world, it is the end of any other day, but inside the Doctor feels it; the day is about to distinguish itself.

A basin clatters somewhere down the hall. "Give me that," Nurse Anne says.

The Doctor places his fingers on top of Albert's head. "Shh, Albert, close your eyes." If the man reading his newspaper in his separate room, pausing for a moment, looked out his window in their direction, what would *he* see? What would he make, the Doctor wonders, of this peculiar, two-headed shadow?

"Shh, Albert, shh." The Doctor's fingers swirl, and Albert's eyes flutter closed. "You are sleeping. You are such a good sleeper. You will stay in the asylum. You will not walk."

"I will stay in the asylum. I will not walk."

"Good, Albert. We only want to keep you safe. Now, Albert, tell me about your travels."

"I will try." Albert's voice sounds strange, as if coming from a great distance, as though he is calling through a long gas pipe.

"That is all I ask."

And Albert does. The Doctor makes notes of each detail: the shoes buried just outside the city of Limoges; the moon disappearing in a public square with the statue to such-and-such great general as a woman poured milk for cats; the horse thrashing in mud. *Dreaming together*—it's an expression he has heard used to describe hypnosis, one he didn't understand until now.

"I'm sorry," Albert says, interrupting himself. "It is in pieces."

"Shh, Albert, you are sleeping."

A gendarme with sparkling buttons on his coat. An angry chambermaid who woke him to catch a train to somewhere else. A child who offered him a potato and a bird that flew out of the holm oak, speared the potato with its beak, and flew away. A hissing woman who threw filthy water on his clean clothes.

The Doctor understands how this must go. Albert is right; he is in pieces. Piece by piece, he will find himself. The Doctor must be patient. He must not be careless. Perhaps if they went back to the beginning.

"Shh, Albert, shh. Do you remember what happened the first time you traveled?"

"I am not sure."

"Shh, Albert, shh. You are sleeping. You are disappearing." Albert's head sways underneath the Doctor's swirling fingers. For a moment, Albert does not speak, and then a slight tremor moves through the Doctor's fingers, up his arm, and into his chest.

"My father could not find the words," Albert says. "Only his hands trembled. His face was so still. *I give you money to buy coke for the gas company* . . . this is where he worked . . . *I give you money* . . . *a day later* . . . *where have you been?* Then he was so quiet."

"Where had you gone?" The Doctor concentrates on moving his fingers in steady circles.

"I discovered myself selling umbrellas for a salesman in the town of La Teste. *Who is this?* my father asked. The umbrella salesman was the very opposite of an umbrella. Not a pointed tip or a sharp edge to him."

"How did your father find you so far from home?"

"It was a miracle, he said. The lamplighter helped him at first. They asked everyone they saw if they had seen a boy. They went in circles, and then got as far as Cestas before the lamplighter gave up, but my father never did. Marcheprime, Mios, he headed for Arcachon Bay, thinking maybe I wanted to see the water or the Great Dune of Pilat."

Piece by piece, piece by piece, this is how the story will reveal itself. "How old were you, Albert?"

"Thirteen. When we returned home from La Teste, the neighborhood women who always brought us plates of food whispered. They whispered about us. *Poor man, he will never remarry, with that face and that odd boy.*"

"Where was your mother?"

"*If you climb the Spanish chestnut trees*, she said, *you will surely die from the bite of one of those filthy rats. And if you don't die, and I discover you, you'll wish you'd only been bitten by a filthy rat.* She laughed and twisted my ear."

"I'm sure you didn't mean to do anything wrong. Where was your mother, Albert?"

"After she died, I told my father I only climbed that tree to be closer to God but I'd rather not speak of that. When my father and I arrived home, Baptiste ran over and threw his arms around me."

"Who is Baptiste?"

"He is my friend," Albert says. "He was my friend. *He must go,* my father said to Baptiste. *He must stay inside. Go to bed,* he told me. He was not angry, though he sounded stern."

"He wanted to keep you safe. We want to keep you safe." It's true. In this moment, all the Doctor wants is to keep Albert safe.

"Yes, he always wanted to keep me safe. He only wanted to keep me safe."

"Albert, this is very useful. There is no need to cry. This is enough for today. We will do this again tomorrow."

"I am so glad," Albert says.

The Doctor blows on Albert's eyelids.

When Albert's opens his eyes, he looks directly into the Doctor's eyes.

"My life was not always without love," Albert says.

"Shh, Albert, shh," the Doctor says, even though Albert is awake now. He is not sure what else to say. The world has shrunk to those large, sad eyes.

He feels a pressure underneath his hand as Albert presses gently into it. Looking down at the top of Albert's large head and the soft hair beneath his fingers, his thin neck and its well-scrubbed poignancy, the Doctor's heart begins to beat quickly; for a moment he believes he is dying. His life—that unruly *there* to *here*, that sequence of minutes and hours and days and months and years of which his father's watch has kept such careful track—is surely leaving him. But then he understands. It is only rushing out of him in order to make room for the life of this man.

The answer often lurks in unlikely places. In the unexpected words spoken by a ship's doctor to a young cargo clerk—a young boy lost at sea—on the Bordeaux-Senegal run: *You have a gift.* But there is never only one answer. Or maybe there are only moments. Moments like this one, moments of relief between who we were and who we will be: You are better *now.* We are better *now.* And *now.* And *now.* And *now.*

18

H E WILL STAY IN the asylum; he will not walk. He is a
citizen held by time; he is a citizen held by a dream.

Ring (shadow ring). It is still time for breakfast; it is still time
to walk with Marian and Walter in the courtyard; it is still time
to put his hands in the dirt of the garden as the veteran digs his
hole deeper and deeper and deeper until it seems he may fall into
it and never return, which would be fine with Albert, since the
veteran will not look at him without hissing, *Deserter*, even
though the Director has told him not to, even though Marian
and Walter assure him he is not ("You are the very opposite,"
Walter says, squeezing Albert's shoulder. "How could you be a
deserter when you are right here with us?"); it is still time to
march behind the Director to the creek; it is still time for exercises. But now—*ring (shadow ring)*, there is a new time. Now,
each day, there is the time for the Doctor's voice to whisper its
way inside of him.

Albert is a house, and each day the Doctor discovers another
door in the mysterious house that is Albert. Turning the knob, he
gives it a gentle push, and there, another room.

Here, his ragged memory.

Here, his lost life not lost at all.

Shh, Albert, shh. Your arms and legs are motionless, and his whole body is heavy. *You are sleeping,* but he is not exactly sleeping. *You are disappearing,* but he does not disappear; he does not vanish.

Instead, *You will stay in the asylum, you will not walk.* In order to hear that voice, he will stay in the asylum, he will not walk. *Tell me about your travels, Albert.* The Doctor's whisper and the swirling, swirling of his fingertips, and then Albert is *here* and *here* and *here.* He tries to put the *here* into words but always, underneath his words, there is more than he is able to bring to the surface; there is so much he is unable to translate.

He is *here,* that first time, the urge to walk filling him until he fears he will burst. At first that terrible thirst, so he drank water, so much water, but it wasn't thirst, so he went outside because he thought it was air he needed. He gulped air until he was dizzy, and when the ache filled his groin, he hid himself at the end of the street and played his cock, his beautiful instrument. Though he played it a number of times, it still didn't bring relief, and then he discovered himself walking through the tight, winding streets of the city, past the ancient amphitheater where the gladiators fought. The urge walked him out of town through the ancient gate of the city, under the giant clock of the church of St. Eloi as it tolled the hour; it walked him until he became a gladiator too.

The inscription underneath the clock read: *J'appelle aux armes. J'annonce les jours. Je donne les heures. Je chase l'orage. Je sonne les fêtes. Je crie à l'incendie.* The earth's tremor rumbled through his shoes and up his shins. He was the whole world and there were the heavens and the angels, there was his mother alive again after being dead for a week that had already lasted years. His bones expanded, making room for it all. He walked until he became ancient; as if he'd always walked, as if all his life his blood had circulated astonishment.

"Where have you been? I have been searching and searching . . ." Albert's father could not find the words. His face was so still; only his hands trembled. "I give you money to buy coke for the gas company . . . a day later . . . where have you been?" his father said when he discovered Albert, and Albert discovered himself, selling umbrellas for a salesman in the town of La Teste. His father was an even-tempered man, stern but even-tempered, certainly not a man whose hands ever trembled as they did now but he was exhausted—the long walk, the searching, believing he had lost his son forever. "Who is this?" His voice had been rough already from the long, late nights spent caring for Albert's mother, who'd been sick for months and unable to ever truly sleep until she finally did and never woke up.

That there were years still to go without his mother in them seemed impossible to Albert, and yet there it was, the fact of it, every morning. No mother, no wife, the neighborhood women said. Pity was stronger than the desire to shun; the flip side of the whispering charity was righteousness, and the neighborhood women started to take care of him and his father. They fussed and clucked: *My duck cassoulet is famous. It cured my brother of cholera! And besides, it is delicious. It is how I am known—for that and for my generosity.* And when the wheelwright's wife was run over by a carriage and the neighborhood women had someone else who needed their attention, Albert and his father were fine because Albert's father had always been a good cook anyway and it meant he and Albert didn't have to be endlessly grateful.

"Who is this?" his father asked again, gesturing to the umbrella salesman. He was a man of folds and layers who seemed to be in the process of swallowing himself.

"An umbrella salesman, sir," and the umbrella salesman held his round hand, all five sausage-fingers, out to Albert's father, who glared until the umbrella salesman took his sausage-fingers back and hid away in his pocket.

"I can see *that*," Albert's father said finally, gesturing to the cart of umbrellas.

"I mistook the boy for an orphan in need of work. I'm only trying to sell an umbrella or two. It helps to have a child." When Albert's father's still face became even stiller, the umbrella salesman changed tack. "But I see now that he could not possibly be an orphan because, well, here is his angry father." In the umbrella salesman's reedy voice, Albert heard the danger he had been in. Albert's father said nothing, only glared, and in that silence Albert heard that the day he had been missing had lasted an eternity for his father.

"Yes, yes," the umbrella salesman said. "No, no, I'm not at all sure what I was thinking," already rolling his cart away.

"Albert?" Albert's father finally looked at Albert, his face a question too.

Albert did not have an answer.

How was he to explain there was a moment while he was walking, silky as mist, when he forgot his father altogether? A moment when he *was* and he *was* and he *was* and he was only *here*. How could he possibly describe the secret silky song of his body? He could not. He could not. He *cannot*.

What does it feel like to walk, Albert?

He could not describe it then. He cannot describe it now.

He says nothing in response to the Doctor's question, the way he said nothing to his father, whose face was still a question, and it was silence for the rest of the way home, where the silence was even thicker with Albert's mother so recently gone.

And then there was Baptiste waiting for them, sweet boy who smelled of apples and dirt, sweet boy whom Albert would abandon when he was no longer a round, sweet boy but a man as thin as a rail.

Who is Baptiste?

What could Albert say? "Baptiste is my friend. Baptiste was my friend."

Albert is a house, and each day the Doctor discovers another door, but sometimes when the Doctor turns the knob, gives it a gentle push, there is a room so full of shame that Albert cannot bear to go inside.

Shh, Albert, shh. Your arms and legs are motionless, and his whole body is quite heavy. *You are sleeping,* but he is not exactly sleeping. *You are disappearing,* but he does not disappear; he does not vanish.

Here, his ragged memory.

Here, his lost life not lost at all, though there are parts of it he wishes would stay lost.

He cannot say. He cannot say. He cannot say how dear, loyal Baptiste was waiting for him and his father when they returned to the neighborhood by the river where the cottages seemed shabby only to those who didn't live there, where the only light at night came from the small gas lamps in the cottages or the gas lamps along the river. When they returned home from La Teste, Baptiste, his smooth round face, innocent of its future, was the only one who would speak to them. He ran over, throwing his arms around his friend, enfolding him in a simple embrace that made Albert want to weep with gratitude.

"You are home, you are home," Baptiste said, jumping up and down, and it was only when he accidentally landed on Albert's foot that Albert noticed his feet were covered in blisters. It was only then he noticed the blood.

"He is home," Albert's father said sharply, "but he is staying inside."

Baptiste cupped a grubby hand over the coil of Albert's ear, whispering so it tickled the inside of Albert's throat. "Later," Baptiste whispered. "Tell me your adventure later."

"Yes," Albert whispered back, but the chasm had already opened between him and the world. "I will tell you later," he lied. There would be no explaining.

"Get inside," Baptiste's father barked at his son. He was usually kind to Albert and his father, grateful that his odd boy had found another boy just as odd to be his friend, but this time he walked away to join the huddle of fathers on the other side of the street—the varnisher, the wheelwright, the fishermen—without a word. All of the wives, including the whispering women, huddled there too. None of them would look across the street, and Albert's father shut the door against the night and his gossiping neighbors. It was only later, when the lamplighter arrived on his nightly rounds, when Albert's father learned what the neighbors' whispering and pointing was about. "Behind the barrels outside the tavern, the varnisher's wife discovered him in the middle of . . ." Here, the lamplighter paused. "In the middle of indulging himself. That's what she claims. Who's to say? She's a vicious woman. Go gently. You've lost your wife, but he's lost his mother too. He's just a boy."

Albert's father said nothing when he came inside. He had lost his wife, his boy had lost his mother, and now they were the man with the disfigured face and his son, already odd, now odd and shamed. What was there to say? There was only protecting his son, getting through the days as best he could. "Go to bed," he told Albert as gently as he knew how; only Albert understood that the sternness in his voice was a form of tenderness.

"Go to bed, he told me." There is such a great distance between the dream and the meager words he can shape out of that dream to offer the Doctor. "He was not angry, though he sounded stern."

He wanted to keep you safe. We want to keep you safe.

"Yes, he always wanted to keep me safe. He only wanted to keep me safe."

Albert, this is very useful. There is no need to cry. This is enough for today. We will do this again tomorrow.

He is glad. He is. These memories are beads strung on a fragile thread that has lasted from then until now. At last, he is here, he is here, he is here. *I am so glad.* He is that *I.* He is an *I* that has lasted from then until now.

The Doctor blows on Albert's eyelids.

"My life was not always without love," Albert says, opening his eyes. What he means is, *Here is love.*

And here: green leaves of the Spanish chestnut trees in the public garden sparkling gold, illuminated by the gas lamps his father installed in the park. *Come climb,* they said to thirteen-year-old Albert, restless in the days before his mother died; so restless he walked over to the cathedral to look up at its soaring arches and buttresses. Looking up at them caused a fire in his chest that felt like the kind of strength that might save a dying mother.

"Tell me about the rats again," he would say to her, because he knew the rats secretly gave his mother pleasure. Sometimes, if he was very lucky, she would describe how much she detested those rats in the public garden, nesting in the soft ground under the Spanish chestnut trees, scrambling and screeching over every fallen chestnut. That rodents had overrun the fancy trees planted by the city at great expense delighted her, a woman who took in knitting for extra money. "We are not a family getting fat off the triangular trade," she would remind Albert whenever he asked for things.

But there were those leaves sparkling gold behind his eyelids. Why couldn't he stop himself? When his mother, so sick in her bed, said, "Don't," why did he hear: *Why not?*

There are some things he cannot tell the Doctor. He doesn't have the words.

Those leaves sparkled gold: an invitation. *Come climb.*

The chestnuts rained down from the spindly branches of the tree. They rained down onto the filthy rats as he climbed, sending them scrambling, but they rushed right back to fight over the soft meat of the nuts. Then he was out on a sturdier branch, clinging to it, and the view was as grand as the one his father once showed him from the top of the Pey-Berland Tower. All of it laid out before him: the slated rooftops of the city, the church steeples, the flickering lights of hundreds of gas lamps illuminating the giant clock of St. Eloi, the ancient gate, the ancient amphitheater where the gladiators once fought.

He clung to the branch as it grew dark, staring into the sky without end, and his life seemed so small. How could it be that his small life could deserve so much love? There was so much love, but since his mother's illness the love was so fragile. In the tree, his body pulsed with that fragile love. He opened his mouth and the fragile love grew strong. He imagined it shooting like flames out over the city, over the countryside, to places he'd never been before. It was so exhausting, this love, and he fell asleep; he dreamed he was a glittering leaf blown by the wind off the branch, tossed and twirled, floating up and up and up. In his dream, he never fell.

When he hit the ground, the filthy rats did not bite him as his mother had feared; they must have run away. Or so he thought. He couldn't be sure. When he woke, he discovered himself some time later, not knowing how he got there, on a bench somewhere else in the city with chestnut-sized bruises down one side of his body. The bruises lingered after his mother's death; he had wanted them to stay forever, a remnant of the time before, but each night the bruises turned a different, lighter color, black then blue then green then yellow. Each night his father sponged the bruises, too tender at first for Albert to touch. "You're scrubbing too hard," he said, worried his father would wash them away. And then one day they were gone.

It was a few weeks after the bruises faded that his father began to tell him stories of the prince with one swan wing who wanted to see the world. After he wandered away the fourth time, they both knew the stories weren't enough. *Listen.* When Albert trembled and shook, when he fell on his way to bed because he was that dizzy, when he was overcome by that urge that he could not find the words for, his father would take him to bed, first swaddling Albert's wrists and his ankles in cloth to prevent the rope from burning. He was always gentle. He always asked, "Is the rope too tight?" The other question was written on his father's face: *What will become of you, Albert?* The same question is there on the Doctor's face when Albert's eyes flutter open.

What will happen when I'm gone? his father's face said. *Who will bring you back?* Albert thrashed in his bed for hours; he tried not to but the urge was so strong. His father's weeping filled the cottage.

Just beyond the weeping, there is another room with another door, one the Doctor hasn't discovered, but Albert keeps this door locked.

"Everything is right here. This is what my father told me," Albert tells the Doctor. "Each night, 'Stay, Albert, stay here with me.'"

19

I S IT POSSIBLE FOR the Doctor to feel even more keenly the pleasure in his system and the system in his pleasure? Since he and Albert began dreaming together, he does; riding around the lake, he feels it in the depths of his beautiful coral bones. Click-clickety-click, ankles rotating steadily with the pedals, he waves hello to the rag merchant and the bicycle doesn't so much as quiver. The ducks quack ridiculously on the shore but the geese sleep on.

Propelling himself above the earth on this simple, true invention—odd wooden hobbyhorse turned gravity-defying machine—makes him feel close to Albert's own willful passage through space and time. *The earth trembling in him. Time passes differently. He is himself and himself. He is no longer only moving toward death; he is no longer only dying. The whole world and the heavens and the angels are in his head, his mother and father too.* Click-clickety-click. Riding his bicycle, the Doctor feels close to understanding the astonishment Albert describes, the astonishment he felt when he walked. There must have been a kind of pleasure in Albert's system too. Why pursue it if it were only pain? If not pleasure, relief. And *now*. And *now*. And *now*. Each step taking him farther into relief but only if he didn't stop moving. Click-clickety-click.

Day by day, the years of appearing and disappearing are adding up to something, swirling into existence underneath the Doctor's fingers: Pneumonia takes Albert's mother and soon after Albert becomes his father's strange boy; the first time he wanders, when he is thirteen, his father miraculously tracks him down in La Teste with the umbrella salesman; not long after, Albert discovers himself slung over his father's back, heading back through the ancient gate of the city; the third time, he wakes to discover himself being dragged through the streets, his father's arms wrapped around him from behind; the fourth time, his father finds him pleasuring himself behind the cathedral, where they had not been since his mother died; and then he didn't walk again for four years until he was seventeen—Albert has not yet said what happened next. The Doctor imagines the fluttering unbuttoned cuffs of the country doctor driving him from his own home when he was a boy. What happens next is death, the Doctor is certain. *My life was not always without love*, but then it was gone.

Click-clickety-click. There are questions that remain to be answered—those four years, how did his father keep him from wandering? There is time enough, his own father said, and now the Director reminds him too. There is no rush, and there has been progress. "Look at him," Nurse Anne said yesterday. There was Albert explaining to Elizabeth how he almost rode the funicular in Lyon. "I always wanted to be that sort of man," he was saying. He is no longer a man comprised only of questions and blanks. Something in Albert's face has changed—no longer always a question. *Am I this man?* Occasionally, there was a flicker of conviction. *I am this man.*

The sun is up, time for the Doctor to go to work. Click-clickety-click. He pedals faster, eager to return to Albert, to continue with the case study he has been fiddling with in his notebook.

It all began one morning when a young man of twenty came from a long journey on foot and was exhausted, but that was not the cause of his tears. He wept because he could not prevent himself from departing on a trip when the need took him; he deserted work, and daily life, to walk as fast as he could, straight ahead, sometimes doing 70 kilometers a day on foot, until in the end he would be arrested for vagrancy and thrown in prison. According to the patient's accounts, the spells of wandering began seven years ago. The patient's father managed to prevent the wandering for four years, but the spells resumed when the patient was seventeen. When he wanders, he is not entirely awake, and when he arrives in another city or another country altogether, he isn't sure where he is or how he got there . . .

The Doctor's bicycle wobbles; he is much improved, but he will never be a great Léotard. *The chaos of gas contained in a perfectly fitted pipe.* Something Albert's father said to Albert when he told him the story of the accident that scarred his face. This is what the Doctor is trying to do—diagnoses are the fitted pipes that contained the unruly, combustible lives, the chaos between the *there* of *before* and the *here* of *after.* But it doesn't end with the diagnosis. *Fugueur.* It is helpful, but it can't hold an entire life. Albert's father taught his son well. A diagnosis is a story like any other, an effort to explain. There is no rush.

And why not slow down? The Doctor still needs to look ten meters in front of him—and never at the road—to keep himself steady. Why not slow down and appreciate the beauty of this morning—the rag merchant waving goodbye, the sleeping geese, the quacking ducks? *The trees, they took fantastic shapes.* To be astonished by the world—Albert's walking has come at a cost, but there is pleasure in his system.

Click-clickety-click, the Doctor pedals past the rows of silent houses shuttered to the wind carrying the eggy smell up from the smoke-spewing gasworks, past the statue of Diana still dragging the fallen stag, past the statue dedicated to the soldiers who die and die and die for their country, through the pushing morning crowd, the merchants and their carts, the narrow streets, past the stony justices who continue to glare, but so what? The Doctor is a man of blood and muscle, miraculously moving through these unchanging edifices. *And?* He is movement. *So?* He is progress. *Now* and *now* and click-clickety-click.

Once he is through the iron gates, the rushing world will fall away, as if it were the fleetingly improvised concoction Walter believes it to be—a scuffle in the public square as a man seeking justice for his nephew grabs the collar of a lawyer, threatening him with a different kind of justice; a woman calling after her friend, "Wait, there is one last thing . . ."; a near-collision of two carriages in the narrow streets, the shrill whinny of a horse and a driver's cursing.

Outside the small stone church, the witchy woman has resumed her watch. "See?" she says, shaking her head, as he rolls his bicycle through the iron gates. "Always on the run."

"Good morning," he says. He will not defend himself. He is fleeing *to* not fleeing *from*.

In the common room, there is the little world to which he has grown accustomed—Walter standing near Marian curled into an armchair, once again exhausted by her vigilance; Samuel, who has shed his large coat, as he has started to do recently with the encouragement of Henri, sits by the fire the Director is stoking. "The fire has nice, sharp edges," Samuel says, though he trembles.

"I realize now what's happened," Walter is saying. "There's been a mistake in the calculation."

"Darling," Marian says, "I am too hungry to listen to your calculations."

"A mistake in the calculation is exactly why we have not eaten our breakfast."

There is Albert speaking quietly to Elizabeth about a town he passed through as if he were a flâneur recounting his travels, "a town whose fragrance I never forgot. They manufactured rose-water there."

"Water made of roses," Elizabeth says, considering.

"Good morning, Elizabeth," the Doctor says, putting a hand on Albert's shoulder. "Good morning, Albert, you look well." He does—so neatly dressed, with his mustache trimmed, and that look of gratitude the Doctor has been anticipating all morning.

It is only when Samuel says, "In death too, no music," that the Doctor realizes what is missing. There is no music. Rachel is not at her usual place at the piano.

"No one has died," says the Director, standing to examine the fire. "We are simply waiting for breakfast to begin. Look how lovely this fire is."

Before the Doctor has a chance to inquire about Rachel, about the breakfast that has not yet been served, or to wonder where the veteran is, or Nurse Anne, or Henri and Claude, for that matter, there is a sound starker than the muted ringing of the bell when the wind is trapped in the tower. Howling, wild, it isn't the wind.

A cry traveling up from the muddy, cold depths of the earth, it is the sound a man makes when the dead brother he abandoned on the battlefield returns to demand retribution. Only the veteran understands the force he has summoned. Standing in the billiard room, he beckons the darkness out of the pockets in the table: *Brother, oh, my brother, there is a deserter among us, but it is not the man I accused. It is me.* Only he understands he is to blame. For the others, the sound coming unwittingly out of the veteran's mouth is the sound of their own singular terror.

"He is here!" Marian shouts, leaping from her chair, pushing

Walter aside. "He is inside. It was *him* all along, the thief. Do you finally see?" She does. The tightness around her eyes is not the usual tightness of something missing; instead, it tugs like a question. Hadn't she known this day would come? Hadn't she sensed a shimmer taking shape after Albert arrived? But how could she know the sun would tuck itself inside *him*? "It is in him," she says, pointing at Albert.

But Walter thinks she means him. Or is, and this is far worse, Marian not real? After all this. It would be just like him to have attached himself to the least real of all. Once again, to have mistaken the portrait for the real woman. His dream of the other night was true after all, a world in which there were only reflections and he was the man walking away from a mirror, or was the reflection walking away from the man?

Down the hall in the women's ward, the wind bangs a door, open and shut, open and shut, open and shut. Rachel lies in her bed, listening to the wind and the shapeless sound of anguish. It is the sound of her frog; he is finally dying. He was sick this morning. He did not want her to get out of bed and Nurse Anne finally threw up her hands. "I'm not spending my morning arguing with a frog." How would she feel if her *life* was arguing with a frog? How would she feel if that argument that was her life was now draining from her? *Tomorrow will bring a new day.* Nurse Anne's words linger, a mockery, as Rachel's frog, the fiery braveness in her belly, goes as still as her mother's hands when the music should have filled her. Why hadn't it filled her? Why wasn't the music filling Rachel now? *Tomorrow will bring a new day. Tomorrow will bring a new day.* Must there be a new day? Why not let her become the ghost she's always known herself to be?

Samuel would be relieved to be something as solid as a ghost. He shivers by the fire because this is his fault for taking off the coat that holds everything together. The shadows have come, and the Director and the Doctor and Nurse Anne and Henri and

Claude, running around the common room, try to gather the shadows before they swallow everyone whole, but they are too late. Samuel will dissolve into that awful sound that is strangely familiar, and then that awful, familiar sound is in front of him, taking the shape of the veteran, and it is reaching for the trowel the Director laid down by the hearth in order to stoke the fire.

If only the veteran could not think about what he is thinking, but he is beyond thinking or not thinking. If only he could dig a hole deep enough and crawl inside, tunnel into it, but there is no hole that is not filled with his decaying brother. The veteran is dead too but not dead enough. He only wants to feel something else; he only wants to feel nothing. When he drives the trowel in, it works as he hoped it might. He does not think, at last he does not think. He does not think, for example, *Am I dying?* He does not think, *Is this all? After all of that terrible life? Is this it?*

After it is over, Henri and Claude will mop up the blood and all that will remain to remind them of this day will be three stubborn coin-sized stains. That, and the Director's hand, the one that laid the trowel down on the hearth, which will develop a small but permanent tremor. The Director, who had always been so careful, but he ignored Nurse Anne's counsel to keep a stricter eye on the veteran. Beauty is an answer to anguish, and years later he will still believe this to be true, but it was he who left the trowel unattended—how could he have left the trowel unattended? No one ever will ever ask him, not directly (Nurse Anne's pitying silence is far worse), but he will never stop asking himself; no answer will satisfy.

And the door continues to bang open and shut, open and shut, open and shut with the wind, keeping time with the weeping and the shouting as the veteran topples over, the trowel embedded in his thigh. Open and shut, open and shut, Albert listens from his room, where he fled as soon as Marian turned on him, pointing, blaming him for the sound he hoped never to hear again, a sound that causes him to sweat and tremble, to feel so dizzy he might fall down, filling him with that urge to walk, so powerful he is afraid he will disappear and wake up in some other place, in some other time. So powerful he will disappear and never wake up at all. He pulls the sheet from his bed and begins to twist it into a makeshift rope.

That night began like any other. The story of the prince who wanted to see the world hovered in the cottage's living room as his father carried him, his sweating and trembling son, to the bed, swaddling his wrists in strips of cotton cloth before binding them with rope. "Is it too tight?" as he tied him to the bed. The same unspoken questions in the worried lines on his face. *What will become of you, Albert? What will happen when I'm gone? Who will bring you back?* Albert thrashed in his bed, as he did each night. But then, instead of his father's weeping, there was a terrible sound that had nothing to do with Albert at all. He wanted so badly for it to be the wind, but it was an animal sound, a roar of protest. Only later would he understand the roar was his father's. He writhed and writhed against the bindings, weakened from all the nights of thrashing, until they frayed enough for him to break loose, but by then it was too late. By the time he reached the living room, the protest was over. His father's pipe lay on the floor near the chairs where Albert and his father sat each night, the tobacco fallen out in the shape of the bowl. Next to it, the beautiful waxy swirls of his father's cheek turned up to the early light.

Falling to the floor beside his father's body, he pressed his cheek against the waxy swirls, not waxy at all but soft and smooth. As the streets began to rattle and hum with morning, Albert's tears ran into the velvety swirls on his father's cold face.

He was there in the cottage with his father and then he wasn't, pushing his way past people and horses, the touch of their flesh cutting and cold as glass. He did not remember crossing the Pont de Pierre, but then he was walking in the countryside on the other side of the bridge; he discovered himself barefoot in a river, his feet numb with cold, his face scratched by holly branches, his fist full of nettles, and he squeezed their poison. To keep from being afraid, he said, *Fascinating! Magnificent! Yet another escapade!* He walked until the flames his father told him blazed underneath the surface of the earth rose through the soles of his feet and he thought, *I will walk until the flames rise up and burn me alive.*

But as often as he implored them to, they would not oblige.

There is only silence now. The door no longer bangs open and shut, open and shut, and the shouting has stopped, but Albert has lost his place in time. It doesn't care for him, a citizen of nowhere, of nothing. He is a shadow. *Shadow ring, shadow ring.* It is all shadow.

"Albert?" A voice begins to take shape in the darkness. "Albert?"

The sheet he has used to fasten his arm to the leg of the bed still holds.

"Albert, what have you done?" Albert inhales the Doctor's warm breath as he sighs. "Oh, Albert," bending town to untie his arm, his one swan wing.

"You are still here," the Doctor whispers.

For a moment it seems possible that Albert never left. Perhaps when he reached the Pont de Pierre he didn't cross it. Perhaps he didn't walk into the countryside until he woke to discover himself standing in the river wishing to disappear. Maybe he turned back. Maybe he walked the winding streets back to the cottage and lifted his father's body from the floor the way his father had lifted Albert's body, bringing him back again and again and again and again. Maybe he carried his father's body to his bed and laid him down as any grateful son would. This is the lost life he wishes for most of all, the one in which he never walked away.

20

A FOX SCAMPERS ALONG THE rough-hewn path to the creek, veering off into the blackberry bushes at the sound of a snapping twig; once it is quiet, the fox returns to the path, padding down to the creek to drink, its red-brown coat dappled by the light through the trees. It is unaware that it is of its hour or that up the hill, across from the small stone church, in the long shadow of the cathedral, the careful balance of the asylum had gone awry and is now being restored.

"We will get you a much better coat," Henri says to Samuel, who is wrapped in a blanket. Claude used Samuel's coat to stanch the veteran's bleeding. "That coat was much too big anyway."

The Director, having tended to the veteran's wound, having given him a bromide, having asked Claude to put him to bed and watch over him, has shut himself in a linen closet to weep for his fellow veteran, who will recover from this wound, which was not grave, but who will never recover from the war. The Director takes this moment but then he will pull himself back together, in order to lead the patients to the creek for the quiet contemplation of nature and beauty, because that is still the point, isn't it? Perhaps they will see the fox again, he thinks, but the fox is long gone.

Marian has become convinced that it is not Albert but the veteran who contains the thieving sun; she perches on her bench in the courtyard to see what the flowers might tell her. Walter stands nearby, having decided he doesn't care if Marian is real or not. She is real enough.

"Your hovering exhausts me," Marian says, grateful for the way he exhausts her. "Would you get me my hat?"

In the common room, Elizabeth has moved on to a different puzzle; the funicular in Lyon may have brought on the violence of the morning. The new puzzle is quite simple, a picture of people drinking in a café—how dangerous can it be? She will begin to put it together soon; for now, she is content to listen to Rachel, who, having announced that her frog is dying, is playing a piece from Chabrier's Pièces Pittoresques, to bid it a bittersweet goodbye.

Soon the frog will be gone, Rachel thinks. "I am tired of this argument anyway," she says. Nurse Anne, setting the table for breakfast, now lunch, may have been partly right after all—no one wants to argue with a frog. But what will be left when the frog leaves Rachel? What will be left when it dies? As Nurse Anne would also say, tomorrow will bring a new day. And so Rachel continued to play.

There is no argument in Albert's room. There is only this: Albert lying on his bed and the Doctor sitting in the chair, which he has pulled up next to the bed in order to lay a hand on Albert's shoulder. The only sound is the tick, tick, tick of the Doctor's pocket watch, keeping track of the minutes, which seem beside the point, and so the Doctor slips the watch out of his pocket and puts it on the bedside table next to the water pitcher.

"My father only struck me once," Albert says, sitting up.

"Shh, Albert. Lie back. You are safe now."

"Because I wandered off. The next morning I pretended to be sleeping when he came into my room. I wanted him to touch my shoulder to wake me."

"Albert." Gently, the Doctor pushes him back.

"He took me down to the river to admire the gas lamps," Albert continues. "'Pay attention,'" he said, because I almost walked into a lamppost. I was still only half awake. He pinched my ear, not hard but firm, as my mother used to. He must have remembered it was something she used to do, because he said, 'She only needed to look at me to untwist me.'"

It's all any of us want, the Doctor thinks. *Mother, I am frightened.* Untwisted and buckled. *You are better now.*

"He started to tie me to make me stay, to keep me from going."

"He wanted to keep his boy safe," the Doctor says. He closes his eyes; there, the faint outline of a ship rocking on a turbulent sea. On the ship, a different boy dreams of safety.

"The night he died, I broke free, but it was too late."

"Shh, Albert, shh."

"I couldn't stay. I left him there."

The Doctor hadn't looked back after he escaped the flapping unbuttoned cuffs of the incompetent country doctor. Not until he was in the Toulouse railway station, but even then he didn't look back for long, because he was on a mission to—to what? He's not even sure; it was so long ago. By the time he hopped on board the *Niger*, there were nights he thought he would hurl himself into the ocean, until the ship's doctor told him what to do.

"Is Marian angry?" Albert says.

"No," the Doctor says. "She was just frightened. Frightened as you were frightened. She's not angry at you."

Albert sits up. "But I came back," he says, as if something has just occurred to him.

"Yes," the Doctor says. "You were right here when I came in."

"No," Albert says. "I came back. I came back, to lay my father in his bed after he died."

"You should sleep now," the Doctor says. He isn't sure if Albert is telling the truth, but the truth seems as relevant right now as his ticking watch. Was Albert returning any more unlikely than walking seventy kilometers in a day? Was it any more unlikely than wandering from country to country? Why not help him tell his story? "You were a good son," the Doctor says.

"Yes," Albert says, lying back. "I wanted to be." He closes his eyes.

The Doctor stays with Albert until he falls asleep, watching his face as he moves through the depths of his own mysterious solitude. What does he dream of? the Doctor wonders. Does he dream of walking? The tight, winding streets pressing in on him until he passed through the ancient gate of the city, the arch underneath the giant clock of the church of St. Eloi tolling all the hours—*les armes, les jours, les heures, l'orage, les fêtes, l'incendie.* Does he dream of walking through orchards with shapely pears that offered themselves to him; apple orchards with knotty branches hanging low; plum trees with fruit so vibrantly blue they are almost black? Does the rhythm of his walking fill his head underneath a sky so blue it swallowed the earth? In his dreams, does he taste the sweetness of the world? The Doctor hopes that in his dreams Albert is astonished by how much more to the world there is than the houses built to keep it out.

As Albert begins to snore, the Doctor's own dream from the night before returns to him—he is in Paris, jostled by crowds of people as he wanders aimlessly down streets that smell of horses and sweat. Where is he going? He walks to the Place de la Concorde, enters a restaurant, and orders a beefsteak, the most delicious beefsteak. Afterward, he walks to the Seine, where somehow he knows he is meant to dive in, but it looks so cold. He does not want to, but the riverbanks are crowded with people whispering, waiting. Are they waiting for him? Through their murmuring runs the gurgle of the river. He is the spectacle they've come to see. And then, the whisper of a familiar voice. He turns, and there is Albert. "Wait," the Doctor says, but his voice is a frustrating dream whisper. "What did you say?" He pushes through the crowd, but Albert is gone.

He puts a blanket over Albert, stepping lightly so as not to wake him as he gathers his father's watch from the bedside table. There is something he needs to do. "I will be right back," he tells Nurse Anne on his way out, and this time he means it.

Click-clickety-click, the Doctor pedals all the way down to the river, where the ships' sails snap and the boats creak as the current pulls and pushes. Tick, tick, tick—was it now? Did his father die now? The Doctor can never go back; he isn't sure if Albert did either. Did it matter? For once, the uncertainty doesn't bother him. He is not a careless man. He rides beside the river's current, his lungs scraped by the air. He imagines his elegant clavicle and scapula; his vertebrae—the subtle curve of the cervical, thoracic, and lumbar; the delicate birdlike bones of his feet—the tarsals and metatarsals; the coral bone of his femur, all of them snapping in two, then four, then eight and on and on, until he is a pile of tiny bones that one of the horses clip-clopping down the street crushes underneath its hooves, grinding him to dust.

But there again is Albert's face, falling away from the world into sleep, into his own peculiar and wondrous mind. The thrillful boy the Doctor once was, his father on one side, his mother on the other, waiting eagerly for the great Léotard to come riding over the horizon; Albert has brought this boy back. The Doctor reaches into his pocket for the warm ticking smoothness. He wraps his hand around it—now, now, now? He will never know, but something has shifted. The restlessness that ached for the precision of the tumbler lock clicking into place has subsided; now he longs to be astonished like that thrillful boy, like Albert. Now? Now? When did his father die? It's the wrong question altogether. As he pedals beside the river, the question blows away, and the Doctor throws the watch as hard and as far as he can. The current is swift and the watch is gone just as swiftly, riding along just underneath the surface of the current and then sinking to the bottom of the river, where it lodges in the silt and is buried.

21

*W*HAT WILL THE WORLD *teach you that you cannot learn at home?*
"*More,*" *said the prince with one swan wing.*

"*More?*" *the king said. He was a generous man who wanted noth-ing more than the happiness of his boy.* "*If you want to see the world, you should see the world.*"

Albert's legs are strong and solid and his heart brims with the world. He will walk out into the hills and dales, and more hills and more dales. He will stuff his shoes with soft blue moss; he will eat berries; he will befriend the squirrels, who will share their nuts with him; he will find trees for shelter and secret animal dens.

Night had not yet sucked the shape out of the earth when, his heart poised for *more*, he set out. He followed his father's voice into the courtyard, into the winding streets, and through the ancient gate of the city. *Walking over hill, over dale, the prince's feet were cushioned by moss and leaves. What would happen now? What next? He can't be sure, but his eyes are filled with something extraor-dinary, something he never knew before he became a citizen held by the days: the future.* He followed his father's voice over the Pont de Pierre into the countryside, where the sky grew dark and darker, where there were stars and more stars as his beautiful feet kept a steady pace. In the woods, he became indistinguishable from the inky blackness, as though he were moving through his own mind. Now the rough bark of the tree he clings to helps him to distinguish his body from the dark.

He is not vanishing. He is not disappearing. He is not nothing. He is a man.

Beneath his feet, the gaseous ejections, the ancient magic of gas, are deep in the earth's heart. The rumble through his feet and up his shins, expanding his bones, causing his blood to circulate astonishment, but even as his feet grow warm, he remains still. The fires blaze forever, but he no longer wishes for them to rise up and burn him to ash.

He will wait for dawn, here on the forest fringe. He will wait for the sun to burn a crisp edge along the horizon, the night rustling all around him—the snap of twigs, the swish of a tail through the forest. He will wait for night to turn into day.

When he left the city the wind blew across the river, stirring up frothy eddies. It pushed at his back; it pushed him along. On the other side of the bridge, he stopped to look back at the gas lamps illuminating the edges of the slate roofs; when he began to walk again the city disappeared behind him in glimpses over his shoulder the size of his forearm, the size of his finger, the size of his fingernail, and then gone, never more his home than right then.

The darting bats keep him company now as he waits for dawn. That darting bat and that one and that one too. That one there is the Doctor watching over him.

In a nearby town, the night watchman walks up one hundred and fifty-three stairs to the top of a cathedral tower. *C'est le guet,* he cries. Every hour, to the north, to the south, to the east, and to the west: *Il a sonné l'heure.*

Albert listens past the wind. All night, he listens.

This is the night watch. The hour has struck.

22

THE DOCTOR WILL TAKE his time writing the case study that describes the diagnosis—*fugueur*—he creates for Albert. Its proximity to the great doctor's Great Neurosis will contribute to the ascent of the diagnosis as well as its descent; it too will eventually fade. After the great doctor's death, those young women who went to picnics and suddenly collapsed in lovelorn fits, who grabbed at their throats as if they were being choked, who suffered from paralysis and complained of a stocking forever slipping down their legs? Some would die from love; some would go home to their families; some would thrash their way into new lives entirely. Sometimes it is better to keep thrashing. Some of those women would pull up their stockings and walk out into the world. In order for a diagnosis to fade it must first appear, and the diagnosis the Doctor is on the verge of creating will appear; he will make sure of that. It will enter the annals of psychiatry, if only for a little while.

But that comes later.

"It is not Claude's fault," Nurse Anne says as she walks with the Doctor to Albert's room. "We had the veteran to deal with. You cannot blame him for leaving the gate unlocked."

"I know," the Doctor says. "I don't." He doesn't. How could he? They are all doing their best; even when they are not, they wish they were, and that is worth something too.

"This is sometimes how it goes," Nurse Anne says. The Doctor knows she is saying it to herself as much as to him. *There, there. You are better now.*

"I know," he says, and he does.

"He might be back," she says. This too she is saying to herself as much as to him, but this he is less inclined to believe. "I'll leave you," she says. "But don't take long. Now that he is gone, Marian has decided Albert is the thieving sun again and he's run off with her liver."

She touches his arm. *We are better now.*

"I won't be long," he says.

Closing the door behind him, the Doctor lies on Albert's bed, listening to the buzz of the street, to the bells and then the bells ringing and ringing. When it is time for breakfast, he will get up.

Albert will not return; the Doctor feels sure. *Il revient.* A frozen river called to him one winter, Albert said. It called him across. The lightning bolt crack in the ice chased him, but still he arrived safely on the other side.

He will not need to return.

At least, that is how the story should end. It is the Doctor's wish for him. *Here, Albert, a story just for you.*

Listen.

ACKNOWLEDGMENTS

Ian Hacking's extraordinary book *Mad Travelers: Reflections on the Reality of Transient Mental Illnesses* was my introduction to the real Albert Dadas. Hacking's translations of documents related to Dr. Philippe Tissié's treatment of Dadas, in particular the exchanges between Tissié and Dadas, were essential in the creation of my imaginary Albert. For this, and for Hacking's imaginative, insightful body of work, I am deeply appreciative. *Charcot the Clinician: The Tuesday Lessons*, edited by C. G. Goetz, was also an invaluable resource.

Many thanks to the editors of the following journals where excerpts of this novel were published: *The American Scholar, Bellevue Literary Review, The Drum Literary Magazine, The Fairy Tale Review, Five Chapters, Forklift, Ohio, The Normal School,* and *Salt Hill Journal.*

For providing vital time, space, and inspiration, I would like to thank Château de Lavigny, the DC Commission on the Arts and Humanities, the Dora Maar House, Fundación Valparaíso, Hawthornden Castle, Ledig House, the MacDowell Colony, the Mid Atlantic Arts Foundation, the Millay Colony, the Passa Porta residency and Villa Hellebosch, and the University of Maryland. A special thank-you to Connie Casey and Harold Varmus for their generosity in this regard.

Thank you to my editor, Kathy Belden, for her keen attention, her insight, and for making this a better book; and to my agent, Alice Tasman, for her unflagging enthusiasm and her wisdom.

For their musical expertise, my thanks to Julia Casey, Alex

Weiser, and especially Jeff Gross. For crucial help and support in the writing of this novel, my deep and abiding gratitude to Jane Barnes, Sarah Blake, Stacey D'Erasmo, Brigid Hughes, Howard Norman, and Timothy Schaffert.

A NOTE ON THE AUTHOR

Maud Casey is the author of two novels, *The Shape of Things to Come*, a *New York Times* Notable Book, and *Genealogy*, and a collection of stories, *Drastic*. She is the recipient of the Calvino Prize and fellowships from the Fundación Valparaíso, Hawthornden International Writers Retreat, Château de Lavigny, the Passa Porta residency at Villa Hellebosch, and the Dora Maar House. She lives in Washington, D.C., and teaches at the University of Maryland.